The Amber Treasure

by

Richard Denning

The Amber Treasure
Written by Richard Denning
Copyright 2009 Richard Denning.
First Published 2010.
This 3rd Edition Published 2011
ISBN: 978-0-9568103-1-1
Published by Mercia Books

A catalogue record for this book is available from the British Library

Book Jacket design and layout by Cathy Helms
www.avalongraphics.org

Copy-editing and proof reading by Jo Field.
jo.field3@btinternet.com

Author website:
www.richarddenning.co.uk
Publisher website:
www.merciabooks.co.uk

For John, Margaret, Jean and Jane

The Author

Richard Denning was born in Ilkeston in Derbyshire and lives in Sutton Coldfield in the West Midlands, where he works as a General Practitioner.

He is married and has two children. He has always been fascinated by historical settings as well as horror and fantasy. Other than writing, his main interests are games of all types. He is the designer of a board game based on the Great Fire of London.

Author website:
http://www.richarddenning.co.uk
Also by the author

Northern Crown Series
(Historical fiction)
1.The Amber Treasure
2.Child of Loki
3.Princes in Exile (coming 2013)

Hourglass Institute Series
(Young Adult Science Fiction)
1.Tomorrow's Guardian
2. Yesterday's Treasures

The Praesidium Series
(Historical Fantasy)
The Last Seal

The Nine World Series
(Historical Fantasy)
Shield Maiden

Northern Britain 597

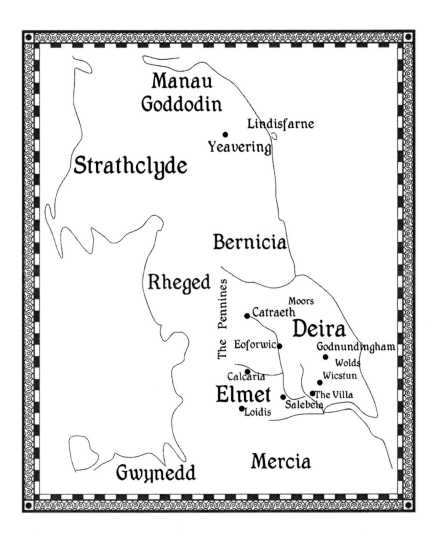

Strathclyde

Manau Goddodin

Lindisfarne

Yeavering

Bernicia

Rheged

The Pennines

Moors

Catraeth

Deira

Eoforwic

Godnundingham

Wolds

Wicstun

Calcaria

Elmet

The Villa

Salebeia

Loidis

Gwynedd

Mercia

Names of nations, cities and towns

The Amber Treasure is historical fiction. As such, I have taken one or two liberties with names in order to make the book more accessible to the modern reader who is here, after all, to enjoy a story.

However, in this book I have tried – wherever possible – to use real place names as well as the names of the real historical characters who existed at the time. All this is difficult, given the scarcity of records for this period – the 'darkest' years of the dark ages. If you are interested, the historical note at the end of the book goes into the evidence about this period in a bit more detail.

Meanwhile, to satisfy those who like to see the use of historical names in fiction and so that you can identify what these places are called today, here is a glossary of the main names:

Bernicia – Anglo-Saxon Kingdom in Northumbria

Calcaria – Tadcaster

'The Villa'/'The Village' – Holme-on-Spalding-Moor

Catraeth – Catterick

Deira – Anglo-Saxon Kingdom north of the Humber

Elmet – Welsh/British Kingdom around the modern day city of Leeds

Eboracum and Eoforwic – York

Godnundingham – Site of Deiran Royal Palace. Possibly modern day Pocklington

Loidis – Leeds

Manau Goddodin – Welsh/British Kingdom around what is now Edinburgh

Rheged – Welsh/British Kingdom in what is now Cumbria

Salebeia – Selsby

Wicstun – Market Weighton

A note about the Welsh and English

If settlement and country names are confusing, the names of the racial groups are even more so.

Historians might call the people left in Britain after the Romans departed, 'Romano-British' or 'Britons'. The invading Anglo-Saxons became the English. I felt that calling the Romano-British 'British' and 'Britons' in this book was going to be confusing to some readers, especially as a lot of the book involves the English fighting the British.

So, I decided to refer to the Romano-British as Welsh, which is what the English invaders called the Britons (originally this was Waelisc – meaning foreigners). The Welsh would probably talk of themselves as Cymry (meaning compatriots).

Likewise the 'English' of this book would probably not have called themselvs that. The Anglo Saxon invaders of the mid 5th century were made up of Jutes, Saxons and Angles. Whilst the Jutes and Saxons settled in the South of England, the Angles colonised East Anglia and Northumbria. In time the word Angles mutated via such words as Anglii, Englisc to English and the country became England. Although this process took some time I felt it was easier to just use the term English.

So for the sake of readability, I decided to simplify these terms and I beg the tolerance of readers.

List of names characters

* Denotes historical figure

Aedann – Son of Cerdic's family slave Caerfydd

Aelle* – King of Deira

Aethelfrith* – King of Bernicia and later Northumbria

Aethelric* – Prince of Deira

Aidith –Village girl

Asha* – Sister of Edwin and princess of Deira

Caerfydd – Cerdic's family slave

Cenred – Father to Cerdic. Lord of the villa

Cerdic – Main character, son of Cendred Lord of the Villa.

Ceredig* – King of Elmet

Cuthbert – Cerdic's friend

Cuthwin – Cerdic's older brother

Cynric – Cerdic's uncle

Edwin*– Younger son of Aelle

Eduard Childhood friend of Cerdic

Grettir – Family retainer

Gwen – Wife to Caerfydd, Cerdic's family slave

Harald – Earl of Eoforwic

Hussa – Village youth from Wicstun

Lilla – Bard and freind of Cerdic's family

Mildrith Cerdic's younger sister

Sabert – Earl of the Eastern Marches

Samlen – Prince of Elmet

Sunniva – Cerdic's older sister

Owain* – King of Rheged

Urien* – King of Rheged and Owain's father

Wallace – Lord of Wicstun

Chapter One
My Uncle

Looking back from old age, when the faith of Christ has replaced the old religions of my fathers, I can recall many times when my friends and I appeared to be at the whim of powers beyond our understanding. Today, we talk of the will of God. In those far off days it was the machinations of the gods or a man's 'wyrd' or fate that affected his destiny. A man prayed to the gods, put his trust in fate and life would go well: unless of course he was fey – unless he had been chosen or doomed to follow some other path.

You know, I am not entirely sure I agree with all that. It implies that nothing we do has any effect, that in the end we are all merely pieces on the game board of the gods; just pawns pushed around by Loki. I will accept that most folk just live and die with little impact on and little affected by the world about them; but some of us, at least, are more than that. We become part of the world, help to shape it and mould it. You can tell we lived, because the world changed whilst we were alive. And in my lifetime the world changed beyond recognition.

I was not long born the day my uncle stood on the battlefield, surrounded by the corpses of his men.

They had died defending this narrow gully through hills which blocked the approach to the city of Eboracum. The city lay to the east under a pall of smoke that arose from a hundred burning houses. King Aelle had taken the army there to capture it but, hearing reports of an enemy warband coming to lift the siege, had sent Cynric and his company around the city to the west to intercept them.

Eighty men marched through the night to reach this sunken road. They planted their flag in the ditch so it streamed in the wind, revealing the image of the running wolf emblazoned upon it. Then, they gathered about it and waited.

They did not have to wait long.

Soon after dawn, over three hundred spearmen came down the road and needing to reach the city urgently, attacked at once. The narrow confines of the gully funnelled the enemy and brought them onto the spears of Cynric's men. Then, the killing began.

The enemy paid dearly for each step they took, bled heavily for each wound they inflicted and three died for each of our own men slain. But, in the end, it was not enough. One by one, Cynric's companions perished and as the company dwindled, it was pushed back down the lane. Time and again, my uncle rallied his men and they charged back into the fray, regained ground and forced the enemy to retreat.

But now, as the sun sank and the sky turned a crimson red matching the bloodstained clay of the road beneath them, Cynric's company were all dead.

All dead, that is, apart from my uncle, Cynric and the grim-faced Grettir. The pair stood on the road in front of their battle standard. Cynric: tall and fierce, with hair the colour of autumn leaves, which in the dying light must have seemed almost like flames; Grettir: shorter, stocky and muscular with black hair and bushy eyebrows.

Cynric thrust forward his great sword and pointed it at the shield wall. It was a magnificent weapon, forged from rods of twisted iron overlaid with the strongest of steel, crossed by a bronze guard and finished with an elaborately patterned pom-

2

mel. With it he now gestured at several enemy warriors, picking out − or so it seemed − his next victims. Strapped to his other arm was his bright blue shield, which was dented and scuffed from a hundred sword and axe blows. Grettir had abandoned his and now both hands grasped the shaft of a fearsome axe that had already today slain a score of foes. Together, they glared down the lane and waited for the enemy to attack once more.

There in front of them many more than one hundred enemy warriors still remained and they, having now reformed their shield wall and seeing that only two foes were standing, came on again. Eboracum lay just a mile beyond this lonely pair standing beside their flag, which now hung limp in the still evening air. If the warband could reach the city they could swell the numbers of the beleaguered defenders and the city might hold. If that happened, more of the Eboracii tribesmen from the surrounding lands would come here. They would save Eboracum, then the Angles and Saxons − like Cynric and Grettir − who had risen up from their scattered villages and come here to capture the city, would be slain. Then, there would be no English city; no English kingdom here north of the Humber; perhaps even no English race anywhere.

All that was needed was to kill these two men and march on to Eboracum.

For Cynric and Grettir, this was equally clear. All they had to do was plant their feet on the bloody soil and survive just a little longer. Cynric glanced at Grettir and smiled thinly at him. Grettir just nodded back. Both men knew they would die here … it was just a matter of when.

The Eboracii advanced again and despite the odds in their favour, their faces were pale and their eyes were flicking back and forth. They were nervous, cautious: some even terrified.

They had seen their friends die and knew these two men were fearsome warriors. So, they chose to come together in the security of wood and iron that a shield wall offered. Nonetheless, they finally reached Cynric and one of them spat at my uncle, then three spear points were thrust at him.

My uncle stepped to his right, deflected two spears with his shield and then slashed the other one aside with his blade, the heavy steel easily shattering the ash stave. Cynric, following up now, stepped inside the spears and smashed his shield against that of a young lad in front of him. His mouth and eyes wide, the boy stared at my uncle, gave a terrified cry, stepped away but then tripped on his own spear and fell, knocking over the man behind.

"I'll kill you all!" Cynric shouted as he jumped into the breach.

"Come on you bastards!" Grettir bellowed and followed him.

Grettir swung the axe to his left and his right; felt its edge cutting into bone and flesh and with cries of agony two men fell – one man dead, the other whimpering as he clawed at his guts, which now spilt out onto the offal-covered ground. Ahead of him, Grettir could hear his lord roaring as he plunged his sword into two more men and then, suddenly, Cynric was behind the enemy shield wall. He turned and cut down another youth, but more warriors now closed in and Grettir lost sight of him. The last that Grettir saw of my uncle was him screaming in defiance as swords and spears lunged towards him. Then, a shield boss thundered into Grettir's middle and with a whoosh of air he was winded and tumbled out of the fight.

He was knocked onto his back and lost his grip on the axe, which spun away. He rolled over, clawing at the ground, desperately trying to reach the weapon. Then, above him, there came a shadow and he looked up to see a huge enemy chief-

4

tain standing astride him. The man was lifting his own blade up, getting ready to finish Grettir. Oddly though, it was not the sword that Grettir noticed, but the man's face. One eye had been hacked away and an ugly, bleeding gash ran from brow to cheek – Cynric had left his mark on this enemy and now the man came to have revenge on Grettir.

As he swung back his sword, there was a sudden buzzing noise and an arrow sped over Grettir's head, striking the brute in the right arm. He gave a roar of pain, dropped the blade and with one eye, he glared over Grettir, towards the city. Grettir bent his head round to look, and almost cried with relief as he saw the glorious sight of hundreds of Angle warriors – English Warriors – charging towards them, up the lane. Cynric had done it: he had held the road and denied it to the Eboracii and now the city of Eboracum had a new name: an English name, Eoforwic.

The enemy fled and after a final venomous glance towards Grettir, the one-eyed chieftain went with them. Grettir took a deep breath and then dragged himself to his feet. He staggered over to where he had last seen Cynric and now he could feel the tears coming. For there, surrounded by the bodies of his foes, he found his lord lying dead in a pool of his own blood and pierced by a hundred blades. His own sword was laid across his chest: although, whether this was the last homage to a noble warrior by his enemies, the whims of the gods, or just chance – Grettir could not tell.

"Gods, what happened here?"

Grettir turned at the voice then bowed his head to his king. Aelle, the King of Deira and now conqueror of Eoforwic, stared at the carnage on the road.

"Sire, we did what you commanded. The Lord Cynric died bravely, as did every other man."

5

Aelle nodded and stood silently for several minutes, taking in the sacrifice that had won him a kingdom. He then glanced down at Cynric.

"Take his body and sword back to his family and tell them I will see he is remembered: he deserves a song."

Grettir also nodded, but then frowned.

"I'm afraid I could not write a song to do him justice, my Lord."

"Ah, but I can," a new voice replied and Grettir saw, for the first time, a strikingly handsome young man, standing next to the King.

"I am Lilla the Bard, Lilla the Storyteller," the man said.

Grettir picked up Cynric's sword, cleaned it and handed it to Lilla.

"I will take care of the body of my Lord and you can carry the sword, storyteller. For all good stories are about a sword."

Chapter Two
The Villa

So, Grettir and Lilla brought my uncle's body home and this was the story that Lilla told my family. It was the year my people captured Eoforwic, when my people became a kingdom. Today, churchmen would call it 580 Anno Domini. I knew it – and still know it – as the year I was born.

Lilla once told me that he became a bard and a poet for purely selfish reasons. It was not to satisfy the demands of a king or his audience, pleasing though that might be, but because he wanted men to never forget him. After he died, he wanted men to say with pride that they heard him speak. Maybe then, if their children listened with awe and envy when they repeated tales Lilla had once told them, well then he would rest content.

I also want men to remember me. It is why, having learned in my later years to read and write, I am setting my story down so that others may read it when I'm gone. I want them to remember the man I was, the kings I have followed and the friends who lived through these times with me. These years were chaotic, dark and bloody. It seems unfair to me – after all we went through – that no one would know our names twenty years after we had died. But it was we who made this age possible: this literate golden age of the mighty Kingdom of Northumbria with its thriving cities, its fortresses, its churches and its books.

Golden ages must begin somewhere though and mine started not in a palace, church or monastery, but in a crumbling stone structure that my family called 'The Villa'. It stood on a small hill and was surrounded by a large barn, the smoking house, animal pens and an orchard. Beyond these were our fields where we grew barley, wheat and rye and where the cattle grazed.

West of the Villa, was the settlement of Cerdham – named after my grandfather actually – but we all called it 'The Village', and it was where the folk who worked our fields lived. My friends lived there too.

At the age of seven, my friends – Cuthbert and Eduard – were a little in awe of the Villa, perhaps even afraid of it. One night after supper, the three of us were lazing about in the orchard enjoying the warm summer evening, whilst playing a game of Tables with stones on a board carved from a plank of wood. I asked them what it was about the building that worried them.

"I reckon it's haunted, or maybe magic," replied Eduard as he moved a warrior stone towards the centre of the board, trapping one of Cuthbert's pieces. He chortled and removed it from play. Cuthbert glared at him for a moment, before he answered me.

"I've been all around the valley and I have not seen another house like it," he said, his gaze flicking towards the Villa. The slate tiles on the sloping roof were just visible between the apple trees.

"What's so odd about it?" I asked.

Eduard now also stared at the house, "I suppose it's because it is made of stone, Cerdic. My father says that none of our people know how to make things out of stone. My house and Cuthbert's … in fact all the villagers live in wooden huts. And it's … so huge. It doesn't feel right, somehow. Syngred, the miller told me that these houses were built by giants."

Eduard's words disturbed me. Since my earliest memory I had always lived there. I had grown up happy with the certainty, which all children share, that the way they have been raised was the right way. Now, at the age of seven, I began to wonder about that certainty and to question it.

Later that same evening, as we sat under the veranda and watched the sun go down behind the trees beyond the village, I asked my father how long we had lived in the Villa.

"You were born here, son, as was I, your brother and sisters, but your grandfather came here long ago and took the land for himself," he answered as he lifted a cup of ale to his lips, gulped at it and then leant back against the wall of the house.

So then, all my family had been born in the Villa: Cuthwine, my brother who was six years my elder; my two sisters, Sunniva − older than me by three years − and little Mildrith who was born the year after me. This, though, was the first time I had heard this story about my grandfather.

"Took the farm?" I asked. "Do you mean he was a warrior?" My mind filled with images from the stories of the bards and poets: stories of heroes fighting demons and monsters with spear and blade. Other stories were told of how our people had come from a country across the sea to conquer this land and make it our own.

My father smiled and the skin around his blue eyes wrinkled as he did.

"No, he was no great hero and did not come here to bravely challenge the previous warlord to single combat."

He finished his ale and then looked mournfully into his tankard.

"In truth, he was a farmer. He moved west when the land was conquered from the Welsh. These fields and buildings were abandoned. Your grandfather and grandmother arrived with my older brother and a dozen hired men. Most of the valley's buildings had been burnt and destroyed. The Villa though, being stone, had survived the fire almost unharmed."

9

Getting to his feet my father walked to the end of the veranda and then turned to look north, where the shadowy outlines of hills could be seen. On one of them, my grandfather had been buried two winters before. I was just old enough to remember the sombre occasion, though I barely understood what death meant then.

"My father could see the land was good and your grandmother used to say he took one look at the Villa and she could tell by the eager expression in his eyes that he had dreams of being a lord in his own great house," he continued, bringing me back to the present. "He moved in immediately. Soon, his men had repaired the damaged fields and built dwellings for themselves and their families."

"So, if he did not build the Villa, who did?" I asked.

My father turned and looked back at me before answering.

"I don't really know − I'm a farmer, not a poet − so you'll have to ask Lilla, or perhaps Caerfydd: he sometimes tells tales of his people and the Romans. Why not ask him, Cerdic − but not tonight. Now it's time for you to go to bed," he added, one hand tussling my knotted blond hair. Then he gave me a slap on the behind and sent me inside.

Caerfydd was Welsh and one of our slaves. The next day, I found him in the kitchen as he and his wife were grinding barley in a hand quern to make flour. He poured the flour into a crock bowl, added fat, water, salt and finally sourdough. As he rolled the dough and cut it into loaves, I asked him if he knew who had built the Villa.

He looked at me for a moment, perhaps surprised I was interested.

"Well Master Cerdic, that was the Romans," he replied as he opened the door to the bread oven.

10

"The Romans; my father talked about them last night. They ruled the land before King Aelle, didn't they?" I sat down on a stool and watched as he checked the heat in the oven.

"Oh long before, Master. The Romans conquered my people five – maybe six hundred years ago. Their soldiers and traders lived here and built many buildings, not just this one. They built cities too – like Eoforwic - and beyond it a great wall to keep the Picts out."

I had heard of the Wall. Lilla the poet had talked of it in a thrilling tale of other Angles battling the barbarians beyond it. Caerfydd's mention of Eoforwic had also excited me.

"I would like to see a city one day. Perhaps, this year, Father will take me with him to market in Eoforwic," I said. Then I asked something that had just occurred to me. "Tell me, Caerfydd, why are you here and not in the West where the Welsh live?"

At this question, Caerfydd blinked and his face darkened. The Welshman did not answer immediately, but he frowned as he appeared to think carefully about what he was going to say.

"All this land was ours once," he said at last. "When the Romans left, your people came across the sea. In time you conquered our land and drove us west."

He paused again and fixed me with an intense stare from beneath his black eyebrows.

"My father's grandfather owned this Villa actually, Master," he said, his voice suddenly defiant: challenging even. Then he looked down at the bread and continued to knead it.

"When the Angles came, all my family were killed, but my grandmother and my father survived by hiding in the hills. A few others survived as well, including Gwen's grandparents," he nodded at his wife. "When your grandfather came, he was strong and we were weak. We submitted to him and he was...,"

11

his lips twitched slightly, "kind and at least he did not kill us, but allowed us to live and work for him."

I heard a snorting laugh coming from behind me and saw that Aedann, Caerfydd's son, was sitting on the floor against the wall. He was a lad of about my age, but we had never been friends. After all, he was a slave and I was the Master's son. He was Welsh too and my friends and I were Angles. Aedann said something in his own language and Caerfydd replied with a few harsh sounding Welsh words. The dark-haired boy scowled and then he turned to stare with undisguised hostility at me and I finally realised that I was treading on dangerous ground.

"Do you not hate us, for what we have done to you?" I asked Caerfydd, quietly. I had never really thought about our conquest of this land from the perspective of the Welsh who had lived here before us. To a seven-year-old, the stories of war and victory seem magical and inspiring. For a moment, I had an image of Deiran axes and spears striking Caerfydd and his family down and found that I did not like the thought.

Caerfydd stopped kneading the next batch of dough and considered my question.

"There are many who do, Master, I will not lie. There are others who say it was the will of God as punishment for my ancestors straying from obedience to Him."

He shrugged and then punched the dough again.

"I cannot change what has been. Your grandfather and your father have cared for us and they are not harsh masters. I'm too old to hold onto hatred, so I accept my life and try to teach my family to accept theirs," he added, staring at his son. Aedann's eyes glittered darkly and I wondered just how well the boy actually did accept his fate.

"Now, Master," Caerfydd went on, "I really must get to my

work or your mother may well be harsh to me, after all," he said, slamming the dough down hard onto the table.

I left him to his work and went out to find Edwin and Cuthbert, taking with me a freshly baked piece of bread I had hidden under my tunic.

The Villa was always a crowded place in the autumn for it was harvest time and the outhouses, barns and rooms buzzed with the constant activities of the estate workers gathering the bounty from our fields. Corn, wheat, maize and barley were brought to the great barn, where they were threshed to separate the grains and then ground to make the flour we needed. Beans, peas and herbs were picked and then laid out to dry in the autumnal sun on the stone veranda that faced south. Mushrooms were gathered, threaded together on a string and hung up like a necklace above the fire in the kitchen.

Apples and pears grew in the orchard, nearby hedges grew berries and behind the barn, there was a large plum tree. All this fruit was collected. Some of it was sliced and left to dry alongside the mushrooms. Other fruit was boiled and the mush poured into crock pots whose lids were sealed with honey and tied on.

One of the outhouses was used as a slaughter house. Here, the pigs, cows and sheep were dispatched with a blow to the head and then the carcasses were roasted or boiled before being suspended from the wooden beams of the smoke house from where the smell of the smoke mingled with that of cheeses, bacon, roast lamb and boiled ham.

When all the work was done, my father always summoned the farm hands and their families to a great feast in the barn, to celebrate and give thanks to the gods for the harvest. Wooden planks were placed between barrels as tables, and other barrels

13

and boxes made do as chairs.

It was only on these special feast days that he would dress in his richest and finest clothes and only on these few days in the year that he would wear the sword. This was not just any sword: it was always one in particular. It was a beautiful blade fashioned by the best weapon-smith in Wicstun. My father had never fought with it, but it once belonged to my uncle, who had, and my father was immensely proud of it. I longed to hold it and feel its weight in my hand, but so far he had never let me.

When all was ready, my father stood at the door of the barn and called everyone to table by blowing a great ox horn. There would be fine white bread – not the rough brown stuff we usually ate – as well as smoked cheese, followed by goose which had been boiled in a floured bag with butter and herbs and hung in a cauldron. Slices of this were served with strawberry sauce. Roasted beef, marinated in vinegar, was delicious and I think my favourite. There was also mead and ale and for the sweet-toothed, some boiled fruit and whey.

Then, having eaten our fill and feeling very relaxed through drink, we pushed the tables back and space was made for a juggler. Some years, a small party of musicians would come with horn, lyre, or drums. Or maybe there would be the asking of riddles. Finally, when night had fallen, a poet would stand up. The candles and braziers cast a flickering light on his face and raised shadows, which would play tricks on the eyes – and the mind.

Then, he would tell his stories: stories of the gods Woden and Thor; stories of the wars with the Welsh; stories of great warriors hunting fell beasts and stories of the world beyond our valley and the lands across the sea.

In my seventh year, the bard Lilla came. He was by then about twenty-five and tall, lithe and agile, with sharp blue eyes and

14

blond hair. He had clever fingers that he sometimes used to play tricks and perform magic with. I remember once, when I was much younger, I had been shocked when he produced a dozen coins from my nose and dropped them into a bucket.

This year, Lilla stood in front of the fire and began his tale. As ever, his speech was formal: the high language of bards and poets.

"I come to you from the councils of the great and the mighty. Only a week ago, I feasted with King Firebrand of Bernicia in his royal hall of Yeavering and joyful and merry was that feast. For, I am happy to relate to you, that the noble king has this very year defeated a great host of Welsh warriors and shown that even the feared and mighty Urien of Rheged can be overcome. English point and English edge can sing their grim song, just as well as the Welsh."

Lilla paused, as we cheered the news that our fellow English kingdom to the north had won a battle. I turned to my father and asked him to explain what point and edge were.

"That's a poetic way of talking about spears and swords or axes – points and edges, you see?" he explained and took another draught of ale.

I nodded and turned back to listen to Lilla.

"Truly this was a great deliverance. For many seasons, our cousins to the north have been sore pressed and forced back by Urien the great king of the terrible land of Rheged across the mountains. From that dread realm a huge army came forth and even the royal hall of Yeavering had fallen. Indeed, for some days, the brave Angles were besieged in the island of Lindisfarne; where Firebrand's ancestors first stepped on the shores of Britannia."

I glanced at Eduard and Cuthbert and saw that they were

intent on the story. I knew that tomorrow we would fight the battle Lilla was describing, in the orchard or the great barn with our wooden swords.

Lilla went on.

"Forward came the host of the enemy to the causeway. And there stood Firebrand with his best and bravest warriors. They blocked the way forward, denying passage to the foe. The brave King drew his sword and pointed at Urien and called out to him.

"'Come no nearer, viper. I tire of retreat. I will die here or I will prevail here,' he said and behind him his men gave a great shout and hammered their spears against their shields."

In the barn, the villagers cheered at this bravado and hammered their cups on the tables. Lilla smiled at this reaction and waited until the noise died down, before going on.

"Urien jeered at the threat and replied, 'Out of my way, little man, little king. I have conquered all before me and killed many kings of your race and those of many others besides. This scrap of land you hide on is all that remains of your kingdom. Like a man extinguishing a candle before he retires a bed, will I snuff out this little flame.'

"At these words, the host of the enemy rushed forward against the causeway. Battle was joined. Swords hammered on shields. Fated men fell on either side to lie dying. Time and time again, as the tides wash upon the shore, Urien and his army charged forth against the desperate defenders ..."

I listened, entranced, to the tale. The crackling of the fire and the dancing of the shadows it created seemed to enhance the story. Once again, I was swept along with the words.

"... yet, all appeared lost: the host was soon to overcome the brave Angles. Even Firebrand could not hold the enemy, it seemed. Urien shouted in joy at his victory and closed in for the kill. Fate, though, cannot be denied and fate that day called for Urien. Firebrand struck and Urien fell dying, into the sea ..."

I did not understand all that was said, but I knew that our English lands, here in Deira and those to the north in Bernicia, were vulnerable. For years the powerful Urien leading his armies from the West had threatened to push us back into the sea and now, at last, he was dead. So, to my seven-year-old mind, as well as to the cheering villagers around me, Firebrand was a magnificent, glorious hero and the greatest man of our times.

Soon, the food and warmth started to make me drowsy. I had just heard Lilla tell us how finally the Welsh had been routed and then fled, pursued by the Bernician king, before I fell into a comfortable sleep, interrupted by dreams of battle.

Throughout all of them, I saw the brave, vengeful and terrible image of the warrior king, Firebrand, slaying his foes: and a great longing to be like him came over me.

Chapter Three
The Warrior's Way

Early on a cold morning, a few days after Lilla's visit, I was summoned to the path in front of the Villa. Here a cart was being loaded with produce from the farm. Jars of preserved fruit sealed with honey were stacked next to barrels of smoked meat. Dried vegetables in pots were also added, along with sacks of flour milled on the Villa. Two large cheeses and a good number of jars of beer completed the collection.

It was time to take the Feorm to Lord Wallace in Market Wicstun. The Feorm was the due and payment Father made to his superior lord. In turn, Wallace would pass on to the King a portion of what came to him. The estates of the more senior nobles and that of the King relied on this obligation. In exchange, the King and his lords offered security and the protection of their swords against any enemies.

Once the cart had been fully loaded, Cuthwine backed our oxen between the shafts and our party gathered for the journey. My father was going, as was my brother, along with two men from the village. I would not be much use unloading the cart, but I think my father felt that it was time for my education in our traditions to begin.

It was half a day's journey to Wicstun – oxen are ponderous creatures and travel but slowly - and we reached it when the sun was high overhead, warming us on this clear, but frosty, morning.

Wicstun had several score houses, two alehouses along with a blacksmith and other workshops. Looking back it seems funny to me - now that I have been to the great cities of Eoforwic, Ceaster and Lunden - that Wicstun seemed such a huge place. Yet, back then, it was with wide eyes that I stumbled along behind the cart.

We stopped outside the largest building in the town. This was the hall of Lord Wallace who was the most important noble in the south of Deira, made even more influential with the proximity of the temples and the royal estates at Godnundingham, just an hour or two further away to the northeast.

My father went inside and came out with an older man with grey streaks in his beard. He was a little shorter than my father, but somewhat larger in the belly. He walked over and patted me on the head and then smiled.

"So, this is Cerdic then, Cenred: another fine son and a credit to you and Hrodwyn. Ah, I see you have a good Feorm for me again this year. Even with the drought and those blasted locusts earlier this summer, you have not failed me."

"We have good land and good men to work it, my Lord," my father replied.

"Well, let's get it inside then," Wallace shouted over his shoulder to his servants and then, quietly to my father, he added, "the usual delivery for Eanfled, I take it?"

My father glanced at me before replying in a rather gruff voice, "As always, my Lord."

Wallace nodded and they passed me to supervise the unloading of the cart, leaving me wondering what they were talking about. Who was Eanfled?

It did not take long to unload the cart, but I noticed that they had left two sacks of provisions at the back of it. When I pointed this out to Cuthwine, he told me not to mind them as they were not part of the Feorm.

19

"What are they for then?" I asked.

"I said don't mind them!" he snapped back at me.

Father then took us to the blacksmith to order some nails and have some tools made that our own smithy could not manage. The blacksmith was a bald-headed man with hugely muscular arms, which strained and bulged as he hammered a rod of steel. He was making a sword: alternately heating the metal in the forge, hammering it on the anvil and plunging it into water, throwing up a cloud of steam and smoke.

As my father entered, the man nodded at him then put the sword and hammer down on the anvil. The two of them, along with my older brother, went over to the corner to examine some nails. The sword was still glowing and it drew me towards it as if by some sorcery or magic. Perhaps, I mused, the blacksmith was enchanting it. I had heard tales of such things. But, then again, swords needed no spells to draw me to them.

I glanced at the others, but they were still eagerly haggling over how many pounds of nails could be bought for a pfennig. I looked back at the sword, itching to hold it and I reached out my fingers and lightly touched the blade. With a yelp, I snatched back my hand and sucked the finger tips: the sword had still been red hot.

Father came bustling across the room, glared at my fingers and then slapped me firmly, but with no real spite, over the back of the head.

"Fool, you've burnt your fingers. They'll blister and fester, if we're not careful. I guess while we are here, we must see if the healer woman is at home and can treat that."

He shook his head and tutted, then stomped back to finish his negotiations. While he continued to haggle, I noticed he kept glancing over at me, as if weighing something up. Finally, he nodded to himself, as if a decision had just been reached.

We soon set off again and I expected us to go straight home but instead, we deviated down a side road. A short way along it, the cart slowed and I could see someone not far away.

She stood beside the road in the late afternoon shadows that formed under the eaves of a house. As we approached, my father, who was sitting on the front of the wagon, seemed to stiffen. I looked at my brother and was startled to see that he wore a scowl. The woman stepped out into the road and my father, jumping down, went over to her. They spoke for a few moments and then he handed the two sacks to her. Without any more words, he then walked back to the cart.

When he had gone only a few paces, she called to him and he turned. She was gesturing into the shadows where I now saw that a boy, perhaps a little younger than I and with brown hair like his mother's, was standing. The lad looked up at my father, eyes hopeful: desperate even. My father stared at him for a long time then he shook his head and turned away. The boy's eyes became wet and he ran over to his mother. She held out an arm and embraced him. They turned back towards us and I could now see that both of them were staring, not at my father, nor at Cuthwine, but at me and upon both their faces was an expression of utter hatred. Shocked and mystified, I looked away.

The cart started off again and we moved away, down the road, towards home. As we passed the last house in Wicstun, I twisted round and glanced back up the lane. The woman had gone, but I could see that the boy was still looking our way. Even at this distance, I could feel the strength of his feelings towards me. Confused, I turned and leant forward, towards my father and opened my mouth to ask a question, but then I saw Cuthwine shake his head and I held my peace, as we returned home.

21

It was only a few days after this that my father came to Eduard, Cuthbert and me, while we were helping Caerfydd repair the roof of the great barn in preparation for the winter storms. This is to say, we were fooling around and he was doing the work.

"Cerdic," he shouted over to me from the Villa, "come here and bring the boys."

I exchanged a worried glance with my friends and saw that the same thought was passing through their minds: we hadn't done anything wrong today – had we? But my father was smiling when we reached him.

"Today, it is time to begin to leave childhood behind and set out on the journey to manhood. You are all old enough to learn the arts of war, for the day may come when you need to defend your family and lands: just as your fathers and grandfathers have done before you."

As he spoke these words, I saw that he had put on his sword – his brother's sword. It was hanging from a baldric – a strap worn over his left shoulder - so that the blade lay against his lower chest. He noticed I was looking at it and pulled it out, holding it in front of his body.

I had admired it often before: it was a great blade of shining steel, which my father polished every evening. It had a bronze guard and a patterned pommel. He swung it swiftly round in an arc, so it cut the air with a faint whooshing sound. Sunlight reflected off the blade and for a few moments, I imagined my father in the role of the heroic warrior in one of Lilla's tales. His voice brought me back from my dreams.

"This," he said, with a proud voice, "belonged to Cynric, my brother and your grandfather's eldest son. Before you were born, there was some fighting in the North. King Aelle was always trying to find a way to defend us against the superior strength of the Welsh kingdoms and make us stronger than they. One day, the chance came. The kings of Eoforwic were not afraid of us, but they saw a threat in Bernicia, Firebrand's lands around the River Tweed in the North. They marched there, but were slain in the battle of Caer Greu," he paused and looked at us, perhaps trying to see if were following all of this. We had heard it all before, of course, but listened attentively. He told it well, but not as well as Lilla.

"Anyway," he went on, "Aelle now saw an opportunity to expand our holdings and secure our grasp on these lands and he summoned the warriors. Your uncle Cynric went away to war and he fought in several battles. In the last one, he was leading a small force of local men from this area. He was sent away from the main army to prevent a relieving force of Eboracii and Elmetae reaching the city. It was a hard battle and all the men including him were slain, save one. However, they had died for a cause, for the enemy army was defeated and ran away to Elmet. So, Eoforwic was finally captured. Aelle won the war and our people have been safe ever since."

I glanced at Cuthbert. I knew his grandfather was one of the men my uncle had been leading that day. The tale was often told on feast days: it was the campaign that finally secured Deira as a nation and had given us peace during my lifetime, just as the recent victory at Lindisfarne had apparently assured the safety of Bernicia, our brethren in the North. Cuthbert looked proud. Eduard, meanwhile, was staring at the sword with longing.

"Now, the main weapon used in wars is the spear, but you will find that some men do own a sword too – particularly men of rank and wealth, for blades are more costly to make," my father was saying, as he put the sword away.

From the Villa came the sound of a wooden spoon being clat-

23

tered against an iron cooking pot and from the kitchen door drifted the smell of herbs and cooked meat. The midday meal was ready. The workers were making their way to the great barn where they sat down to broth, bread and a goblet of ale. My father glanced that way and gestured with a finger.

"Right, off you go for food now, but tonight after the evening meal, come to the east paddock and we will begin," he ordered.

The afternoon seemed to last forever but finally, after a meal that held little interest for us, Eduard, Cuthbert and I rushed to the east paddock. We were the first there, but shortly afterwards my father arrived and with him came Grettir. He was one of the older men from the village and owned some land to the north, granted him by my grandfather. My father turned to us and spoke.

"Grettir here was with my brother in the wars. He brought his body back for burial. He is the most experienced fighting man in the village. I have asked him to teach you about weapons and fighting, in the time he can spare."

We turned to look at Grettir. He was a broad-shouldered man in his late forties with black hair and a beard, both of which had wisps of grey and silver. He had not said much to me when we had met before around the village, but had usually nodded and given a grunt of acknowledgment. He was carrying a pair of wicker shields and some wooden mock swords.

My father went over to the gate and climbed up to sit on it, so he could watch us. Grettir walked over and tossed Cuthbert and me a sword and shield each. The shields had a strap behind the centre and we grasped these.

"Now boys: step apart about five paces and face each other," Grettir ordered. We moved to comply. He went on, "Now, attack each other."

Cuthbert and I exchanged glances and shrugged at this. I braced the shield against my chest and extended my right arm, so my sword was pointing at my friend. Cuthbert tried a different approach and ran straight at me. That took me by surprise, but the threat of the attack was blunted when he tripped over the sword and ended up rolling head-over-heels straight into me, knocking me flying, so that we both went down in a heap. From the gate I heard Eduard collapse into a fit of laughter. Sounds of giggling from beyond the wall hinted that some of the village girls were watching this. My sister Mildrith bobbed up over the wall and back again. Then I saw Aidith, Cuthbert's cousin take a quick peek at me. My father turned a stony face towards them and they disappeared again, with more giggling.

"Get up," boomed the voice of Grettir, like a wave hitting the rocks.

"You!" he said, pointing at Cuthbert. "If this had been for real, you would be dead now. You must learn self-control; you are not in one of the sagas now."

Cuthbert's face was now glowing bright red and his hands were shaking.

"As for you, Master Cerdic, your posture was all wrong. He should not have knocked you over. You should have been in a position to take advantage of the folly of your foe – not end up in a tangle of legs and arms."

Grettir picked up my shield from the ground where it had fallen and then took my sword. He held the shield away from his body, in front of him so that it was turned towards Cuthbert, who was staggering to his feet a few yards away. He then twisted his whole frame, so it was facing to Cuthbert's left. He held his right leg straight, but bent his left knee a little, so he was leaning forward. Finally, he thrust his sword into the air,

25

slightly above and to the right of his shield.

"This," he said, "is a warrior's posture. Observe how I advance."

He moved his left leg, still bent at the knee forward a pace and then brought his right leg forward still straight. He advanced again, left leg bent and right leg straight. While he moved forward, he still held the shield braced away from his body and had his sword at the ready position above the shield.

"In this way, a whole army can stay together, advancing as one with shields ready to protect you and your fellows and swords ready to strike at the foe," Grettir told us, as he continued to move towards Cuthbert. He reached my friend, who had now got himself into something resembling the warrior's posture. He looked terrified at the arrival of Grettir in front of him and half closed his eyes.

I heard a derisive snort from behind the fence and saw that Aedann was standing there watching us and looking scathingly at Cuthbert. My father saw this as well and his face hardened. He then lifted one finger and pointed back towards the house.

"You, slave! Get away, this is no place for your sort!" he shouted. Aedann flinched at that as if he had been struck and slunk away, humiliated. He waited until my father turned his back on him and then shot him a glare full of spite and hatred.

Grettir continued his instruction. "You can now strike the foe in three places. You cannot hit the body, as it is protected by the shield. You can strike down onto your foe's head thus," at this he moved the wooden blade down to just above Cuthbert's head. My friend gave a whimper, which caused Eduard to giggle again, this time earning him a clip over the head from my father.

"Or," continued our teacher, "you can angle the blow to his

26

right arm; his sword arm. The third target would be his left lower leg which is visible beneath his shield." Swiftly, Grettir knocked Cuthbert's sword out of his grip and then slapped his shin. Cuthbert yelped again and hopped around rubbing his leg, whilst sucking his fingers. Grettir grunted at these antics.

"You will endure greater pain than that in battle, if you do not learn to pay attention. Now, pick up your sword," said Grettir. Cuthbert, obviously fearing another blow, moved quickly to comply. Our instructor turned back to me and threw me the other sword and shield.

"Begin again," he ordered, "and this time try and use your shield to block the other's attack."

I adopted the posture that Grettir had done and found that I could advance on the opponent in steps, while holding the shield ready for defence and the sword for attack. As we closed, Cuthbert tried to bring his sword down on my head. I shifted the shield up and deflected the blow. I then returned the same blow and as I expected, Cuthbert shifted his shield in imitation of the defence I had used, so I adjusted the angle of attack and brought my sword down onto his left shin and was rewarded by feeling it hit home.

"Good work, boy," said Grettir. My father and Eduard applauded, whilst Cuthbert groaned again and looked even more miserable.

So, I began to learn the trade of the warrior. Over the next seven years when Grettir was free to teach us, we received instructions in the art of warfare. We learnt about the use of the bow, sling and the small throwing axe – the francisca. These weapons were used by skirmishers to break up enemy shield walls. We also were taught about how the long knife, called the 'seax', was the basis for the other name the Welsh sometimes

27

gave to our race: Saxons.

"But, you will not see the seax used much in battle except in dire need. It is more useful in hunting," Grettir commented.

Grettir proved to be an enthusiastic teacher and took to his task with zeal. There were times when he got together boys of families from around the nearby villages. My brother, Cuthwine - who was also being taught by Grettir - along with three older boys, my friends and I, would form a shield wall and defend against teams of youths our tutor had invited along.

"Individually, you are weak and vulnerable and no one protects your rear or flank, but together you are strong. Your fellow warriors defend you and you them," Grettir would say.

So the years passed and we boys grew up. Eduard and I developed into tall youths, although Eduard was broader in the shoulders than I. Cuthbert, being three inches shorter and much thinner, lagged behind us. Eduard would always win games of strength, such as wrestling and lifting weights at festival times. However, Cuthbert began to show greater agility. He became accomplished at juggling – a skill I was never able to master. As for myself, while I was not as strong as Eduard or as agile as Cuthbert, they both deferred to me in decisions about what games to play, or where to go exploring. As the years went by and the boys we had been became young men, I found that I enjoyed leading them.

Of course, it was not just the boys who grew. Mildrith, my sister, began to change from the rather clumsy, slightly plump girl to a slim but tall adolescent. We were past fourteen by now and I noticed increasingly that my friends' eyes began to linger in her direction. They strenuously denied this when I asked them about it: Eduard always had a joke to explain staring at her. "I was just thinking that from the side, when she holds her arms out, she looks like a scarecrow!" he said with a snigger one afternoon when I had caught him watching Mildrith walk past. Cuthbert, however, would just blush and turn away, or rapidly change the subject. I sneered with derision at them both.

"You boys make me sick! I'm going to be a warrior one day. Do you think I am going to have time to pay much attention to girls?" I said, feeling I had scored a point. At that moment I turned my head and saw Aidith running after Mildrith. She wore a loose-fitting green gown that hung from her shoulders and as she ran there was a mixture of bouncing and swaying within the dress that was ... well ... quite distracting. I stared at her, open mouthed and I felt a tightness come to my throat as well as a stirring of interest between my legs. She saw me looking, smiled at me and then waved, before running off. I knew my ears had gone bright red.

"Ah! I see that now, Cerdic. Girls clearly have no effect on you at all," said Cuthbert dryly and Eduard roared with laughter.

Aedann was also maturing. Being a slave, he was not permitted to join in the training for war, but I'd often see him lingering in the shadows beside the barn, or sitting up a tree watching us, unless my father caught him. If that happened, he would be sent away with a clip to his head. Aedann's eyes were darkening to a deep green, his hair to jet black. I hardly ever heard him speak and whatever thoughts he was having, he kept to himself and just studied us in silence.

We boys called him Loki because, like that god, Aedann seemed to be able to disguise and conceal himself, appearing suddenly from the shadows. Loki was also the god of trickery and deceit and we began to think of Aedann that way. We started talking about this quietly, when he could not hear us, but over the years he had stumbled into us as we joked about him

29

and he must have heard what we said, because we could see him getting angrier with the passing months.

Aedann was a slave so had no rights or recompense for any hurt he suffered. He could do nothing and did nothing, save bite his lip and stomp off away from us: until one day, when Eduard, Cuthbert and I had been practising with swords and were coming back to the Villa hoping to steal some bread. Aedann came rushing out of the kitchen door and collided with Eduard, knocking him down on his arse.

"Clumsy Welsh bastard: you should watch out for your betters," Eduard snarled at him, then shoved Aedann from off the top of him and tossed him down into the mud, outside the door.

Aedann's tightly bound fury exploded. Like a snake leaping up to bite at its prey he surged up from the ground, punched Eduard and then kicked at his shin, all the time swearing and cursing in Welsh. Eduard was stunned for a moment and then swung his fist round to connect heavily with the slave boy's chin. Aedann was heaved through the air, hit the door with a splintering crash that knocked it off its hinges, then slid down it to the ground.

The noise must have been heard all over the estate. My father and Grettir came running from the barn and Caerfydd emerged from behind the ruined door and bent to examine his son: a crumpled heap on the ground.

"What in Woden's name happened here?" Grettir demanded of Eduard. My friend was standing glaring down at Aedann, breathing fast, his fists clenching and unclenching.

"This little runt hit me; that's what happened," Eduard shouted, pointing at the Welsh boy. My father turned to question me.

"Well, son," he said, "is this true? Did Aedann attack Eduard?"

Everyone now looked at me and their faces each wore a different expression: Cuthbert's shocked at the sudden violence, knowing that this was not the full story but unsure whether to speak; Eduard's demanding I back him up. 'This is about loyalty, Cerdic,' his expression was saying. Caerfydd's face was tense − afraid for his son − and hoping I would say something to help him. Grettir, impassive: watching how I would deal with the situation. Finally, I saw Aedann's face. He looked at me like a warrior looks at an enemy who has captured him in battle. There was defiance and there was hate, but there was no hope of mercy.

I hesitated. Maybe this then was the moment for mercy; the moment to show Aedann that his blind hatred was wrong. I could speak the truth; say it was an accident and flared tempers, but nothing more. I could have said that we had teased the slave and called him names and that was why he was angry, but I did not. I kept silent and just nodded my head and I let Aedann be punished. Now, so many years later, I still regret the choice I made.

Father's face darkened as he turned to Aedann. "On your feet!" he hissed.

Aedann did not try to defend himself. He stood sullenly, not speaking or saying a word, his dark gaze fixed on me.

A slave hitting a free man could expect death but, after his temper had died down, Eduard stepped in and actually defended the boy, saying perhaps he had spoken harshly. So, instead of being hung, Aedann was thrashed by Grettir. Our tutor used a birch branch and with every swing you could see Aedann wince in agony, but he never cried or yelled out, not even once. He just kept on looking at me as if all of it was my fault.

He was right of course ... which only made things worse.

31

Chapter Four
Lilla Returns

That incident happened in the autumn of my sixteenth year and soon afterwards it was time to pay the Feorm again. I was strong enough to go with my father alone this time, leaving Cuthwine at the Villa. Wicstun was familiar territory by now and once the work was done, knowing that Father and Wallace would spend some considerable time talking about gossip and news, I wandered around the town in the rain stopping at the blacksmith, as I always did, to look at his swords and axes.

Grothir, the blacksmith, nodded as I entered and let me examine a blade. Whenever I visited, it was always one sword above all that attracted me: the same one, in fact, on which I had once burnt my fingers. He had used the finest metals and ores and taken the greatest of care in its creation; forging a weapon of dark-coloured steel with highlights of bright gold and bronze on its guard and grip, which made it a thing of beauty. As such, it was expensive and even though years had passed since its making, he had not yet sold it and I hoped he never would; not until I was ready for it. Narrower, but longer than my uncle's sword, its balance and elegance were perfect. Grothir let me take a few practice swings all the time wishing, as I always did, that I could afford to buy it and longing for the day when I might use it in battle.

I was just putting the sword back on its rack, when I felt the hairs prickle on the back of my neck and I sensed that I was being watched. Turning round I saw, lurking in an alleyway across the road, the dark-haired lad who had watched me from the shadows each time we visited Eanfled. He had grown since last year, but not quite as much as I. His hair was more a dark chestnut brown. His shoulders were not as broad and his arms not as muscular as mine, yet there was something of the wolf about him as he stood lightly on his feet, seemingly ready to pounce. I took a step towards him, wanting to ask who he was and what he wanted, when my father stuck his head out of Wallace's hall and called me over. As I ran across the street, I glanced back at the alleyway – but the boy had gone.

My father and Wallace had been drinking and Wallace offered me some ale as I came in. The hall was dimly lit from what little light penetrated from the door or the smoke hole in the high roof, but the gloom was made more cheerful by a welcoming fire burning in the central hearth. The air outside was damp and I happily took the offered drink then sat close to the fire to dry off.

"Well, that's the last of those Welsh rabble we'll hear about, you mark my words," Wallace was saying, as he topped up my father's goblet and then mine from a jug of ale. I sipped some of the strong brew and sat staring absently into the flames. I was sullen and quiet, still bothered by what had happened to Aedann a few days before and also wondering what problem this brown-haired lad seemed to have with me.

"This is good beer, Lord Wallace," my father said. "What's that you were saying, Lord?"

"It's just what I hear," Wallace replied. "A wool merchant from the mountains passed this way last week and he told me that he heard it from a Welshman, who spoke to Aneirin himself."

"Aneirin?" said my father, in an awed tone.

Even I had heard of the poet and bard Aneirin. He was Welsh and still young, but Lilla said he was a genius. I'd had to ask

33

what that meant and Lilla had said it was someone highly and uniquely talented, unlike me. Aneirin travelled the Welsh kingdoms west of the Pennines: Strathclyde, Gwyneth and Urien's Rheged. I had heard he even came east once to Elmet, our neighbour and the only Welsh land on our side of the mountains.

"So, what I hear is," Wallace slurred his words and then belched, "... what I hear is that Firebrand has led his army out of Bernicia and gone into Rheged. Killed loads of Welshmen. Urien's son – er, wot's his name?"

"Owain," I said, stories of battle bringing me back to the conversation. Owain had succeeded his father and was now King in Rheged.

Wallace beamed at me like I had won a prize.

"That's the chap. Anyway, wot's his name is trying to get the Welsh together again into an army after most of them got killed a few years back up north. What I heard is, he ain't doing very well and Firebrand is looking to finish him off," Wallace concluded, before sliding down off his chair and starting to snore.

My father winked at me and slurped some more beer.

When we got home, I found Eduard and Cuthbert out in the orchard. Cuthbert was trying to teach Eduard how to shoot a bow. Eduard could never get the idea. The problem was that although he was fearsomely strong, he was clumsy and a bit of an oaf really and he could not manage to get the hang of aiming it. Arrows would fly out in random directions. As I approached, I heard a twang and then Cuthbert screamed at me to drop. I did so and felt the arrow shaft pass by my ear.

Standing back up I glared at my big friend, who looked back at me aghast; his face pale and his hands shaking.

"Sorry, Cerdic," he said at last, then passing the bow rather sheepishly to Cuthbert added, "look, you'd better have this,

Cuth. I don't think I'll ever quite get it." Cuthbert was also shaking gently and he, still staring at me, just nodded.

"Anyway, forget about all that and let me tell you about Firebrand …"

So this was how it was. The three of us soaked up any news of war and battle like a sponge. More than that, we were of an age when we needed heroes. Firebrand might be Bernician, but he was still English − my race − and he had defeated an overwhelming army of Welsh in a last ditch battle to defend a tiny spit of land, which was all that remained of his kingdom. He was then my father's age and fearsomely strong. Rumours spread that he was merciless in battle. Over the following years he pursued his enemies with an almost holy zeal. No Bernician opposed him. He unified the Anglo-Saxon kingdom and forged a powerful army, which he now led to ravage the lands of Rheged.

My friends laughed and cheered at the story I told them, then we got the wooden swords and shields and practised a little. Suddenly, I became aware we were not alone. Aedann was sitting on a fence nearby watching us and we fell silent, although we had no reason to. We were free men and in my case, I was the son of the Lord, whilst he was just a slave, and yet we felt awkward near him.

"Aedann …" I said, but was then at a loss, not knowing what to say.

It was Aedann who broke the silence. "I heard what you were talking about − about Firebrand and Owain."

"That's right, Firebrand is going to kill Owain and defeat the Welsh for good," I stared at him.

Aedann actually laughed. It was the first time I could recall him doing so. Then, he boldly walked forward and picked up one of the practice swords and examined it. Eduard looked darkly at him. Slaves were not allowed swords and it seemed wrong somehow for him to pick up even a wooden one.

Suddenly he swung the sword round and pointed at my throat.

"Owain will kill Firebrand and then come and kill every Angle between the mountains and the sea. Then I will be Lord of the Villa," he said and smiled. He was teasing us, goading us with words he knew would challenge us. I looked at my friends and winked at them and as one we brought our swords up and lunged at Aedann.

Aedann had not been trained alongside us, of course, but he was fast on his feet and moved to the side and caught, of all people, Cuthbert, a clip on the back of the head and laughed as he trotted past.

"See what I mean; you English are a sorry lot if an untrained slave can beat you."

Eduard bellowed at that and charged the Welsh boy, who slipped and fell but, in so doing, dodged my friend who ended up floundering in a ditch. Now, it was my turn. Aedann got back to his feet, picked up his sword and eyed me warily, weighing up this new opponent. We circled each other, both looking for that chance opening or error to seize upon.

He looked the part, I'll give him that. Not allowed to train in warfare as we had, had he spent lonely hours watching us, listening to Grettir and taking it all in? Unnoticed, even ignored, had he picked this up, just by himself? If so, he was a fast learner.

Aedann moved first, lunging with his sword at my throat. I flinched back and then brought my sword up to block the move. Aedann was feinting, however, and recovered his balance faster than me and now angled his blade down towards my belly.

Yes, Aedann was good, but I still knew a thing or two. I twisted violently and let Aedann's momentum carry him by, fetching him a sharp tap on the backside as he passed. Eduard howled with laughter, as the slave ended up on his knees.

"Enough!" bellowed a voice from behind me. I did not need to look to know it was Grettir. I looked anyway and saw that he was not staring at me, but at Aedann and with eyes that now blazed with anger. We all fell silent and I could feel the gloom descend, like the feeling in the air when a thunderstorm closes in.

"So, what is going on, boy?" he said to Aedann. "Are you bothering your betters? Need I get the birch again – or the noose?"

He emphasised the last word by slapping the sword out of Aedann's hand. I knew Grettir and how much he valued tradition and custom. My father felt the same way. I was treading on thin ice, but I did what I should have done before – I spoke out for Aedann.

"Aedann is helping us train, Grettir. He's pretty good and could make a fine warrior, given the chance."

Grettir's eyebrows bristled like the fur on the back of an agitated cat.

"That is not what is done; you know that, Master Cerdic!"

My heart was pounding from something close to terror, but I knew that what I did next was critical.

"That is not for you to tell me. If I say it can be done; then it can!"

Grettir's eyes bulged. I could see that inside him, tradition was fighting against itself over two opposing points of view. On the one hand he knew that a slave should never be armed and taught how to fight. On the other, I was the son of his master, Cenred of the Villa. That meant I was due respect and obedience.

He nodded, gruffly accepting what I said.

37

"What you say is fair enough, Master Cerdic. However," he continued in a smug tone, "your father might have something to say about that."

With a final glare at Aedann, he stomped off, carrying the rain clouds of gloom with him.

We waited a heartbeat and then I let out the long breath I had been holding inside me. Eduard chortled and slapped me so hard on the back that I winced.

"Cerdic my lad, that took balls; balls of bloody iron in fact!"

Cuthbert said nothing and was shaking with the same anxiety he always had around Grettir. Yet, he nodded in agreement.

Aedann was still kneeling, but he was not staring where Grettir had gone. Instead, he was looking at me and for the first time the look was not one of loathing or mockery – but gratitude.

"Thank you," he said, as he picked himself up.

Father, of course, sent for me immediately. He told me bluntly that no slave on his land was allowed to carry weapons or become a warrior.

"That is the tradition, so that is that."

I told him that I thought tradition was a pile of fetid horseshit, but that earned me a vicious slap across the cheek, which sent me reeling.

"Tradition is everything," he bellowed. "It tells us who and what we are and where we come from. Tradition, honour and fate – it is all men are. Lose sight of that and we are nothing. Do you understand?"

"Yes, Father," I mumbled.

"Grettir knows all this ..."

"Grettir is a bit of an old battleaxe, Father."

"Maybe he is, but he was still impressed by you today."

That surprised me.

38

"I thought he went off in a huff."

My father nodded, laughing now.

"Oh, he was mad as a demon, but he soon calmed down. Grettir is the salt of the earth and a very good man to have on your side, but he expects someone to be in charge and giving the orders; your grandfather or uncle in the past, then your brother, me or you. He respects authority – but more than that, he demands authority. Leadership is not just a right; you must earn obedience and loyalty by taking command. Today was the first time he saw that in you and he was impressed."

I felt myself colouring, unused as I was to compliments.

"Even so – don't get carried away. I rule here and that means no more swords or practice for Aedann."

"Yes, Father."

But, maybe something of Loki was about Aedann after all and maybe some of that had rubbed off on me: Loki the trickster and deceiver of the gods. So, I knew even as I promised it, that I was lying. Loki looked down upon me and laughed as I plotted and planned.

Strange the way things go in life. Aedann had seemed to be an enemy and someone who did not want me about and I had felt that way about him. Now, Eduard, Cuthbert and I were suddenly quite fond of the boy. Only a few days before, our teasing and name calling had led to him being punished and now his name calling and challenges to us had made us want to be with him.

So, we planned ways to smuggle swords and shields out to the woods a little way from the Villa and he practised with us, despite my father forbidding this. He was good with all the weapons when he got the chance, even, much to Eduard's chagrin, the bow. However, it was with a sword that he excelled.

We were ever watchful of Grettir and kept our eyes on the woods in case he or Father would find us. One day, I was keeping watch whilst Eduard and Aedann fought. Aedann was goading Eduard by telling him that he was Owain and Eduard was Firebrand and that soon he would be victorious. Suddenly, I saw the bushes move.

Quick as lightning, I pushed Aedann into the undergrowth close at hand and then signalled to the others to throw their swords away. We then stood, breathing quickly, our gaze fixed on the bushes. Yet no one emerged, so Eduard circled round to come at the suspicious thicket from the rear. Nothing happened for a good few minutes. Then, we heard Eduard give a load bellow and with a scream, two girls came tumbling out of the bushes: Mildrith and Aidith.

"You were spying on us!" I accused them.

Mildrith stood up and glared at me indignantly.

"No, we weren't. We were … erm," Mildrith replied, with some hesitation.

"Picking fruit?" suggested Aidith. Mildrith nodded vigorously.

I looked at the hazel thicket doubtfully.

"It's midwinter and that is a hazel tree. There is no fruit anywhere."

"Oh, that explains it then," Aidith said, with a giggle.

"Yes, no wonder we did not find any," Mildrith added.

"It's a … an easy mistake to make. A … a … anyone could make it," Cuthbert said to my sister. She smiled back at him and I sighed. One day, my friend might get the courage to say something about his feelings for her.

Just then, the winter sun broke through the dark clouds lighting up the glade. It caught Aidith's red hair and I felt my throat go dry. Maybe, one day, I would get the courage up as well, I thought.

With a crunching of leaves and snapping of branches, Aedann pulled himself back out of the bush.

"I would think you could give a man some warning!" he complained, spitting out holly leaves. Then, he saw Mildrith and Aidith and he smiled at my sister.

Mildrith looked surprised. Like me, she was not used to seeing him do this. After a moment, she smiled back.

"Hello, Aedann, you with the boys?"

"No!" I said, quickly.

"Yes!" said Aedann, just as quickly, striking a manly pose with the sword he carried. Mildrith giggled.

"Well, don't let Father catch you, will you?" she said with a wink and then dragged Aidith away.

As they left, I noticed that Cuthbert was studying Aedann, his eyes narrowed and dangerous. I smiled to myself. So then, Cuthbert has a rival, I thought, and Cuthbert knew it too. Oh well, might do him some good.

Lilla came to us again at the start of the spring. He brought shocking news from distant Rheged. What Aedann had jokingly predicted, had come true.

Lilla had the lights extinguished in the barn, save one that lit up his face and he spoke in a sombre, mournful tone.

"The Warlord, Owain, ambushed the great Firebrand in a rocky, barren land. His army was surrounded as it passed through the mountains and slain to a man. Last to die was the great warlord himself. Ten score he killed before they killed him, but die he did, pierced by many blades and arrows."

A groan broke out across the barn as we took in what he had just said. Firebrand, the great Anglo-Saxon warlord who had

41

kept the Welsh on the back foot for many years, was dead. The lands he had conquered and occupied, Lilla told us, had now risen up in rebellion. Bernician lords vied for power and civil war had broken out. But that war did not last long, for Firebrand had an heir. His son, Aethelfrith, was as strong and fierce as his father and had put down the rebellions and civil war with a vengeance.

The shocks of the campaigns in the North and West were felt even in the Villa. During this time, Deira remained neutral in the struggles and concentrated on assimilating the new lands King Aelle had conquered years before. However, the fighting in the North drove scores of people south. Thus, leaderless men and bandits deprived of land and livelihood came to Deira and the countryside became a dangerous place. Small groups of travellers and, in particular, traders were their prey and the people soon became afraid to travel. The King took action and called up the Fyrd – the local levy of a portion of the warriors in each district – and set them to clearing the woods and abandoned farmsteads of the bandits.

So it was that Cuthwine went off to fight. He was passing twenty-two at the time. Father gave him my uncle's sword to carry. He left tall and proud, leading two other youths from the village and accompanied by Grettir and was gone many months. When he returned, late in the summer, he bore several scars and told stories of skirmishes and battles amongst the Wolds. Once again, my spirit burned with longing to take my place in the sagas. The Villa seemed dull indeed, compared to these strange and exciting places. In the end, the bandits had been dispersed or slain and the King discharged the Fyrd. The sword was hung up again in the Villa and we went back to daily life as farmers, expecting that peace would last.

This was not to be. When Yule time came and we feasted on roasted lamb and beef and drank the best ale and mead to stave off the winter cold, Lilla came again to stay with us. His courage rising after the victory over Bernicia, Owain of Rheged had – so Lilla had heard – been gathering an army. It was not just from Rheged over the mountains to the west, but from other Welsh lands like nearby Elmet and more distant Manau Goddodin, up towards the land of the Picts.

"For, all these are in fact one race and one people. Owain would unite them all and lead them against his enemies," Lilla said, standing in front of the fire, so that he again cast disturbing shadows on the walls of the barn.

"I cannot say in truth who their intended enemy is," he went on, "but my heart tells me it is we Angles he aims to attack."

By 'we Angles' he meant slowly recovering Bernicia, weakened and broken by civil war or Deira, the land of farms and market towns, which had not fought a war in my lifetime: both vulnerable kingdoms. Both might struggle to raise enough spears to oppose such a horde; both were ripe for invasion.

War was coming: my heart told me that this was the last winter of my youth. Fool that I was then, I felt joy and a desperate yearning for the glory of battle. Had I known what would happen soon, I should instead have felt dread.

Chapter Five
Hussa's Grudge

War was coming and King Aelle had sent word that all areas should arm and train the Fyrd and be prepared for battle, when and if it should come. In our area of southwest Deira, the responsibility lay with Lord Wallace of Wicstun and he took to the task with vigour. As well as the town itself, there were a dozen or so villages like ours under his lordship. Each of these would be called upon to provide him with a handful of warriors. The Villa and Cerdham contributed the largest single contingent outside the town, with twelve men and boys old enough and fit enough for duty.

Wallace kept the local warriors training while he gathered arms and equipment. He also sent word that there would be a gathering of the entire Wicstun Company in a few weeks. My father had agreed to hold this at the Villa where there was space for us to learn to fight as one company. Prince Aethelric, the son of the King, was coming to inspect us.

This time of year was not a popular one to be taking men away from the land as it was spring and a time to be ploughing, sowing and planting. Wallace told my father that he had some resistance to his call to gather at the Villa, but this summons had the authority of the King behind it and come they would.

Father and Grettir were determined that Cuthwine, myself and the others would put on a good display and so kept us practising late into the spring evenings, after the work on the fields was done for the day.

So, one evening in April – the first month of spring when the rains came and the weeds grew fast – Grettir had again gathered together the men and boys from the Villa. Some from Wicstun had also been sent over to learn from the veteran. We were being taught about spears and stood in an arc round him in a clearing in the woods, west of the Villa. The day had been particularly hot and so we took shelter under the outspread branches of an ancient oak tree, which Caerfydd had once told me dated back to the years when the Romans lived in the Villa.

"Whilst the sword is often the mark of rank and wealth, it is the spear that defines a warrior. Slaves cannot bear arms. If a man owns a spear he must be a free man," Grettir was saying looking at me, making me wonder how much he knew – or thought he knew – about us and Aedann. He was holding a spear, made of ash and topped with an iron head shaped like a leaf. The opposite end of the spear was capped with an iron ferule.

"There are two ways to use a spear," Grettir went on. He put the spear down against the gate and picked up a mock version. He also picked up a shield and indicated that I should do likewise. I assumed the normal warrior's pose and braced the shield.

"I can hold the spear over arm gripped about halfway down its length."

He raised his right arm straight up and angled the spear end slightly downwards.

"Thus, I can attack over the foe's shield against his face and upper body, or," he said, dropping his right arm down and bending the elbow, "you can hold it under-arm. The shaft is grasped further back and supported against the forearm. This method gives you greater reach and you have more strength behind the point. You can use the spear to knock aside the enemy's or to push against his shield and force him back."

45

As he said this, he pushed the spear against my shield and I had to shift my weight to keep my position. "But clearly it is more difficult to wound your foe – protected as he is."

Grettir turned and leant the spear and shield against the trunk of the tree and then turned back to us. "Now, break up into pairs and practice," he instructed.

Cuthbert, ever the optimist, paired up with Eduard. I turned my head away but was not surprised to hear, a few moments later, a dull thud and a yelp of pain from Cuthbert as yet again he was beaten by my other friend. Cuthbert's best chance was to use his natural agility to protect himself, but he always tried to stand up, like a warrior from the sagas, usually to unfortunate results.

Smiling to myself, I looked around for a partner. Of the lads present all had paired up, apart from a red-haired youth. I nodded at him and walked over. He looked familiar. Then I realised with a start that this was the same youth I had seen every autumn over the last several years, standing beside the road in Wicstun and again near the blacksmith's about six month before. His hair seemed to be getting redder, if anything.

"Hello, I'm Cerdic: it looks as if we have to pair up. Who are you, then?" I asked.

The boy did not reply at first. He studied me for a moment then shrugged, before finally answering.

"I'm Hussa," he mumbled.

He might have said more but at that point, Grettir appeared at my elbow and shouted at us.

"Stop talking and practice. Don't think I won't make you run to the Humber and back, master's son or not."

I looked at Hussa, quickly took up my spear and shield and prepared to advance on him. I moved forward feinting a thrust with the spear in order to draw his shield to his left, then quickly pushing forward with my own in an attempt to slam it into his unprotected side. Hussa, however, was too quick for me. He stepped back, allowing me to stumble past him and then ramming into me with his own shield, sending me tumbling to the ground. Then, the red-headed lad followed up and jabbed the wooden spear end into my ribs. Nearby, I heard a clapping of hands as his manoeuvre was appreciated by Grettir.

I got up and rubbed my bruised side. I nodded at Hussa. "Nice move," I said. Hussa did not acknowledge the compliment but looked about him, as if seeing if his fellows from Wicstun had noticed. Ah, I thought. Perhaps vanity might be a weakness in this one. I will remember that.

"It seems noble blood or not you can be beaten, Master Cerdic," he muttered emphasising my rank in a way that left me in no doubt he did not respect it in the least. I tried to ask him what I had done to offend him, but Grettir again appeared and urged us back into the mock fight. Hussa proved a skilled opponent. Maybe he was not strong like Eduard or agile like Cuthbert. He was, however, cunning and surprised me more than once with a sudden change of attack.

It was a little before dusk when Grettir called us together. "You have done well today, lads. You all deserve ale and meat. Even Cuthbert here," he grinned at the rather bruised Cuthbert, who looked surprised. But, then again, I think this was the first time Grettir had ever praised him. After a moment, he grinned back.

As I watched the group disperse, I suddenly realised that Eduard and Cuthbert were not the boys I once knew: we were growing up and were now almost the warriors we had always dreamed about. I had longed for the day when I would go away

47

to fight, but now it seemed certain that we would, I began to think about how I would react when battle came at last. Idly, I thrust my spear forward in a heroic stance imaging myself, as I often did, as a hero. I was roused from my day dreams by a sarcastic taunt from behind me.

"The great warrior, huh!" It was Hussa. I turned to see him twenty yards away, lurking in the shadows beneath a beech tree. I walked over to him.

"Hussa, what is it with you? I've never done you wrong. So why do you sneer and snarl at me like this?"

Hussa stared back at me, his dark eyes failing to hide what seemed like an ocean of hate, though his face was still blank – expressionless.

"Oh no, you have never done any wrong, how could you – the beloved son of your father – ever do wrong? But your father, ah ... that's another tale," he replied.

"My father, what's this to do with my father?"

"It has everything to do with your father! How it angers me to see him strutting about as a lord and a close friend to Lord Wallace. Even due to play host to the Prince tomorrow. Yet, if we go back seventeen years he was a philanderer and a seducer of women. Women who saw in his strong, muscular form, something they yearned for. Women like my mother!"

"What are you saying, Hussa?" I demanded.

"Were you hit in the head today? Certainly you don't seem to be thinking straight. What I'm saying is that your father is also my father. I was born from a summer's fling. Your dear beloved father mated with my mother when your mother was with child – with you."

I stared at him, unable to accept what he was saying.

"No, it's not true!" I exclaimed, shaking my head.

48

"Why do you think your father gives us food? Your mother found out and insisted that he cut all ties with my mother. Wallace discovered what had happened and it was agreed that it would all be kept a secret if your father would supply food and other goods during each Feorm. Mother and I always hoped that one day he would acknowledge me. But as you will recall, he still refuses even to talk to me."

He turned away, but not before I had seen the tears that had come to his eyes.

So, this is what those deliveries of food down that side lane had been about all these years. But, if my father was Hussa's as well ...that made us half-brothers. Hussa was the rejected son, turned away from the family and deprived of the affection and warmth I had known as a child. I could see why that would anger him.

"Hussa ... I'm sorry, maybe though I can talk to Father and he will, oh I don't know, be kinder to you and your mother." Hussa laughed hollowly at that and still faced away from me.

"For some of us, that would be too late," he said.

"Why?"

"Because my mother died last winter – with a fever. Your father never even sent a message, the bastard."

"Hussa, I'm sorry – I didn't know, really I didn't," I said and his head snapped round to look at me. A scowl came to his face, giving it at last some animation.

"I don't want sympathy, Cerdic, from you least of all," he said.

"Hussa, I said I'm sorry. We do not need to be enemies."

"Ah, but we do. For two people's share of pain and rejection for seventeen years we do. For what I could have been – son of a lord and not the bastard of a peasant – we do. It's your fault, Cerdic. Ah, to hell with you ...," his voice trailed off. After glar-

49

ing at me a moment longer, he turned and went away, leaving me staring after him wanting to say something, but really not sure what and burning with resentment, for how could it be my fault?

The day of the muster came at last and we were kept busy from early dawn, getting the Villa ready. Prince Aethelric was coming and like everyone else, he would be staying the night. My parents gave their room – the largest and best in the Villa – over to him. It had to be swept clean and Mildrith and Sunniva were sent to the river to collect fresh rushes and Aidith to the meadows to pick new flowers to perfume the room. I was ejected from my room, which I shared with Cuthwine and that was given to my parents, whilst Lord Wallace got Mildrith's room – she was moving in with Sunniva for the night. Cuthwine and I would be finding a bed in the barn, with the rest of the company.

"Not that I expect we will get much sleep tonight, Cerdic," Cuthwine said, "far too much ale to be drunk."

At this moment, Aidith passed with the flowers and I let my gaze linger on her as she walked by.

"Maybe tonight you won't get sleep for another reason, eh brother?" Cuthwine said with a wink and an elbow in the ribs. I was still looking the way Aidith had gone, suddenly aware that there was more to being a man than just swords. Maybe tonight I would be lucky, I thought.

Two lambs and a calf were slaughtered and a huge fire pit dug to roast the animals, which were suspended over it. They would roast all day and be ready for hungry men at nightfall.

At noon, the men started to drift in from the villages, followed soon after by Lord Wallace, who was mounted and leading his thirty warriors from the town. We joined them in a field and for the first time, just short of one hundred men were gathered, all armed with spears, axes and knives and carrying shields. A few had armour and even fewer, swords. They looked tatty and far from ready for war. But this – what was to be known as the Wicstun Company – would, before the first leaves of autumn fell and with me in its ranks, achieve glory and fame amid the blood and horror of a battlefield. The naive youth that I was would have been thrilled to know this. Now that I know the truth, when I think back on that summer, a lump comes to my throat. For the truth is that half these men would be dead or wounded before those same leaves fell.

Hussa was also in the company, but he avoided me and stood towards the other end of the line. That afternoon, we marched back and forth and practised moving as one body, three ranks deep and with shields locked behind other shields and spears held high, as Grettir had taught us.

Aethelric arrived mid-afternoon, with a small escort. He was older than I expected: a man in his mid-forties, with grey, balding hair, more weight about his middle than you would want and a slightly nervous look about him as if he was afraid he would get it all wrong. Not exactly the image of a great warrior prince. I muttered this to Cuthwine, as we stood in our ranks waiting for him to inspect us.

"That's the problem when your father lives a long time. A king should inherit when he is young and strong. That's what I think. But Aelle though old, just keeps on going. He must be not far off seventy now."

"Even so, you'd think the Prince would try to look after himself a little more. Wallace is getting on a bit too, but look at him."

We did. Wallace was as old as Grettir, both of them older than Aethelric, but both looking muscular despite a predilection for ale, at least on Wallace's part. Wallace was telling the Prince

51

about how he had organised the company and was pointing out veterans like Grettir and Cuthwine.

"Think about it," Cuthwine went on, "Aethelric was my age when Aelle led the armies to capture Eoforwic. Since then we have had no wars and only a few raids or bandits to contend with. There is only so much hunting a man can do. Don't suppose he ploughs many fields, do you? After a while of sitting on your arse, it all goes flabby."

I sniggered at that.

Aethelric was likeable enough, though, in person. Cuthwine and I were called forward with Father to be introduced.

"Splendid looking chaps you have got there, Lord Cenred," the Prince said, eyeing us both. Do a father proud. Strong and tall like my own son," he said.

Father thanked him. The Prince just stood there, nodding and smiling cheerfully, waiting for something else to happen. My father waggled his eyebrows at Wallace to get his attention.

"Maybe, your Highness, you would like to inspect the company?" Wallace suggested, taking the hint.

"Erm, what's that? Inspect? Yes, that seems fair. It's what I am here for. Check the army and make sure it is ready," he intoned, as if he was repeating orders from the King.

To be fair by him, he made a good job of this bit. He did not seem much of a leader, but he was friendly and cheerful and would stop at a man and ask him where he came from and soon they would be deep in conversation about planting beans and what the apples would be like this year.

I wondered if Cuthwine was wrong and whether he did know how to plough a field. In fact, once I had thought it, the image of Aethelric as a cheerful ruddy-faced farmer stuck in my head: a man who was born in the wrong place and just trying to do his best.

With him stopping and chatting to every third man, it took a good hour to inspect us and my legs and arms were aching from standing and holding a spear for so long. Eventually though, he returned to the front and looked expectantly at Wallace.

Wallace had arranged for a small grandstand to be built in one of our fields and he, Father and the Prince, along with his party and my family took seats there. The company competed in tournaments for the next couple of hours. Cuthbert shocked everyone, apart from Eduard and me, by winning the archery competition. There was no surprise, however, when Eduard defeated all comers in the wrestling.

The finale was to be a grand melee with sword and shield. Only then did I discover that the prize was to be the magnificent blade crafted by Grothir of Wicstun: the very one I had long coveted. The blacksmith handed it to Prince Aethelric, who held it aloft so all could see. A barely audible sigh emerged from the company as every man in its ranks observed it, wanted it and longed for it, each man having the same thought: just win today and it will be mine.

We were paired up and fought with mock swords and wicker shields. The winner was to be the first to achieve a hit with his wooden blade on the torso of the other. Cuthbert and I were paired first and it was no surprise when a few moments later, I landed him a nasty smack on his ribs. He went off glaring at me and rubbing his side. As each pair's fight was decided, the vanquished withdrew and new pairs were created. The bouts went on for over an hour but, slowly, we were whittled down to a handful.

I started to think that I might manage to reach the final pair, perhaps even to win. Glancing around, I saw there were now only four pairs left.

Cuthwine was fighting a lad from Little Compton, who was about my age. The young boy was outclassed and Cuthwine stepped to one side as he attacked, deflected the lad's sword and then brought his blade back to deliver a blow in the poor fellow's stomach. I grimaced as I heard the air rush out of the lad and then, with a groan, he collapsed to the ground. Cuthwine helped him back to his feet, smiled at him, added a quick "Well done, good try," and looked for his next challenger.

Meanwhile, I had taken on a huge blond-haired brute from a farm near Wicstun. He was a terror to all the local lads when we were younger, relying on fear and intimidation to get his way. He roared at me, but when I stood my ground and did not flinch, he seemed to have exhausted his options, so when I moved inside his blade and lightly tapped him on the chest, he just looked at me stupidly and stomped off the field.

Eduard was still in the fight, but met his match in Grettir who, despite his age, had a lifetime's experience. Eduard was big and strong and relied on that to batter down a foe's defences and then, when the enemy was staggering, would look to land the killer blow.

Grettir just absorbed the blows on his shield looking, frankly, a bit bored. Then, when Eduard paused to catch his breath he suddenly struck, thrusting the sword forward with a vicious stabbing motion that caught my friend by total surprise. Grettir nodded at him as he stomped off and the look seemed to say, 'Not bad, but you can do better.'

Hussà was still in the melee, moving lithely back and forth, dodging this way and that. His opponent was a dull-looking man in his twenties, who looked confused and bewildered. He tried to swing his sword down onto Hussa's shoulders, but

54

Hussa was too quick and was already past him, then clouted him on the back.

It was now Hussa's turn to square up against the old veteran, Grettir, in his semi-final match. It was a good contest: wisdom and experience against youth and agility. In the end, Grettir, tiring after the five previous bouts, was flagging a little despite his stamina and Hussa, who still looked fresh, kept moving until Grettir made a tiny error and paid for it. A good loser, Grettir slapped the boy on the back and smiled before stomping off the field. Hussa stepped to the side to wait for his final opponent, which was to be either Cuthwine or me.

Cuthwine and I had trained together many times over the last few months so, although he was more experienced than I was, I knew most of his moves and was also slightly quicker. As a result, we were well matched and exchanged thrust and counter thrust, parry and swing for a full ten minutes, until we were both getting exhausted. In the end, I tried to finish the fight by rushing him. It was a mistake and I felt my foot slip from under me and I fell. Ironically, that is what saved me as I passed under his attack. Somehow, as my arms flailed about wildly, my sword managed to connect with his body. He just stood there, glared down at me and then shook his head, not believing what had happened.

"You lucky bastard!" he groaned then reached down to pull me to my feet, whilst all around us the audience howled with laughter. When I took my place for the final round, a rueful smile was on my face.

So, that left just me and Hussa. Just one more fight, I told myself. Just one more win and the sword would be mine. I glanced over at my parents. Father was talking to Aethelric and pointing at me. He seemed to be avoiding looking at Hussa, but then I caught him glance at him for a moment and in his eyes I saw, what: guilt, pain? I was not sure.

Then, I looked at my mother and a chill shot down my spine. She was not looking at Cuthwine or me, but straight at Hussa and it was a look of implacable hatred.

Here, she seemed to be thinking, was living proof of her husband's infidelity. For years, she had managed to keep that distasteful memory remote from her life but, today, here was her husband's bastard son, Hussa, in plain view of all. I wondered how she knew it was he, for he was not much like Father, but there is never any point in trying to fathom a woman's instinct. I turned back to Hussa and saw that he had seen my mother's expression and returned it. Of course, he might resent me and our father, but it was this woman who, in his eyes, had ruined his life and destroyed his mother.

His face took on a dangerous expression and he now fixed me with an appraising stare, as he swung his sword in a gentle arc and shifted the weight of his shield. Then, in a flash, he was on me. I might have expected fury and as a result recklessness, but there was none of that. His moves were calculated, driven by ice cold anger: which focused his mind on the fight. As a result, every attack was threatening and any one of them could have potentially won the bout. Forced onto the defence, I just blocked and parried each attack as I watched him and waited for my chance.

He lunged at me and I caught the blade with my shield then followed up with a swing from the side. He danced out of the way and my momentum took me past him. I could feel my heart pounding as I turned to face him, just in time to see the thrust coming towards my neck.

I flinched back, staggering away from him, but I had to open

56

my arms to balance myself so he came on again, attacking the gap in my defences. This time, it was he who overstepped and I slammed my shield into his side sending him sprawling onto the grass, trapping his own shield under him. I was over him now, ready to finish the fight. In my moment of triumph, I looked away to see if Aidith was watching. She was and she smiled at me and gave a little wave, so I smiled back feeling a surge of elation. Maybe, Cuthwine was right and today my luck was in.

Then: disaster! I had wasted that moment of chance: I had done what Hussa had done in the woods and looked to see who was watching me and now I paid for my pride. Hussa sprang to a crouch and at last red hot fury did show on his face as he thrust the wooden sword violently up into my belly. I crumpled into a ball of agony and fell on the grass.

Hussa howled out his triumph and pointed his sword towards my parents. Beneath him, I rose to my knees and retched. Then, I slammed my fists on the ground in frustration, staggered to my feet and limped off the field, feeling my face burning. I was not really hurt – but I was angry, very angry. But not at Hussa – I was fuming at myself for the mistake I had made. If only I could go back a few moments: if only I had just finished the fight, rather than wallowed in the glory. Then, I would be the victor. It was a hard lesson to learn, but learn it I did. Never again would I allow pride to trip me up.

That day, though, Hussa had won. He swaggered up to the Prince who, oblivious of all the anger and hatred on this field, just beamed at him.

"Well done, young man, what is your name?"

"Hussa, Sire."

"That was a good fight and you deserve this sword," he said, and then he raised his voice, "I give this sword in honour of a great victory to Hussa, son of … erm," with a whisper he added, "what is your father's name, boy?"

My parents' faces went pale and, close by me, I heard Cuthwine gasp. Hussa looked over at my father and smiled a mirthless smile and for a heartbeat, I thought he would say what had happened seventeen years before, but he just shrugged and then looked back at Aethelric.

"I have no father, Sire," he said, his voice bitter. "He abandoned my mother when she was with child."

"Ah well," Aethelric coughed, "I give this sword to Hussa of Wicstun. Well done."

Hussa bowed, then took the sword and held it up so we could all see it. The Wicstun boys cheered at this and Wallace applauded too, although I saw him looking at my parents and biting his lip. But I said nothing and neither did I applaud. I was staring at the sword. I wanted a sword so badly: I had wanted that sword so badly and now Hussa had it! I could almost hear the gods laughing.

That was the end of the tournament and it was now time to eat. I wandered over to my friends and Cuthbert patted me on the shoulder as a consolation.

"Bad luck, come on, let's get some ale," Eduard said and I nodded. Then I froze, because I had just seen a girl go over to Hussa and examine the sword with him. Hussa said something and she laughed. I felt hollow inside, because I had just realised the girl was Aidith. Hussa pointed towards the barn and Aidith nodded her head and they went in together. Jealousy raged within me and I gasped with the pain of it, as though a mule had just kicked me in the belly. Cuthwine came over to me and pushed me after them.

"Come on, brother, looks like you lost the sword and the girl

58

tonight. Never mind, there's always ale."

The feast that night was spectacular. Mother had made sure the finest food and the best of our beer was served by Caerfydd, Gwen and Aedann. There was roast beef and lamb, fresh and warm bread, fruit preserved in jars through the winter, sweetened with honey and our most delicious cheeses. The ale was outstanding: warming, bitter and very strong.

My mother revelled in the evening. This was her moment, when she showed the world the wonders of her tables and made sure that tonight was a feast no one would ever forget. She was dressed in a startling emerald-green gown, trimmed with gold thread. Father had bought it for her a while ago, but she had never worn it before, saving it, she always said, for a special day. This, at last, was the day.

The coming of a Prince, along with such a large gathering of warriors, was worthy of such a dress, but what really drew every man's eyes to her was a fabulous set of jewellery. It was a necklace, bangles and headdress of priceless amber, mounted in a setting of exquisite silver. The set was given by King Aelle in recognition of my uncle's valour in battle against the Welsh of Eboracum. In gratitude for his victory, the King gave it to the widow of the great hero. My aunt had died childless a few years ago and the set then passed to my father, who gave it to my mother. Of all the men at the feast, only Cuthwine, Father and I had seen it before.

A hundred men and more sat, ate and drank and as the cups were filled and refilled, they started to forget the clouds of gloom that lay over the future and they laughed and sang. They laughed and sang: but I did not. I was on one end of the high table and from there, I could see Aidith pouring Hussa some more ale and laughing again at his jokes.

Every so often, I would see him glance up at our table. He would look at me with a smug smile and lean closer to Aidith. Or, he would stare with spite and loathing at my mother and father, whose food and drink he now enjoyed. I once saw mother glare back at him, but then look away. The gracious hostess could not deny him being there – the champion of today's games and so, nor could I. So, I sat alone, sulking and sipping my ale.

Lilla, of course, was present. Once enough ale had been drunk, men called for the harpist to come and sing and tell his tales and Lilla obliged. He told the tale of my uncle and his battles against the Welsh, of Aelle and the conquest of Eboracum. Then, having seen the firelight reflected in Mother's amber jewellery, he told tales of the distant Baltic Sea, from where the jewels came and wherein the sea serpents lived.

He then told us that the tales must go on and he was now waiting to sing songs about us; of our battles and our glories so that, a thousand years from now, men would still talk about us and remember what we had done. It's what the men wanted to hear and they hammered on the tables so hard that many jugs of ale fell over and Aedann had to bring more, so the men could go on drinking long into the night and I – miserable because I had lost both the sword and the girl – joined in, until I remembered no more.

The next morning, I felt sick and my head was pounding when Eduard kicked me awake.

"Go away, you bastard!" I yelled, but he just laughed.

"Come on, Cerdic, everyone else is up and ready for the hunt!"

The hunt! I had forgotten that Aethelric had given permission for the company to go boar hunting in the royal forests. These were west of the village and ran right up to the river, which was the border with Elmet. Groaning, I dragged myself to my feet

60

and was promptly sick.

Eduard watched me for a moment.

"Better now?" he asked.

I nodded.

"Yes actually."

"Let's go, then!" Eduard roared and I groaned again, holding my throbbing head. Outside, the company was assembling and I saw, from the number of green faces, that I was not the only one to have had too much ale last night. I searched the crowd for Hussa noticing with distress that he looked fresh and was now swaggering about, wearing his new sword. Aethelric and Wallace soon arrived and we were off.

It took us an hour to reach the woods we were to hunt in. Once there, we separated into small groups, each man taking a boar spear. This was shorter than a war spear and designed to be much more mobile. A small cross piece, just below the point, is welded on to stop the beast carrying on towards you if you manage to skewer it.

Wild boar hunting is dangerous. A fully grown adult can weight much the same as a man. The beast is armed with fearsome tusks and is enormously strong and powerful. In short bursts it can cover ground with breathtaking speed. There was a very real danger of injury or death, so we hunted in pairs: each looking out for the other. The forest was dense and Eduard and I – hunting together – soon lost track of everyone else.

We crept along, searching the undergrowth for movement, for what seemed like hours but without success and I had just turned round to tell Eduard we should head back, when there was a snort from behind me. Spinning round, I saw a flash of a red and brown mass for an instant, before something huge and hard thumped me in the abdomen – still a little sore from the previous night's fight – and knocked me over, stunned and with stars flashing in my eyes.

Eduard shouted something and then I heard him charging towards us. The next few moments were all flashing steel, the roaring of the beast, grunts from my friend and finally a squeal of pain and then: silence. My vision cleared and when I could see again, I saw that the beast was dead and Eduard stood triumphantly over it. I dragged myself to my feet and staggered across to him.

"Nice work," I said.

"Yes, it was, wasn't it?" he answered with a grin, never one to be shy of self praise.

We took the boar back to the glade and soon afterwards the other groups started to arrive. Aethelric drifted around us, stopping at each man or boy who had killed a boar and congratulating them in his vague but enthusiastic way and then he stood, looking a bit lost, before Wallace suggested that he and Cuthwine escort the Prince and his party back to Wicstun.

After he left, we prepared to carry the wild pigs home, strapped to long branches. Eduard was still proudly showing Cuthbert the boar he had killed, when Wallace looked around the company and asked where Hussa was. We all looked up and searched the faces around us. None of us knew where he was; indeed, no one had seen him since soon after the company had split up some six hours before. No one, it seemed, had been his partner, as it now emerged that he had been bragging about his sword until everyone got bored and he went off in a sulk.

"Oh, bother the lad: we'll have to go and find him!" Wallace was saying, when there was a rustle of undergrowth nearby and Hussa emerged from the trees. He looked pale, blood was drying on his face and he had lost his boar spear.

"Where the hell have you been?" Wallace demanded.

Hussa collapsed onto the ground in front of him then lay there panting for a moment, before replying.

"Went off on my own, didn't I ... my Lord? Thought, I could kill a boar by myself."

"Did you?" Eduard asked.

Hussa gave him a blank look.

"What do you think? I found one alright, but it charged me. I missed it with my spear and suddenly it was on me and I was knocked backwards, tripped on a tree and landed half way down a slope on my arse."

"Dammed idiot, you could have got killed. Don't be so foolish in future," Wallace said. Hussa nodded.

"No Lord, I won't."

Well, I must admit I felt better. Hussa had been strutting around the night before, showing off his sword and the gods alone knew what he and Aidith had got up to. Now though, his reputation was tarnished. Fool that he was for getting knocked down by a boar, no one would mind that. Going off in a sulk though, that's what folk objected to.

We shuffled off towards home, tired, but on the whole, happy. Many men had daring tales to tell and after all, roast pork was on the menu. Soon we were laughing and joking, exaggerating our own glories whilst snorting in light-hearted derision at the others' stories.

We reached the edges of the forest, where we paused for a moment to rest and drink from a stream before the company separated – us to go due east to the village and the rest bearing northeast for Wicstun and beyond.

As we rested, Cuthbert confessed to us that he had cheated and taken his bow, but had still managed to wound a pig and slow it so his partner could kill it. He laughed as he told us the tale.

Then, his grin faded and his eyes widened as he stared over Grettir's shoulders, through the trees to the east. I turned to follow his gaze. Beyond the trees, I could see the dim, red glow of fire and the spring evening sky was heavy with dark, black, smoke. Yet, there was nothing else in that direction for many miles, apart from ... my home. I felt my heart sink with the grim realisation that it could only be Cerdham and the Villa. Around me, the company had spotted it too and were rising to their feet, alarm spreading.

Eduard and Cuthbert set off at once through the undergrowth, followed by several other boys from the village. Grettir screamed after them to stop, but it was no use: they had vanished to the east. Grettir seemed about to pursue them, when suddenly Hussa pointed further to the north.

More fire. More smoke.

"It's Wicstun: Wicstun is on fire!" he shouted, sounding not just shocked, but almost affronted as if it was a personal insult. A moment later, he set off that way, followed by most of the other boys. Again, Grettir tried to stop them, but it was no use. The boys were now just worrying about their families and their homes and blind panic had set in. I spun round, staring at Grettir, then in the direction my friends had run, and then towards Wicstun.

Wicstun was on fire!

Cerdham was on fire!

What, in Woden's name, was going on?

64

Chapter Six
Raid on the Villa

Grettir turned to me and shouted, "Master, please follow the village lads and I'll find you later. I'd better go with these town idiots and make sure they reach home safely."

Nodding, I turned and ran east in the wake of my friends.

"I'll find you at the Villa – or here if Cerdham is not safe," my instructor shouted after me, as I crashed through the branches. I saw him head off northwards, running surprisingly quickly for a man of almost fifty odd summers and then he was gone, invisible among the oak and beech trees.

My friends had a few moments' lead and were already out of sight through the trees, but I could still hear them up ahead and I set off in pursuit. While I ran, the branches whipped at my face and then snagged and tore at my clothes. I almost tripped over a large log buried deep in the undergrowth, staggered a few steps, managed to keep upright and was off again.

Ahead of me, there was a sudden yelp of alarm, followed by the sound of something heavy hitting water. I pushed a willow branch aside then it was I who cried out, as my feet seemed to sink into the ground and then slip away from under me. I just managed to hold onto the branch to stop myself falling and then looked down to see I was standing on a sandy bank of another stream that ran through the royal hunting woods. I had slipped on the sand and would have ended up in the stream, were it not for the branch. Eduard, it seemed, had not been so lucky and had ended up on his back in the water. Beyond him, I could just see Cuthbert disappearing through the woods on the far side: he had obviously managed to react in time and leap over the stream. I could not see the other lads from the village, so I figured that they must have become separated in the woods.

"Cuthbert – wait!" I shouted after him but, whether he heard or not, he continued running.

"Woden's arse!" I cursed and looked down at Eduard who sat in the stream, drenched through. I frowned at him then reached down and gave him my hand and heaved him up. We crossed the stream and took to the chase again, with Eduard lumbering along behind me.

Soon, the trees began to break up and become sparser and the undergrowth vanished. I could now see the west end of the village and the orchard. Several of the villagers' huts were burning. One of them – I feared it was Eduard's – was fully ablaze. Behind me, I heard my friend give a shout and then a cry of despair and we paused and both stared in horror at the scene before us.

Cuthbert was a hundred yards ahead, approaching the fence around the village. Past him, I could now see figures silhouetted by the fire moving about and I could hear screams of agony and shouts of panic. What puzzled me was that no one seemed to be trying to put out the fire: why was no one getting water from the stream to the south and how was it possible that the whole village could be on fire? We started off again.

Suddenly, Cuthbert stopped running and dropped into a crouch. I caught up with him a few moments later and he turned to me, signalling for silence – one finger moving to his lips. He then pointed the same, trembling finger, towards the village.

I peered through the gloom, squinting to make out details against the glare of fire. Along the main street of the village, there were shapes lying in the dirt. It took me a moment before the realisation came to me that these lifeless lumps were the bodies of some of the village men folk. A number were lying face down in a pool of their own blood, whilst others looked like rag dolls that some careless child had discarded and which had landed on a barrel here, or a sack of flour there. The screams and sobs we had heard were from half a dozen women and as many children, who were, even now, being rounded up by a mob of dark-haired warriors, who each carried a spear and a shield: spears which now dripped with the blood of our own men.

"Who are they, Cerdic?" Cuthbert whispered.

"I'm not sure, but I guess they are Welsh – from Elmet," I answered. "They must be a raiding party. It looks to me like they took the village by surprise."

I glanced again at the bodies in the street, noticing now that some of them had spears and axes lying nearby and I added, "Mind you, some at least of our men tried to fight."

Suddenly, I thought of my family and I knew that I must get to the Villa. Eduard joined us at that point, puffing a little he stood and stared at the sight in front of us. Then, a moment later, he set off towards his hut. I had been right: it was his hut that was burning so heavily. If he reached the hut, he ... we would be spotted. I had to stop him! I launched myself forward, knocking him onto his front. He hit the ground hard, air whooshing out of his lungs.

"What in the name of Thunor's balls ...!" Eduard hissed.

"Quiet Eduard, we must be quiet or we will get caught."

"Let me go, I'm going to kill the bastards," Eduard threatened, as he thrashed about to get free from me. I sat on him, struggling to hold him down whilst I tried to work out what to do. Eduard, though, is the strongest man I know and he was beginning to push me off when I noticed some activity in the village.

"Stop it, Eduard: look over there."

Three Welsh warriors had rounded up all the women and children and had tied their wrists behind their backs. Our people looked miserable and terrified and most were crying. Several of the women's clothing had been torn and some were showing their breasts. For a seventeen-year-old lad that gave me an odd feeling: seeing in the middle of all this smoke, blood and death that which at another time would have been arousing, seemed to emphasise the horror of what was going on.

A scream from a young woman brought me back to hard reality and I felt ashamed. The Welsh were prodding the captives with their spear butts and forcing them to begin walking towards us. One of the young women – I think it was Aidith – had slipped and fallen and the lead warrior, a tall stocky fellow with hair as black as night and cold unfeeling eyes, had kicked her and snarled some words in their outlandish speech. Almost I broke cover, so angry was I at this outrage, but something held me back. Common sense or cowardice? I have never been sure.

Aidith got up slowly, holding her side and began walking again, towards the setting sun. The others, wailing and sobbing, followed along behind like sheep afraid of a dog. No wonder they cried, I thought, they knew they were being taken away into slavery. I thumped the ground in frustration. How on earth could this be happening? We all thought we were safe here. Where was our army?

Then the realisation hit me: by Woden, we were the army!

The enemy warriors came on towards us, leading their captives along and I realised we would be discovered as soon as they passed through the fence. Eduard had begun to struggle again, beneath me.

"Come on, Cerdic, we can't let them take our people," he said. Nodding, though still looking terrified, Cuthbert agreed and so did I.

I glanced past the captives and their guards towards the Villa.

I could see no more Welsh, but the sound of the crashing of sword on shield and the screams of wounded men told me they had moved on over there now. I spared a brief thought for my father, mother, brother and sisters. Were they alive? Were they dead?

There was no time to think about my family for long, because the enemy warriors were now getting very close and I felt my belly become all knotted up, so I prayed to the Valkyries to keep my bowels from emptying. The look of fear on Cuthbert's face told me that he felt the same way. Eduard, however, showed no fear; instead his expression indicated that he had just one thought: murder!

The three Welsh warriors all looked alarmingly strong. The lead fellow's arms carried scars that spoke of many battles. The other two were younger, but looked just as confident. Our only hope here was surprise. If the raiders had come from the west, they must have missed us as we hunted our wild pigs in the woods. As such, they would not expect an attack from this direction. I indicated to my friends to follow me and then ran south a little way, to where the grass in the meadow was long. I then crouched down. The others did likewise. I pointed at Cuthbert's bow and then at the lead warrior. I then held up my fore and middle fingers. I wanted two arrows fired at him. Cuthbert gulped hard, his lips twitching, but he nodded and then pulled the bow from his shoulder, strung it and took the three arrows he had thrust through his belt. These he stabbed into the ground in front of him so as to have them ready for use. He took one and loaded it onto the bow string. I held my hand up to tell him to hold fire a moment and he pointed the bow down to the ground.

I now drew out my long seax. It was a gift from my grandfather when I was just four, although Father had not let me carry it until I was eight. I had no sword, but this was sharp and broad and would have to do. Eduard was not armed and I was worried about that. Indeed, I was worried about the whole situation. We were just three seventeen-year-old boys. Our village's strongest men had been killed: how could we hope to defeat even three experienced warriors, the youngest of whom must be five years our elder. Eduard seemed to sense my hesitation. He made a fist and punched it against his other palm – clearly he was ready.

The warriors and their miserable booty were now quite close. They were moving more southerly now. I looked around and saw that the grass behind me was trodden down, so the Welsh had come up from the Humber. They must have followed it from Elmet before striking north and east to the village.

I whispered to Cuthbert, "Now!"

My friend nodded and then rose out of the grass. He brought his left arm up and locked the elbow, then drew back on the string. He aimed the arrow head at the lead warrior, who was now only thirty paces away. Cuthbert held his breath for an instant then let the arrow fly. There was a look of startled horror on the face of his target and then a sickening sound as the missile punctured his chest. He gave a brief cry of pain and fell forward onto his knees. For a moment, I didn't move. Despite the years of training for war, this was the first time I had seen a man actually hit by bow or blade. Then, to my right, Eduard burst up from the grass and charged straight for the second guard.

I recovered my senses as Cuthbert's second arrow left his bow and flew towards the wounded foe. It hit him in the throat and the man's hand flew up to grasp the arrow, shock and disbelief showing in his wide eyes. Then he tumbled full length onto the grass; already dead. I ran forward ten yards behind Eduard, feeling the blood pumping through my veins and my heart pounding like a blacksmith's hammer. Suddenly, the fear was gone and all I now wanted was to kill these bastards and make them pay for what they had done to us.

The women and children started screaming and crouched down in the grass, shielding their heads with their arms. As yet they did not recognise us: and why should they? We were bellowing and screaming in fury, faces distorted with rage and vengeance – hardly the friendly lads they all knew from around the village.

The second guard, a man of maybe twenty summers, looked more puzzled than surprised, as if he could not quite understand what was happening. Eduard was five yards from him, when the warrior finally spotted him and quickly tried to bring his spear point to bear. He had been walking along with the shaft leaning casually against his right shoulder and it took him a few moments to swing it down to point it at Eduard. Moments later, Eduard arrived in front of him, running so fast that he could not slow down in time. Had he arrived a heartbeat later, he would have taken the point firmly in the chest and his own weight would have impaled him upon it.

Fate and the Valkyries must have been watching him that day for the point was angled still slightly up so, although it hit him, it was deflected off his shoulder, piercing muscle and ripping a gash right up to his neck. He gave an agonizing cry at the pain but then ploughed headlong into the warrior. They both tumbled over and landed heavily on the ground, which knocked the wind out of them, the guard ending up underneath my friend.

I now arrived at the floundering pair, knife in hand. The Welsh lad was looking up at me, eyes showing the fear he must now feel. Realising that I must thrust my blade into him, my rage dispersed and all I could feel was the bile rising into my throat.

71

I knew I had to do this thing: think of Aidith, think of Eduard, I told myself and I moved towards the enemy.

Fate now took a hand again and spared me the choice. For, at that moment, the third Welsh warrior bellowed a war cry full of hate. He was a dozen yards away, following the line of villagers. I could see that he was some twenty-five years old and had the same dark black hair as the other two. Indeed, there was a shape to the face and a look in his eyes that was similar to the older warrior whom Cuthbert had shot. The thought occurred to me then that these three might all be brothers.

I had no time to debate such matters: he was already moving towards me. He had dropped his spear and drawn a sword, whose blade gleamed and shone red under the sunset light. He swung it from side to side as he closed upon me, a man set on revenge for a dead brother. He was close now: just five yards away. I glanced down at my short knife and sighed. So it would end here. I would be just one more youth slain this day. After all, he was a strong and fierce warrior; I was just a boy who, only yesterday, was practising with wicker shields on the last spring afternoon of my childhood.

I should run, I thought. Get away, survive – but I could not. Whether I was frozen in terror or held by some feeling of honour and duty, I cannot recall. I tried to think of some ferocious battle cry or threat to intimidate him, but it was already too late. He moved in and swung back his blade to cut down on my shoulder. I moved my knife up to block the blow, realising as I did, that he would knock it aside with ease.

Then, I heard a buzzing noise past my right ear. An instant later, I could see an arrow embedded in the warrior's left arm. He gave a cry of pain, moved his right hand across as a reflex and dropped the sword. In a flash, I was on him. I thrust the

knife hard into his upper abdomen, beneath his ribs and felt it
ram home. Blood gushed out of the wound and ran hotly down
my arm, drenching my tunic. He stared at me in horror, grabbed
my shoulder with his hands and pulled me towards him. Even
with a knife in his gut, the strength he had was surprising, but it
began to drain away as his life blood ran down me. Finally, his
hands released me and he slumped down, first onto his knees
and then, with a groan, onto his front.

Turning round, I could see that Eduard was still punching
the other warrior with his good arm. The Welshman's head hit
the ground with the sound of splintering bone that told me he
had hit a rock or stone and he now lay completely still, perhaps
dead, perhaps knocked out. Eduard, holding a hand over his
still bleeding wound, slumped down next to his enemy then
he looked up at me for a moment, eyes unfocused at first. He
blinked and dragging himself over, collapsed on the ground
beside me. We glanced over at Cuthbert. He was still crouching
in the grass, bow in his left hand staring open-mouthed at what
he had just seen. Then, suddenly, he laughed.

"I wonder what old Grettir will say about this!" he said.

We had done it! Three youths barely out of childhood, had
fought their first battle and won. For a moment I just nodded
at Cuthbert and then the sound of a baby crying in the arms
of a village woman brought me back to the present. The villagers were still staring at us, fear yet lingering in their eyes then,
Cybilla – Cuthbert's mother – bustled over.

"Woden bless you, Master Cerdic, you've saved us all from
this filth."

She rushed past me and over to her son, who cut her bonds
with his small dagger and then embraced her. A moment later,
we were surrounded by crying and laughing women and chil-

dren. We cut them free and Aidith tore a strip of linen from her dress and used it to bind Eduard's wound. She then came over to me and without warning, gave me a brief but intensely passionate kiss that left me staggering. I stared at her, desperate for something to say, but lost for words.

"Do I get one of those as well?" Eduard asked. Aidith laughed and bending over pecked him lightly on the top of the head.

"Don't think much of that," he grumbled.

"That's the best you're getting, so don't complain," she muttered.

Reaching down, I picked up the Welshman's sword from the ground. It was short, compared to my uncle's, but felt heavier: a weapon made for the cut and thrust of a shield wall. It was well made and sturdy too. Not as pretty as Hussa's new blade, nor as legendary as my uncle's, but it was a sword taken in battle from a foe and that would do – for now. I examined it more closely. There were signs of dried blood along the blade and around the guard and I tried not to think which of the villagers had been struck down by it. That thought made me think, with sudden horror, about the Villa and my family. It was out of sight at present, beyond the orchard and the still burning village. I wanted to go there and find out what was going on, but then I looked at the villagers. Even though we had rescued them, they still looked scared and vulnerable and I could not just abandon them, could I? I bit my lip, realising that I was in two minds.

It suddenly occurred to me that we were all being rather too loud. We were standing in an open field only a few hundred yards from our burning village. Somewhere, not far away, there were more raiders and I did not want to get discovered here. I turned to the women.

"Quiet now, everyone," I ordered and was then rather surprised that most of the noise ceased. Was I no longer just a boy to them? Did they see me as their leader?

"We must find somewhere for you to hide. We cannot return to the village yet, it is far from safe," I began. I pointed with the sword towards the west, into the woods we had run through earlier.

"Through there the woods get denser. There is a stream some way into them. You can hide there and you will be safe overnight. By morning the raiders will have gone," I advised them.

At least I hoped the raiders would be gone. Perhaps I was wrong. Perhaps they were part of an invasion force. This land had been theirs before it had been ours. Maybe they had returned to reclaim it and drive us Angles out. In that case, no place would be safe. I prayed to the gods that I was right.

"But, Master Cerdic, you're coming with us, surely?" asked Cybilla and she looked at me imploringly. "It's not safe for you at the Villa and in any case ... we need you to protect us."

I looked east again, towards the Villa. In my mind, I saw an image of it burning and the Welsh rampaging all around it. I could imagine them looting my mother's food store and then dragging away cattle and poultry. Had my father used my uncle's sword to defend it? He was not a warrior. Had he fallen at the door to the house? Was he dead? What of Cuthwine the warrior and Sunniva my older sister? Images of her and Mildrith slain or raped flashed into my mind and I felt cold with fear for them all.

I then considered the women and children who stood around me here. Dark thoughts came again to me. What if they were found in the woods and dragged away to serve masters in Elmet? Some to be slain, others to become the playthings of Welsh warriors. I could not allow that. I was torn, all my instincts urged me

75

to go to the Villa, but common sense told me that it was already too late and that by now, whatever was going to happen had happened. I hesitated a moment longer then reached a decision: I could not leave these people prey to the Welsh. I had to protect them; what else could I do?

I turned back to Cybilla and I nodded my head. "Yes, Goodwife, I'm coming with you."

It was now getting quite dark. The moon was rising and I could see several stars. The village still burnt close at hand as, like a shepherd with his flock, I gathered the village folk to me. We then set out: me leading the way with the women in single file behind and Cerdic and Eduard following up in the rear. We walked back into the woods and pressed on into its depths. Soon, we had come back to the stream where Eduard had fallen, although it took half an hour for our slow moving party with its children and wounded. We halted there, washed away the smoke and blood and drank the cool water.

I scouted on ahead through the dense undergrowth. By now, it was full night and I had great difficulty seeing the way, but I was searching for a place to rest; a place to hide. I soon came to the stream where the company had rested just before we spotted the smoke. It was quiet and deserted; the abandoned kill from our hunt still lay where we had dropped it. I decided we would sleep here and go back to the village in the morning and find out what had happened to my family.

Suddenly, I saw movement up ahead behind a beech tree: a glint of metal in the moonlight and the crack of a twig snapping underfoot. I raised my new sword and braced myself, whilst my eyes strained to see in the gloom. Were there two eyes staring at me through the branches? My heart began to pound, then a voice spoke and I half jumped out of my skin with fright.

76

"I thought I taught you the warrior's pose better than that, Master Cerdic," said Grettir grinning and coming out of the deep shadow under the tree.

"Grettir, thanks be to Woden. How long have you been here?" I asked moving towards him. I then stopped when I noticed his left arm was in a sling and was bandaged. The bandages were oozing blood. He saw me examining his wounded limb and grunted.

"Don't worry about this, Master. I got careless and one of the Welsh raiders stabbed me in the arm, but it's just a scratch, really. I took his head off for it, so I think he learnt his lesson. I've been here only a few moments. I saw the lads back to Wicstun and then I returned to look for you."

Suddenly, he slumped against the tree, appearing exhausted and extremely pale: so perhaps he had lost more blood than he thought. I ran over and helped him to a tree stump that stuck up out of the undergrowth. I unwrapped the bandage and examined his wound: it was quite deep, several veins had been cut through and the wound bit deep into his muscle. I cleaned it with a little water and then bandaged it with torn cloth from my own shirt. I then fetched the villagers and the sorry looking band of dirty, bloodstained women and children staggered into the clearing and collapsed under the trees.

Grettir told us that the raiders had been attacking Wicstun, but they had been driven off by the townsfolk by the time he and the youths drew near. A small band of the enemy had encountered the boys as they fled west and there had been a brief fight. One of the Wicstun boys was hurt and two of the raiders had been slain, whilst the others had made their escape. My tutor, though, could not tell me what had occurred at the Villa, as he had not been there, so I still had no idea if any of my family still lived.

Cuthbert, Eduard and I took turns watching the trees for signs of the raiders while the villagers slept. Throughout the short spring night, my thoughts were of my family and the Villa. As I sat alone, staring into the gloom, the whole evening came back to me. The fear, the rage and the excitement echoed around my mind which, combined with the anxiety I felt about my family, brought on a sudden attack of nausea: a terrible hollow, gnawing feeling inside that made me want to retch and I wandered a few yards into the woods to find a bush to vomit into.

Just as I had finished, I heard a rustle of movement off in the woods, away to the south and I sank back into the shadows under the trees and froze. Nothing, though, came from that way and after a moment I breathed out slowly, but then caught my breath again when I heard a clear voice calling out. I was not sure … but it sounded Welsh.

My shield, sword and spear were back in the clearing. All I had was my knife and I drew it as I crept slowly towards the noises. Now I could hear more crashing in the trees and exchanges of conversation in an alien tongue. Soon, I came to the edge of another clearing, perhaps a hundred paces from where the villagers and my friends slept and I heard the voices again, but this time right in front of me. Startled, I crouched down quickly and hid behind a tree.

In the glade, five Welsh warriors were standing in a small group leaning on spears and drinking from clay pots that looked like the ones father stored his wine in. Behind the men, I could see a group of women and children being herded along by yet more warriors. Their hands were tied and a rope linked all the prisoners together in a long, miserable line. I did not see all the faces but, I was sure that one of them was the wife of the blacksmith from Wicstun and two of the children were from the village. So, we had not saved everyone – or so it seemed.

I raised my knife and then put it quickly away again. Clearly I could not hope to fight ten enemies alone. I thought about going back to fetch my friends and Grettir, but even then we would be outnumbered and by the time I roused them, it would be hard to find this group in the dark.

I watched the nearest group of warriors gathered around a huge man – easily a head higher than his fellows and broader than Eduard. He was dressed in leather armour overlaid with iron rings and plates sewn onto the leather, and on his head was a helmet of bronze and iron. Only the wealthiest men could afford armour, but that was not what most struck me about the warrior, rather it was the man's face.

It was cruel, his expression menacing as he watched the poor wretches trail by. The image was made all the more terrifying in the moonlight, due to the fact that his right eye was missing and his face was scarred, horribly, by what looked like an old axe or sword wound. Something stirred in my memory then – something from one of Lilla's stories. For a moment the warrior's one eye turned towards the woods where I lurked and seemed to search them. Had I made a noise, or had the moonlight caught my knife blade and betrayed me? I tensed and was ready to spring up and flee if needs be, but he glanced away from my hiding place and muttered something to the other men, which they laughed at.

After another few minutes, they drank up and tossed the empty pots towards the trees, cheering or jeering as each man hit or missed a trunk. One landed and shattered by my foot and I jumped, almost giving myself away, but they were moving off behind the prisoners and in moments were gone. I was just about to return to the villagers, when I saw another man emerge from the trees, going the same way as the others.

This was no warrior: this man I knew and I stared at him in confusion as I realised that it was Aedann, our slave. He was carrying a spear as well as a shield, which bore the Welsh Christian God's symbol upon it. I stood up and was about to yell after him, when two more Welsh warriors emerged, twenty yards behind him. They must have been able to see him ahead of them, across the glade, because they shouted a challenge at him. Aedann turned, answered them with a few words in Welsh, before passing into the woods ahead of them and was gone. Minutes later, they followed him and finally, the glade was silent. I was left alone to ponder what I had seen. Firstly: the prisoners – some from the village and some from Wicstun – being herded westwards, towards Elmet. Then Aedann, carrying a Welsh shield. Had he joined them? Had he taken advantage of the raid to make his escape? I turned back towards the villagers and found them still asleep. Should I rouse them and tell them? No – let them rest – dawn would come soon enough, with the sorrows it must bring. Then, we would go home and see what had happened.

In the middle of the night, Cuthbert relieved me from watch. I lay down on the ground next to the snoring Eduard and waited for sleep to take me. As I grew drowsy, images from the day flashed across my mind. I saw the horribly scarred face of the one-eyed Welsh warrior chieftain leading our people into slavery and in my dreams he looked at me, his face mocking, as if saying that I had failed these people and that he had won. Then the chieftain vanished and next I saw Aedann, walking along with a spear leaning against his shoulder. He glanced over at me with those brooding, dark green eyes and then, after a moment, he laughed. '*You thought I was your slave,*' he seemed to say. '*You*

80

fool: now I am free.' A moment later and then he too was gone and the last thing I was aware of, before oblivion came, was the terrified expression in the eyes of the man I had killed and the warm, sticky feeling of his blood running over my hands.

Lilla never mentioned that in his poems.

Chapter Seven
End of Childhood

In the morning, we led our charges back through the woods, eastwards towards the Villa. From yet some distance away, we could see a cloud of thick, black smoke and fumes hanging in the air over the smouldering huts and hovels of the village. One of the buildings was still burning: the cracking and popping sounds the only ones we could hear as we approached. At first I could see no sign of life: no villagers, or indeed any Welsh raiders. As we crossed the meadow in which the day before Edwin, Cuthbert and I had fought our first fight, we passed the bodies of the warriors we had slain. They still lay in the long grass with flies buzzing about them. A raven hopped about on one of the youngest men, pecking away at his face. Then, when it brought its head up, I could see a glittering scrap of bloody flesh dangling from its beak and I felt my stomach tighten again, a surge of bile burning my throat.

Quickly, I led the women and children in a wide arc, trying to avoid the horror of that scene, yet when I glanced behind I could tell from the pale faces that some at least had seen it. Oddly though, most of the women seemed undisturbed by what they could see and I caught the fierce look in Aidith's eyes, which seemed to say the dead raiders were getting only what they deserved. Then, when I recalled the previous day and the terrors that Cybilla and Aidith had suffered, I thought that maybe she was right. Leaving the corpses to the scavengers, I halted outside the village and sent Cuthbert ahead to scout it out. He returned after a moment and waved at me, so we walked on through the gap in the west fence.

As we entered, the villagers emerged from the hiding places they had run to when they first spotted us approaching. There was a moment's pause as we looked at each other, then a cry of relief from Eduard's young brother, Tomas, who was only five and now, oblivious to everyone else, he hurtled over and flung himself at my friend. Eduard winced in pain, but gave a huge roar and he dragged Tomas off the ground and spun him round. Suddenly, this released the tension and we rushed over to greet each other, embracing loved ones and sobbing with relief. Cybilla moved past me to hug her sister, Audrey, and then held her at arm's length, examining an ugly gash on her cheek. Aidith and her mother were on their knees, holding hands, both talking at the same time. I watched as, for a short while, our spirits lifted as families were reunited. Then, one by one, we would search the faces for others we knew: others we loved and as it became obvious how many had died and how many were missing – the tears started.

Eduard's father and his older brother were both dead. He stood now in a huddle with his mother and little brother, looking down at their bodies, laid out alongside the others behind their hut, awaiting burial. It was the first time I could recall him ever crying, but he was not alone. A half dozen men and young boys – those too young to quite yet be in the Fyrd, but who had picked up weapons and fought the raiders nonetheless – had been slain. As many other women and children had been dragged off as captives – away to the Welsh lands to farm their fields or lie in their beds. These were the terrified faces I had seen in the dark last night; the ones I had been unable to save.

Was this war, I thought? Was this the glory and the joy of battle that Lilla spoke of? All it seemed to be was tears and death.

I had longed for war to come and now I wished it never had. Some hero I was, I thought: away hunting boars and playing at being a warrior whilst here, our people had died and I had done nothing to prevent it. Then, I felt a hand on my shoulder and turning round, I saw Cybilla and Audrey.

"Master Cerdic, I want to thank you for fighting bravely and for bringing my sister back to me," Audrey said. Behind her the villagers were gathered and despite their sorrow, they surrounded Eduard, Cuthbert and me and thanked us for rescuing their folk and protecting them. Eduard wiped away his tears, then smiled and nodded: how so easily he accepted the fate that the gods had brought him. Cuthbert looked shy, but I could tell that he was touched. As for myself, I felt sick. I knew I did not deserve the praise and yet I nodded. In the end I realised that they needed to do this for us and that they in turn expected something from me. As frantic as I was to get away and see how my own family had fared, I forced myself to make a little speech.

"We thank you all and I want to say that I know how you feel, your loss is my loss. We will find those that are missing and we will make those that did this pay."

There was silence as the villagers looked at me with an odd respect. Audrey's eyes filled with tears again, but there was something about her reaction that seemed strange. She had not lost anyone – now that Cybilla had returned – so why was she so emotional about what I had said. Unless ... I felt a tension leap into my chest ... unless ...

I turned now and looked towards the Villa and at once I spotted Sunniva, my sister, moving down the street peering into the huts and searching among the villagers. Her face was pale and her eyes red, so she could not have had much sleep and it looked like she must have been crying. I moved towards her and she turned her head, saw me, gasped and then ran over and hugged me.

"Cerdic! There you are. Thanks be to Woden," she said, with a faint smile. "We had feared the worst when one of the other lads told us that he had last seen the three of you running towards the village last night. We thought you had run into some of these bastards in the woods. I could not stand to lose you as well ..."

Suddenly, her face darkened and she moved towards the Villa.

"Come, Cerdic. Leave your friends here!" she ordered.

I nodded at Eduard and Cuthbert then hurried after her, her words 'as well' echoing in my head.

"What is it Sunniva, is someone hurt? Is it Mother?"

She stopped running but did not turn to look back at me.

"No, Cerdic, Mother is well, although she wishes that the gods had chosen her instead of..." Sunniva's speech stumbled to a halt and then she sobbed and when she looked at me, I could see that her face was screwed up as she fought back the tears.

"Instead of who - is it Father?" I asked, aware that my voice was trembling. The tension in my chest was worse: an almost unbearable tightness, as if my heart would burst.

"Father is injured, but not too badly and he will live." Sunniva answered, wiping her hand across her face.

"Who then, Sunniva?"

She now looked utterly shattered: her spirit burned away by sorrow. She sighed.

"Cerdic, it's Cuthwine: Cuthwine is dead!"

I opened my mouth, but aghast at what she had just said, no words came out. It couldn't be true, could it: Cuthwine, my brother − dead? Of all my family, he had been more the warrior than the farmer, unlike my father. He had always seemed so strong and so able. Yet he had died last night, fighting to defend our home.

"How ...when ...?"

"During the raid, a group of Welsh stormed the Villa. I hid beneath my bed as they burst in, but Mother took Mildrith and the slaves out through the kitchens to hide in the fields to the east. The raiders stole what they could, including Mother's beautiful amber jewellery. Cuthwine, Father and some of the villagers who were around when the attack came, tried to delay the raiders to give the others a chance to escape. Our people fought the raiders in the courtyard," she explained, then for a few moments her face distorted once more as fresh tears forced their way out. Eventually, she spoke again.

"I crept out to the balcony and peeked down at them and from what I could see, they had almost seen them off and three of them certainly won't be going back to Elmet, if that's where they were from. Then, Cuthwine and Father seemed to have got carried away and pursued the others out of the door. I went to your room and looked out the front of the house and I could still see what was happening though ... though I wish I had not ..."

She cried a bit more and it took almost a minute for her to be able to talk again. I was too stunned from what I was hearing to say anything, so I let her take as long as she needed.

"Well, then what happened is the raiders rallied around their chieftain, a great brute with only one eye and a scar where the other should be. He charged forward and ... he ... oh, Cerdic ... he cut Cuthwine down with a great axe – just hacked into him. I think he was dead before he hit the ground. Father went into a fury then and attacked the chieftain with a wood axe and a seax. I think the anger of seeing Cuthwine killed gave him strength and he managed to shatter the chieftain's axe shaft."

86

My heart was pounding inside me and I could still say nothing. I was thinking back to the night before, when I had seen just such a man going back through the woods – all the time unaware that this man had just killed my brother.

"Well, that made the beast furious and he smashed his shield into Father's ribs and I heard them crack," she shuddered. "Father just collapsed and I thought he was dead too ... then the one-eyed man picked up Cuthwine's sword – the one that Uncle once had. I think he would have killed Father with it, but just then one of the villagers arrived and he had a bow and shot a few arrows at the raiders forcing them to back away. They then took off, north towards Wicstun. But, Cerdic, the one-eyed bastard took Cuthwine's sword with him."

It struck me as odd that my throat could feel so dry and my eyes so moist at the same time. Cuthwine had always been such a strong part of my life. I simply could not believe he was dead. Sunniva and I had never been that close, but sorrow brought us together and there between the Villa and village, we held each other and wept. Eventually, I pulled away from her, my hands gripping her shoulders.

"How are Father and Mother now ... what about Mildrith?"

At Mildrith's name, Sunniva looked away and gave another great sob.

"Oh Cerdic, I don't know where Mildrith is. Mother said she stole back through fields to get a look at the warriors."

"What?" I cried, stepping away from my sister.

"Mother tried to stop her, but you know what Mildrith is like! She just scampered away. Mother went after her, of course, but just then some warriors came close to the fields and she had to hide again. When she finally came out, she could not find Aedann, Caerfydd, or Gwen. But ... she could not find Mildrith

87

either. Cerdic, no one knows where our sister is!"

I stared at her and she looked right back at me. The horror of the moment seemed too vast to bear. Cuthwine dead and Mildrith missing: I just shook my head and holding hands, we both walked up the track to the Villa in silence and despair. As it came into view, I gasped. The white walls were charred and blackened where they had been set on fire, although, being stone, it had fared better than the hovels in the village. We went in through the main door, which was hanging from one hinge, smashed and irreparable.

In the entrance room, which Caerfydd had once told me was called an 'atrium', I stopped short. A chill shot down my body when I saw Cuthwine lying in state there. He had been decked out in his richest clothes and to my eyes he looked like a warrior god, slain in the last battles that were yet to come at the end of the world. I walked over to him, stared down at that cold, pale face where once such life had dwelt and again my tears came.

The next day or two went by in a blur. Only a few days before, I would have given anything to fight as a warrior, for the songs of the poets told of the glories of battle. Now, those words seemed almost lies to me. All those ballads and great sagas told little of the reality of war. The burning huts in the village; the charred Villa; Mildrith missing and the body of Cuthwine brought that reality home to me.

We buried Cuthwine the next day, up on the north ridge, near to my grandfather. I helped my father and Sunniva lower him into his grave. He was dressed in his finest clothes such as he had donned for feasts and holy days. He wore his trousers and a blue tunic fastened with a belt, from which hung a knife and a flint box. His best soft leather boots were on his feet and he was wrapped in a great green cloak. At his feet we laid his seax, shield and a bow. Alongside him was an ash spear. A nearby priest came and spoke of our brother going to be with Woden, to feast with his fellow warriors whilst he waited for the great battle that ended all days.

The words failed to bring much succour to me. I looked around at the others. My father and sister were staring down into the grave, their faces the colour of marble. My mother was sobbing, totally lost in grief. Nearby, most of the village had turned up out of respect for the family. Almost all of them looked distant; surrounded by their own grief or worried about missing loved ones, just as we were.

After Cuthwine was buried, six other men from the village were laid into their own graves. We stayed on that hill top whilst all were interred. My father's expression grew grimmer with each inhumation. What was he thinking? Was he angry at the Elmetae or at himself? It was his duty to protect these people. That was the price of their service to him. Did he feel he had failed in that duty? If any of the villagers thought so, none of them said a word. Indeed, several came over to offer their condolences and compliment Cuthwine's skills as a warrior. After the end of the service, we then returned to an empty Villa, which felt too cold and too quiet, the blackened timbers stinking of smoke and soot.

Gradually, over the next two days, we began to get an idea of what had happened. Some hundred raiders had come from the west, over the border from Elmet. It seems they had passed very close to where we were hunting boar in the forest but had, somehow, missed us. They split then: thirty headed for the village and the rest curved to the north towards Wicstun.

They had killed half a dozen in the village as well as Cuthwine – all those we had buried. As many again were wounded including my father. Then there were eight or nine missing – mostly villagers, but also Mildrith, Aedann and his parents.

The last three vexed us: Welsh slaves missing after a Welsh raid. One of them I had seen armed and walking westwards, towards Elmet. It did not take much for many in the village to conclude the obvious. Aedann and his parents were spies and in league with the Welsh and had taken advantage of the raid to escape.

Aidith looked small and sad as she sat on a stool in the Villa kitchen where Mother and Sunniva had been preparing food when she had come to find us. She told us that when the raiders arrived in the village there was a brief fight with the few men there who, not being in the company, had not been away with us in the woods. These were too young or old, too ill or unfit to be warriors. None were given any mercy and most died there and then, though some had fled towards the Villa.

"Then the raiders started searching the village," Aidith said. "They took anything of value, but they seemed to be looking for a specific item. They kept babbling on about something, but none of us could understand what it was they were saying."

"Do you know what it was they were looking for, child?" asked my father.

"Not at first, my Lord, but then that horrible big brute with one eye started asking us questions in English. He said he knew we had a great treasure and he wanted to know where it was. Well, I didn't know what he meant. Then he slapped me hard and said something about ..."

Aidith hesitated and looked at my mother.

"Go on," urged Father.

"He kept saying, 'Amber treasure, where is the amber treasure?' Then he went off with his men and we were rounded up and led away. Cerdic found us soon after that, of course," she nodded, her gaze flicking over towards me.

We sat in silence for a moment and exchanged glances, but I could tell from the look in the eyes of all my family that we were thinking the same thing. Aidith had said One Eye asked about the 'amber treasure'. He could have meant only one thing: my mother's priceless amber and silver set of jewellery. It was indeed a treasure; brought from the distant Baltic by traders to Deira, where it then became a king's gift to a great warrior: my uncle.

Mother started crying. She had never worn it before in public and now, the day after she had proudly displayed her jewellery, the raiders had come looking for it and they had killed Cuthwine and taken Mildrith because of it.

"It's my fault ... it's all my fault," she sobbed. Father went across and took her in his arms, rocking her gently as if she was a child. Then, even whilst showing such tender love to his wife, he turned to me and his eyes now burnt with terrible anger as he whispered to me a single word.

"Aedann!"

I nodded. Aedann the slave, bitter at his lot in life, was a spy. He had somehow passed news of the great treasure that lay hidden at the Villa and the prize drew a warband looking for it. He had escaped with his parents and though his treachery had lost us the jewels, it had taken two far more precious items from us – Cuthwine and Mildrith.

"Aedann!" I replied.

The next day, Lilla arrived at the Villa with news from Wicstun. When it had been attacked, Aethelric had still been there and alongside Wallace, had fought bravely enough to repel the raiders. Even so, Wicstun had suffered losses too, as well as having more prisoners taken away. Aethelric then dithered about what to do, but Wallace persuaded him on a course of action and in the end the Prince had agreed.

"So, I am sent to summon the Wicstun Company to muster to Lord Wallace, immediately. You are going to strike back against the bastards. You are going to get our people back and make these Elmetae pay for what they did ... you are going to Elmet!"

So, there it was: war at last and Cerdic, son of Cenred of the Villa was going along. I gathered my spear, bone helmet, sword and shield and as I prepared to say my goodbyes, I wandered over to the burial ground, knelt down and I swore an oath over the grave of my dead brother.

"Cuthwine," I whispered, "I'm going away now. I am going away to war. I will come back, I swear it: but I have work to do first and promises to keep."

Firstly, I thought of my little sister, Mildrith, taken as a prize of war: as loot in fact and dragged back to be a slave.

I would find her and bring her home.

I thought of Aedann the betrayer. I had treated him as a friend and that mistake had cost me dearly.

I would find him and he would pay.

Finally, I thought of that ghastly scarred face with one merciless eye, coldly looking at his victims. This was the man who had slain my brother and taken my uncle's sword.

I would find him, kill him and bring the sword back home!

Chapter Eight
Muster at Wicstun

The next morning, the official summons arrived. Lord Wallace was ordering all the company to muster at Wicstun. Father called me into his room where he lay in his bed, still recovering from his wounds. He looked me up and down for a moment.

"Son," he began at last, "I must ask you to grow up fast. Lord Wallace has called for the men of the village to go to him and that means they must have a leader."

I nodded feeling with a growing sense of anxiety that I knew where this conversation was going.

"With Cuthwine ...," he started then paused, unable to say the word 'dead', "... with Cuthwine ... gone and me injured, you must do it."

"Father I ... I'm not sure I can. I'm afraid I will mess it up."

"You must do it!" he said abruptly, then just as suddenly realising he had spoken harshly, he smiled at me. "Cerdic, you are my son and I know that you can do this. You can depend on Grettir: he will advise you wisely. The men are brave and will fight well, but they need a leader. That has to be you: lead and they will follow."

So it was that ten men got ready to leave the village that noon. There was Grettir, Cuthbert, Eduard - groaning as he lifted a spear and leant it against his injured shoulder - six other villagers and myself. We collected our weapons and we were supplied with ale, smoked cheese and meats as well as some bread.

The village folk gathered to see us off. I looked for Aidith, hoping to say something to her, but I could not spot her. The mood around the Villa was bleak. Only a few days before, the village had lost twelve members and now another ten were going away. No one argued – we were going to get the others back after all – yet the fear hung in the air that morning, unspoken but palpable, that there would be yet more loss, more death and more sorrow to cope with in the days ahead. Some families parted emotionally, others without a word. Mother hugged me as tightly as she had not done for many years and Sunniva kissed me on the cheek. Neither said much, but in the expression in their eyes I read the words: 'Come back, Cerdic'.

As we marched towards the Roman road that would take us to Wicstun, I chanced a glance behind. I could just see the Villa in the distance and – standing there, still watching us – my mother and sister. As I reached the main road, the Villa disappeared from sight and I felt an aching, maudlin feeling in my heart. This was it: I was going to war. Through childhood it had been this moment I had dreamt about and waited for. Lilla's warriors were always brave and valiant, so why did I feel scared and homesick?

Just then, I saw a shadow under a large beech tree beside the road. The shadow detached itself and came into the light and I recognised, with a jump of the heart, that it was Aidith. She moved towards me, looking bashful, yet eager to say something.

"Cerdic, I wanted to say … that is I need to say…," she stammered. This was new. Aidith was usually self-assured and full of laughter. She blushed, then, taking a step forward, kissed me on the lips.

Before I could say a word, she ran past me – without looking back – and on down the lane to the village. I stared after her for a few moments, before realising I was standing on my own in the road and that I was now fifty yards behind the rest of the men who were still heading north, towards Wicstun. Turning away from sights and thoughts of home, I ran and caught up with the rest of our band and marched with them, off to war.

It was early afternoon when we reached Wicstun. From a distance, we could see a pall of smoke that still lingered over the town. Many houses were damaged and not a few burnt down completely. The townsfolk were walking around with the same dazed expression that the villagers of Cerdham had worn the last few days. In the market square, a few dozen men were already gathering. Men and youths from the company were cleaning and sharpening weapons. From the nearby smithy, the sounds of forging and hammering could be heard, whilst the womenfolk were organising food supplies on carts. In the centre of the chaos, on a dais outside the main hall, stood Lord Wallace wearing a well made, but slightly rusty, chain shirt and a sturdy helm.

Grettir stopped walking and we all gathered up behind him. I waited to see what would happen next, but then noticed that everyone else was looking at me and I realised that they were expecting me to talk to Wallace. Gulping and feeling the gaze of every man in the square upon me I walked up to him and made a slight bow.

"Lord Wallace, how are things in Wicstun?" I asked.

Wallace looked at me blankly for a minute, as if not sure who he was expecting to see, then he blinked and spoke.

"Ah, Cerdic, it's good to see you again – but not like this. I'm sorry to hear the news about your brother: he was a brave warrior," he said.

I just nodded and thanked him for the sympathy.

"As you see," Wallace went on, "we were hit hard here also. About fifty warriors – the bulk of their force – attacked us. Maybe

95

another twenty raided farms and villages to the north: a heavy raid indeed. Twenty of our men were killed and as many again wounded, but we drove them off, the maggot-ridden scum."

His eyes unfocused, he paused to think, then mused, "I wonder what was behind all of this. Why did they attack right now? I mean, the Elmetae have not attacked in my lifetime. Oh, I know about the rumours of an alliance with Rheged and I guess I knew that one day it would happen, but we have heard nothing to suggest an agreement has been reached, nor less about attacks elsewhere. Just one warband – say one hundred men – from Elmet attacking alone: it does seem odd."

Wallace looked at me then, his eyebrow raised as though he thought I might have the answer. So, I told him about the amber treasure and the news that the warband's leader – a one-eyed warrior chieftan – had been asking for it. I told him about Aedann and how I thought he had betrayed the news of that great prize to them.

He nodded and looked thoughtful. Then, sitting back on a cart loaded with spears, he rubbed his chin and squinted at me.

"Of course, Samlen One Eye could not resist that," he said. Then, seeing the quizzical expression on my face, he explained. "Prince Samlen is brother to Ceredig, the King of Elmet. He took that wound to the eye years ago, in the fighting near Eoforwic, when Elmet sent an army to help hold the city - it was your uncle Cynric inflicted it, so Grettir told us - since then Samlen has hated us and wanted revenge. It seems, from what I hear, that he is trying to persuade his brother to ally with Owain and is desperate to make his name in the war against us. He is proud as well as cruel. He does however have a weakness: he loves plunder and loot to levels bordering on obsession."

"So, he would be likely to go after my mother's jewellery?"

Wallace looked at me and then nodded.

"Yes. Yes he would, perhaps even if Ceredig had not yet agreed to fight us. But he is jealous of his treasures. Therefore, he attacks in many places, so that the rest of his men are occupied ransacking poor farms and our town. Meanwhile, he led a much smaller group – maybe those most loyal to him – to the Villa, to claim his prize."

Around us the carts had been loaded now and more of the company had assembled. Wallace looked at them for a moment and then back at me.

"This could alter things. Ceredig hesitates because he has little money. Wars cost money and he will need a lot to attack us. That amber necklace and the rest; it's worth a fortune. It could arm and keep an army in the field for months."

I began to wonder if the jewels were cursed. They seemed to bring nothing but death and disaster. In any event, it looked like I now had a fourth reason to go to Elmet.

"Then we must try and get them back, my Lord!"

Wallace nodded.

"Yes, Cerdic, we must."

The company assembled and Wallace asked the leader of each contingent to join him in a council. I represented the Villa. Wallace had laid out a map on the table. It was made of cured vellum, now cracked and torn with age. I had never seen one before and looked at it curiously.

"It's old that map. When we attacked Eoforwic, when I was young, we took plunder and treasure. One of the Welsh lords had some scrolls and this was with them. I think it was made by the Roman army just before they left," Wallace explained.

I peered at it again, but it was all lines and letters which I could not understand. Looking around at the doubtful expressions on the faces of the others present, I knew that I was not alone. So, Wallace interpreted it for us.

"See that picture that looks like a castle? That is Eoforwic – the Romans called it Eboracum. Wicstun does not seem to have existed at the time, but all the Roman forts and villas are on it. Look, Cerdic: that is your Villa," he said, pointing at a small square near the Roman road that ran past Cerdham and on to Eoforwic. He then waved his hand at another part of the map.

"Now, everyone, look over here. That's the River Derwent and that is the Ouse. Our scouts report that the trail left by the raid went that way, over the river just west of the Villa, and Cerdic here thinks he saw Samlen and his band go past the royal forests there just three nights back."

I nodded and then I had a thought. Cuthbert had told us that he occasionally went hunting with his father in the border lands west of the Derwent. They had, out of curiosity, once strayed to the Ouse and reckoned that it had been a day's journey from the village to the border and back again. If so, it would take us a good half day to reach the border from where we were. But, what he had also told me was there was a ford over the Derwent just near where we were boar hunting and another crossing the Ouse further to the west. I told Wallace this.

"Right then," he said, biting his lip, "I think that is where they were heading. If so, we should be able to follow them easily enough. After that – I don't know."

"The biggest settlement in that area is Salebeia," one of the other men said.

Wallace nodded and pointed and we could see a small town just the other side of the Ouse. He tapped his hand on the map, further over.

"The Welsh capital is at Loidis there, but that is twenty miles and more beyond the border. We must hope they have not gone that far!"

Our fears were that we might be captured in Elmet by the warriors of King Ceredig of that land and be taken off to slavery or even killed outright. We would have to travel quietly, through hostile territory, which was going to be hard for one hundred of us. Yet, if we could manage a surprise attack on wherever our people were being held, we might be successful. Wallace told us to be ready at dawn and sent us to get some sleep.

I was just leaving when there was a knock on door and one of Wallace's older veterans entered; a wild looking man called Sigmund. He stepped up to Wallace, who nodded at him to speak in front of us all. He had been compiling a list of the dead, wounded and those missing from the town.

"Apart from the twenty men who were slain, I reckon thirty or more folk are missing, my Lord. Some of them were seen being dragged away. Others we have no idea about, like Molly Baker, the lad Hussa ... my sister Emma, Ken the farrier ... and several others, besides."

So, Hussa was missing as well as Mildrith. In all likelihood they would be taken to the same place. Wallace was thinking this too.

"Well, maybe we will find them all in one group if we move quickly. Right," he said, clapping his hands, "I think it is time for sleep now and then we will see what fortune tomorrow brings."

Bowing, we left Wallace alone in the room with his map and I went to find a place for the villagers and me to bed down.

The company departed Wicstun at first light, amongst scenes like those of the previous day at the Villa. The anxiety felt by their relatives for the men about to depart and the hope that we might find those taken from them, mixed as one in embraces and

99

final words. Then we were off and following the trail left by the raiders, which was still visible in the mud and damaged crops through the fields southwest of Wicstun.

As we marched along I was surprised to see the bard Lilla amongst the ranks. He was chatting to the men, telling jokes and singing little ditties. Catching my glance, he came over to us and greeted me by name.

"Sorry again about your brother, Cerdic. Good man he was – I thought. I'll tell you a story sometime about what he got up to when he was away with the Fyrd a year or so back. Make your hair stand on end it will," he said, with a sad little smile.

"Thanks Lilla, I would appreciate that one day, when the pain is less raw. But tell me: what are you doing here?"

"Oh, looking for songs," he replied cheerfully.

He saw my quizzical expression and sighed, as if talking to the village idiot.

"Sagas don't just pop up in bards' heads, you know. We try to be where stories are happening and then we know what to put in them."

"Can't that be a bit dangerous?"

"Well ... yes, but I've been lucky so far."

"I hope your luck lasts – for all our sakes," I muttered.

Mid-morning saw us cross the Derwent near the Villa – itself out of sight in the woods and hills to the east. By shortly after noon, we had reached the approaches to the Ouse and we slowed our pace to make a more cautious advance. Finally, we halted and Wallace sent out scouts across the river to trace the direction taken by the warband.

Whilst they were away, we rested and ate some bread and meat as we crouched in low scrub overlooking the Ouse. About a mile to the west and a little way down the river, we could see the smoke from a small settlement and beyond it a larger town – Salebeia. Further west, the hills rose higher and higher, until they became the mountains of the Pennines.

After about an hour, our scouts returned to us.

"We are in luck, my Lord," a bright-eyed woodsman from the Wolds reported. "I don't think there can have been any rain here these last few days, for the mud on either side of the ford still shows the tracks the raiders left. Several score feet passed that way and seem to have veered northwest, away from Salebeia."

"Northwest? That's a surprise. What's in that direction?" Wallace said, as much to himself as to the scouts, and pulled the rolled up map out of his tunic. He squinted at it for a moment, grunted, then looked up at the company.

"There is an old Roman fort northwest of Salebeia – perhaps five miles from the ford. Its name is," he brought the map closer to his eyes, "erm ... Calcaria, I think. I would guess Samlen was going that way. If so; we should find him there."

"If he is still there, my Lord," I pointed out.

"Indeed, but we will only know by going," he said and stared at the slate grey sky above us. "Well, there may not have been any rain since the raid, but we might have some soon. Best press on. I would like to get to some shelter near this fort and take a look at it today, if we can."

To begin with, all went well. We moved down to the river and found the shallow crossing point. There, we waded through the clear, icy waters and clambered up the far bank. We had now left Deira and I gazed back over my shoulder with a sudden feeling of anxiety. My home – what was left of it – was back there. Eduard and Cuthbert saw me looking and paused too.

We were now further away from home than I had ever been. It could only have been ten or eleven miles and looking back now, over the thousands of miles I have wandered since, it was just next door. But there and then, to the young man I was, it seemed a very long way indeed. Cuthbert and Eduard agreed with me. Indeed, Eduard had an excited expression of wonder at each new hill we climbed and each new valley beyond it. Cuthbert, on the other hand, looked a little afraid and glanced around at the woods we passed as if he expected a horde of goblins to attack us at any moment. I grinned at him and he looked away, his face flaring pink with embarrassment.

"I never expected to leave the valley, you know," Cuthbert said, "and here we are attacking another country."

"You a bit scared?" I asked.

"Well, yeh, you?"

"A bit, but I'm excited as well and keen to get this job done. Find Mildrith and the others and sort out Samlen and Aedann. So, because of all that, it does not seem so bad." I turned to my other friend.

"Eduard?"

"What?" the big lad asked.

"Are you afraid?"

Momentarily forgetting his wound he shrugged, then winced, but nothing bothered Eduard much, big strong lad that he was. He just took life as it came and got on with it. I sometimes envied him that ability.

We finally turned away from our homeland and rejoined the company. The land on the other side of the river was much the same as on our side: woodlands and fields in the low lands, then hills rising gently away from the river. The scouts reported that the tracks we were following joined a narrow road or path heading northwest and so, we followed it.

We were cautious and travelled quietly with scouts out ahead of us and on each flank to look for the Welsh but, as yet, we had seen none. After a few miles the path turned sharply north towards the River Wharfe, passed between two woods then emerged in flat open fields, before turning again back to the west. The river was now immediately on our right. Ahead of us, no more than a mile away, was a small settlement – perhaps a dozen huts clustered round a larger one – the headman's house most probably.

Wallace gestured for me and Sigmund to go with him and sent the company back into the woods. We slipped down into the ditch that followed the road and then through a thorny blackberry hedge that separated it from fields running down to the river bank. Some cattle were grazing in the meadows there. Following the hedge, we approached the village until we were hidden in a small copse, barely a hundred paces from it.

From where we were, we could see the villagers going about their daily lives. Some were building a new hut near us and were pounding in the upright posts to make a frame from ash trunks. Beyond them, some women were gathered together round a well and were filling jugs and pots from it. Out of sight, I could hear hammering and banging from a blacksmith or carpenter. The village was at least as big as Cerdham and so there could be over fifty men and women here. The men that we could see looked strong and while we could easily take the village, there would be some resistance and many of our men would die.

"Blast," Wallace cursed. "We will have to go round it. We can't go through – someone in the village will surely alert Samlen and that's our surprise gone."

"I say we attack the village, burn it down and kill them all," Sigmund said, "serves them right; revenge for what they did to Wicstun."

Part of me agreed – why not inflict pain and suffering in measure for what we had suffered? Yet, another part of me knew that was not right.

"These villagers did not burn the Villa or Wicstun or kill any of us," I pointed out. "It's Samlen we want and he is not here."

Sigmund looked at me like I was sticking my opinion in where it was not wanted, lord's son or not, and argued that we needed a base to operate from. By now, however, I was not listening, because I had just noticed something. Something that made my blood boil.

Standing in the centre of the village were two men. They appeared to be haggling over a barter. The goods concerned were food and a shield: a Welsh shield with a Christian symbol on it. Well, there would be many such shields around – one looking much like another – but the man who was holding the shield did not look just like any other. He looked like and was, without a doubt, Aedann: Aedann the slave, Aedann the traitor who had sold his countrymen with news of the amber treasure and as a result had caused the death of Cuthwine and many others.

There, in front of me, was my father's Welsh slave, bartering for food like none of that had happened, like he did not care. Like none of it mattered. But, it mattered to me and I drew my knife and started running towards the village with one thing on my mind: I would kill Aedann.

"Cerdic, what the hell do you think you're doing?" hissed Wallace, "Get back here now!"

The voice was full of authority, but I ignored it and carried on running. No one in the village had seen me at first. I was only fifty yards from Aedann and now I swerved, so I would be able to pass between two huts. Suddenly, my legs were swept from under me and I fell, full length, knocking my chin hard against the ground, so that I bit my lip and tasted blood.

Head spinning like it did if I'd had too much ale, I felt someone pick me up, so I struggled and hissed at them to let me go, but then I received an agonizing punch to the belly which doubled me over. I was heaved up onto this someone's shoulder and carried away. I heard a high-pitched scream. Was that me, I wondered? Then I passed out.

When I came round, I was back in the copse and Sigmund was leaning over me. I groaned and spat out blood. I looked up at them both. They returned the glance with disgust.

"What were you doing boy, trying to give us all away?" Sigmund asked nastily.

"What made you go running off like that?" Wallace added.

I dragged myself up onto my knees and coughed, spitting up some more blood.

"Aedann, it was Aedann."

"Your escaped slave – the one you think told Samlen about the jewellery?" Wallace asked.

I nodded and looked back at the village. One of the women by the well was pointing at the gap between the houses where I had been knocked down by Sigmund. Two men had armed themselves with short spears and were peering through the gap. They glanced at the copse, but did not seem to have seen us. A few of the villagers had started running around in panic, looking this way and that. We could see Aedann, still in plain sight, completing his trade and taking a sack of food off the villager then, heaving it over his shoulder he walked out of the village and away from us towards the Roman fort and Samlen. As he left, I was certain that he glanced towards our hiding place.

Wallace insisted we stay in the copse for two full hours and

105

then, as it started to get dark, we scampered back down by the river and so found the company in the wood.

"My Lord, we were worried about you and were about to come and look for you," Grettir said.

Wallace glanced at me before replying.

"We were seen and had to lie low for a while for the fuss to die down," he said.

"Seen? But my Lord if you were seen, Samlen might know we are coming," Grettir pointed out.

I thought about Aedann glancing towards us and the villagers running around in panic. Feeling very foolish, I looked at Sigmund who was watching me to see what I would say. I might as well come clean and confess, I thought.

"It was my fault; I saw Aedann and went to confront him. I was not thinking straight."

There was silence as everyone in the company stared at me. Even Eduard and Cuthbert gave me a strange look.

"I'm sorry. I know this is not just about my own revenge, but the sight of him just ..." I shrugged.

I could not look at them and sat down on a log feeling miserable.

Wallace told the company that because of the time lost, we would now camp in the wood, post plenty of sentries and carry on at first light.

Eduard and Cuthbert came over to me, but seemed unable to say anything and I ignored them. I then felt a hand on my shoulder. It was Sigmund.

"Well lad, you sure buggered up today. But I will say one thing for you. It took guts to come out and admit that just now. Don't make things any easier today, of course, but folk mostly feel better about a man who will admit a mistake," he said.

"We'll see. I hope that Samlen doesn't know about us yet and we can carry on in the morning, without trouble."

Sigmund shrugged.

"We can hope," he said, but his tone was doubtful.

Hope. It drives men forward and keeps them struggling on, whatever the odds: whatever the difficulty. But the gods don't deal in hope. They mostly deal with fate – what destiny has in store for a man. But Loki, the trickster God Loki: he deals in mischief and that night he was abroad mixing up his mischief. The winds carried his laughter far and made sure that news of our passing reached the ears of the one man we hoped would not hear. Perhaps Aedann was his agent or maybe it was one of the villagers – it makes no difference, really.

Whoever was the messenger, it seems Samlen heard about us and – sharing Loki's laughter – he sent his men out to look for us and now, only a few miles away, they were waiting for the chance to pounce upon us.

Chapter Nine
Ambush

It happened in a field between two woods. The corridor of open land was perhaps two hundred yards long and fifty yards wide; we had chosen it to avoid the Welsh village to the north. Wallace, with most of the Wicstun lads and Sigmund were in the lead, followed by those from Newbold, Sancton and Compton, whilst the men of the Villa brought up the rear. The whole company was tired, having slept poorly in the damp wood the night before and perhaps this had made us careless, so as a result, we were strung out in a loose, dawdling line, a hundred yards long.

We were almost half way across the field when, without warning, there was a guttural cry from the northern wood. The shout was taken up by a hundred voices and then two score men charged out from the trees to our north, blocking our path. We all stopped, startled by the suddenness of it but before we could respond, another forty Welsh warriors ran out behind us this time from the other wood – the trees to the south – preventing any thoughts of retreat. Finally, a further dozen emerged on each flank and lined the edge of the wood. These, being armed with bows and without giving us a chance to react, sent a volley of arrows spitting towards us. Most of these, mercifully, missed us although one unlucky man from Wicstun fell dead with three arrows sticking out of his chest.

"Men of Wicstun to me," Wallace shouted, drawing his sword. We all moved in that direction, but the Welsh closing in from either side and pelting us with arrows, divided the company in two.

Grettir looked grimly at the Welsh and then at me, expecting me to take command. Father's parting words came back and I heard him speaking.

"Lead them and they will follow ..."

I drew my sword and then thrust my spear up in the air, like a standard.

"Men of the Villa ... from Compton: to me!" I yelled. For a moment no one did anything and they still milled around confused and bewildered, like so many frightened sheep, so I yelled again.

"Come on, you bastards, to me!"

Eduard and Cuthbert reacted at that and moved to my side and Grettir followed. Cuthbert quickly strung his bow and reached for an arrow. Eduard braced his shield and spear and prepared himself for the fight. The other men took a moment or two to move, but another bellowed order finally brought them close.

Glancing towards Wallace, I saw he had his men ringed round him and I decided to copy the idea.

"Form a ring," I yelled. They looked doubtful, as this was not a formation we had practised, yet they could see the danger coming from both in front and behind us. Soon, we had almost forty men in a ring, twenty in the front rank and twenty behind them.

The enemy were close now – only two dozen yards away. So, I thought to myself, here at last in this field is where I would first command men in battle. I prepared myself for the blow to come, unstrapped my shield and put away my sword. Then, I readied my spear, all the time praying to the gods that today would not be my last fight.

"Spears over shields!" I bellowed and the men obeyed, forty spears now pointing out at the enemy, who in just a few moments would be upon us.

Yet, the clash did not come. The enemy, having hemmed us in two rings, halted and surrounded us. Their archers moved up and threatened us with arrow fire, but did not attack. A broadshouldered chieftain came forward out of the enemy ranks and inspected first my men and then those round Wallace.

"Saxons," he shouted in strongly accented English, "I am Peredur, chieftain of these lands. Your presence here, armed and secretive, is illegal. My Prince will want to see you and know what you are doing here. We have you outnumbered and surrounded. Surrender and you will not be harmed. If you fight, many of you and many of us will die today. We will take you to Prince Samlen."

I figured the odds and sighed. Peredur was right. We were tired, damp and hungry. I was stiff from sleeping last night in that copse. Eduard was clearly suffering from his wound and Cuthbert had only a few arrows and there were not many other bowmen in our ranks. Few of us had fought a battle before and if we fought one today, it was obvious that most of us would die. As much as I hated the idea, if we surrendered we might survive.

Wallace glanced over towards me and then at the Welsh surrounding us. Sigmund and he spoke for a moment then Wallace nodded his head and dropped his sword and his shield. A moment later, with a great clattering noise, the rest of us threw our weapons to the ground. The Welsh came forward and collected them and as one of them picked up my new sword, I felt an ache in my chest. I had taken the weapon from a vanquished foe only a few days before, but somehow it already felt like mine.

After gathering up the spears, shields and swords, the Welsh herded us together and led us away.

Gloom descended on the company as what we had feared came true: we were now captives! No one said anything, but I felt the gaze of many lingering upon me and their thoughts were mine too: had my foolish act the night before betrayed us? A few moments of anger and now our chance of revenge, along with all hope of rescuing our families were gone – maybe forever.

No one said anything: they did not need to. I already knew it was my fault.

The Elmetae took us north and west, along a mud track that meandered through dense forest, which covered much of Elmet. Here and there, we saw swirling smoke rising from what were presumably villages and hamlets in woodland clearings. Eventually, we reached a stone Roman road running from the distant south and – I found out later – via Loidis across the south Pennines to Eoforwic. Strange how roads play such a large role in one's life: armies march along them. Folk use them to go to market and back. As a boy I dreamt of where the road that ran past the Villa would carry me. Well, I did not know it then, but I was going to spend a great deal of my life on one road or another.

We turned northwards and as the sun began to fall behind the mountains we saw the fortress of Calcaria. It was an old Roman fort such as Caerfydd had told me their legions once lived in. It stood to the east of the road at the end of a short path, backing onto the river. The fort itself was oblong in shape with the short sides parallel with the main road. In the centre of the southern wall was a gateway accessed via a bridge, which led over a ditch. The ditch had once been quite deep, but had clearly filled up over the years with the debris of nearby trees and decades of mud that no one had tried to clear. Beyond it was an

111

earthen embankment topped by a stone wall, which had once encircled the entire fortress. However, in the two centuries since the Romans left it had decayed and fallen down in many places. Here and there, I could also see signs that it had been attacked more than once since their departure. These defects were partially repaired by wooden palisades or loose rocks and bricks.

We marched through the crumbling gatehouse, closely observed by sentinels standing watch upon the walls and above the gates. Beyond the gatehouse, we entered a road that ran between two rows of long low buildings on either side.

Lilla was walking besides me and pointed at them.

"Those were barracks for their legionaries, or stables for their cavalry. Now look, see there," he continued, indicating a number of large, square two-story buildings on the other side of the wide open space we had arrived at. "One of those would have been the Headquarters building for the legion or regiment that was barracked here, maybe that larger one. The slightly smaller one now, that would have been the Commander's accommodation."

We looked at them both. Massive they seemed to me, compared to the Villa which I had always thought to be a palace. Clustered around these, there were other, more diminutive structures and beyond them all, even more buildings. Like all Roman structures, these buildings were well-made, but once they started to decay, the Welsh, like the English, did not possess the skills to maintain them. But whereas we generally avoided such places, the Welsh still lived in them.

"What about those?" I asked, indicating some other buildings.

"Um ... maybe granaries, storehouses, possibly a workshop and those further on are more barracks."

"More? Just how many men did the Romans have here?"

"Hundreds, maybe thousands, if they needed them: and this was just one of many forts they had."

We stood together, staring round at the impressive sight.

"They must have been giants!" Cuthbert said: reminding me of a similar conversation we'd had about the Villa years before.

Lilla shook his head.

"No, men just like us. They were just men but conquered the world. Then they died and their Empire is gone and these places are all that are left."

It was a sobering thought. As if to emphasise the briefness of glory, a tile slid off a nearby roof and smashed on the ground. We all sank into gloomy silence, each maybe thinking how short our own lives might be, right now.

"Makes you think, don't it?" Eduard muttered, after a moment.

"Silence! You'll be silent!" Peredur shouted at us. While Lilla had been talking, he had left us under strong guard on the parade ground and gone into the smaller of the main buildings. A few minutes later, he came back and was standing in front of us, glaring. He turned to Wallace.

"You are the chieftain of this warband?" Peredur asked in his accented English.

"I'm the Lord of Wicstun and this is the Wicstun Company," Wallace said, defiantly.

Peredur glanced at us all appraisingly and smiled.

"Some army, we caught you half asleep blundering around the countryside. I doubt you can even fight."

"Give us our weapons back and we'll show you," Wallace countered.

Peredur looked amused but shook his head.

"I don't think so. Now, bring your senior captains and come

with me."

"Where are we going?"

"Prince Samlen wishes to see you and talk to you. I warn you to show respect, or you'll regret it."

Wallace nodded at Lilla, Sigmund and three of the village leaders and finally, after a pause, myself. My youth would cause him hesitation and maybe my rash behaviour at the village was still on his mind, but I did in theory command the largest number of men, after him.

Peredur, accompanied by five huge warriors, led us across the ground and up the steps of the largest building. We walked through a small passageway, which opened into a central courtyard similar to the one at the Villa, only much bigger. To either side were small rooms: offices, Lilla told me later. Opposite us were two large double doors, a Welsh warrior standing on either side. They opened it as Peredur approached. It led into a rectangular room in the corner of which were two statues of Roman gods, their once bright gold and red paint peeling off. To the left was another door and yet more guards. Peredur opened this and entered.

Samlen One Eye sat on a chair raised upon a small platform against the opposite wall. To either side more Welsh warriors and chieftains stood staring at us as we came in. We shuffled forward to stand in front of Samlen, who studied us in menacing silence much like a fox watches a goose waiting for the moment to strike.

Finally he spoke. He, like Peredur, knew and spoke English with a strong Welsh accent.

"Who are you and what are you doing on my land?"

Wallace stepped forward.

"Prince Samlen, I am Lord Wallace of Wicstun. King Aelle of

114

Deira sends his greetings and bids me bring a message and a gift for you."

Samlen rose and stood on the platform. Already tall, he now towered above us.

"Wicstun, where's that?" he asked and then muttered some words in Welsh to Peredur, who replied.

"So, you rule that miserable shit heap full of hovels and filth, a day's walk east of here? Bloody awful place that was, with very little of value," he sneered.

"Still, you took something of value to us – our families and friends." Wallace's tone was cold.

Samlen laughed.

"Miserable and feeble lot those are as well. You should have been grateful I took them away and got on with life – found yourselves some new women and had new children with them."

"We find we prefer to have them back."

Samlen looked at his chieftains and roared with laughter now and they joined in, though many plainly were not following the English.

"What? You thought you would just walk into Elmet and take them, just like that. You really are fools. Well, you can be reunited with them soon: one big happy slave family."

Wallace did not reply and just stood his ground, staring at Samlen.

"Well then, what is this message from the mighty and aged Aelle?" Samlen asked. "Is it to say there will be another delivery of slaves next Tuesday?" he asked and then he laughed again.

"No, I had to deliver a gift to you, so that you will not attack us again."

"What gift would make me agree to that? It would have to be impressive!"

Wallace now smiled, but there was no humour in it.

"It is this," he said and stepped closer. Peredur looked across at him now, anxiety etched onto his face and he moved towards Wallace, but he was already too late. Wallace had slipped a dagger out of his sleeve and quick as lightning, swung it up towards Samlen's belly. The Prince's arm lashed out like a snake's head and grasped Wallace's arm by the wrist. With strength like the jaws of a wolf he twisted the arm viciously, there was a crack. Wallace screamed and dropped the blade.

Peredur now arrived and punched Wallace in the stomach, so he collapsed winded on the ground. Sigmund and I started forward, but the guards ran out and rammed the butts of their spears into our guts and we too were forced to the ground. The spears swung around and now sharp points pricked at our throats.

Samlen was glaring at Peredur.

"Did you not take their weapons?"

"Yes, Sire, but he must have concealed this one, forgive me," Peredur said, showing his own fear of the one-eyed chieftain, but now Samlen had turned his fury back to Wallace. He kicked him in the stomach and then slammed his foot down on Wallace's broken arm, so that he screamed again in renewed agony.

"So, that is Aelle's plan: to assassinate me and maybe stop our army marching. He knows we have armies gathering does he? Much good it will do him: I will burn his little country and make him pay."

Wallace was back on his knees and spoke in a weak voice.

"It was not Aelle's doing. It was my idea. I tried and I failed so, if you must burn someone, make it me."

Samlen smiled at that.

"I may do that. Burning an English lord, eh? Yes, my warriors

116

would like that. Take them away, Peredur, and lock them up while I decide their fate."

We were abruptly herded out of the door. Peredur snapped out an order and his men pushed and shoved at us with spears and shields. The Welsh chieftain was angry at us now, perhaps thinking that we had tricked him and also feeling aggrieved that the botched assassination of Samlen was being blamed on him.

Around the side of Samlen's hall there were a few large buildings that may once have been workshops. One of these had large double doors. We were pushed through and the doors were slammed and barred shut behind us. The rest of the company was already here.

Sigmund examined Wallace's arm, then looking round the room he found a small length of broken pole – perhaps a table leg or a spear once – and taking strips of cloth from the bindings around his legs, strapped Wallace's arm to it, having first had Eduard pull hard on the lord's hand to straighten the bones as best as he could. Wallace grimaced and gave a slight groan at this, but stood the pain well.

Sweating and his face pale, Wallace now quickly told everyone about what had transpired in the other building.

"Well done, my Lord, for trying to kill him," Eduard grunted and everyone nodded their agreement.

"Now what do we do?" Cuthbert asked loudly. Grettir growled at him to hold his tongue and wait to be told and so my friend went off in a sulk to the far side of the room and sat down alone.

"Cerdic?" Eduard said, just visible in the dark room to my side.

"Yes, Ed, what is it?"

"While you were in that room, some Welsh villagers came in

117

bringing food for the garrison here."

"Well, what of it?"

"I recognised one of them."

I felt my heart miss a beat, my hands bunching into fists.

"Do you mean ..."

"Yes, it was your slave: here in the fort."

"Um ... well, if we can escape, I look forward to breaking the little runt's traitorous neck," I hissed.

With a scraping and juddering noise, the door swung open and a dozen armed guards moved into the room followed by Samlen. He too was armed and I gasped as I realised that he was carrying my uncle's sword. Standing in front of us now, he glanced around the room and then at Wallace.

"You were fools to come here hoping to attack this place and rescue your people. Nevertheless, there can be courage in foolishness and your act," now he pointed at Wallace, "showed me you have guts, so I offer you a choice." He opened his arms to include us all. "In fact, I offer you all a choice."

He pointed his sword, my uncle's sword, at us.

"Your people – the Angles are doomed. You came to this land like a tidal wave and swept away all in your path. But the tides are turning. The seas are now going east and it is you who will be swept away. My people will reclaim what once belonged to us. What will become of you then? Will you be destroyed? You need not be: there is an alternative. You are warriors. Join me and you will write your names in glory in our songs and our stories. Our children will grow up knowing your names. That is the offer I give: be a warrior in my army. Forget your past and seize a new future."

He stood, waiting for a response but none of us answered him. Eduard spat to show his feelings. Finally, Lilla came forward and everyone looked at him and I was not the only one holding my breath.

"You said that our names will be written in stories and poems and those songs will be known to your children. I agree." Samlen looked with interest at the bard but Lilla shook his head. "You are right, but for the wrong reasons. These men will not betray their homes and their king for such a promise of false glory. If their names are written in song and poetry, it will be because I wrote them and it won't be about Welsh victories over the English, but our revenge over you, Samlen."

Samlen stared at him coldly and around at the rest of us. Then, he moved another piece on the table of our game with him. This move had me stunned.

"There is yet more to my offer that you have not heard. All of you can save your lives and those of any family I hold here, if you will just join me. Your families will be freed and if you serve me you will be given land to farm."

So there it was. If I just stepped forward and knelt and swore loyalty to him, I would be a warrior in his army. I would have land and Mildrith would be safe. But, I thought I could now hear Loki laughing and I knew then that Samlen could not be trusted.

No one moved.

"There, you have your answer. Do with us what you will, but we will not join you," Wallace said.

"You fools ..." Samlen started to reply, but then I just lunged at him with my bare hands, face snarling like a madman, fists flying and feet kicking. Samlen did not move but just smashed the hilt of the sword into my face, knocking me down. Then he swung the sword up and it looked like he would kill me.

"Fight me!" I shouted. The sword hesitated and Samlen looked down at me.

"Who are you, then?"

"That sword is mine, it belongs to my family. I will fight you for it."

The one-eyed chieftain examined the blade for a moment. Then he laughed.

"I don't think so. I killed the man who owned this sword and took it from him. Took his sister as well and brought her back, here."

"It was my brother, it was his sword. She is my sister, Mildrith: fight me!"

"You are nothing. You refused my offer. You are no longer free: in fact you are a slave. I do not fight slaves. The sword is mine and I may take more from you − I may take your sister to my bed," he grinned his ghastly smile, the knotted purple scar wrinkling the empty eye socket. I felt a brief gleam of satisfaction knowing that my uncle had done that to this man's face with that very sword. It was on the tip of my tongue to tell him so, but then he laughed and started to walk away.

"You should have taken my offer, fool!"

I was angry now and desperate to kill him. "Coward! You're just a coward!"

He spun round and thrust the sword point at my throat.

"No, you do not get to call me a coward. You seem to think that I will want to defend my honour and meet you in single combat and that to refuse that challenge would be cowardly. Indeed it would, coming from a warrior of my race, coming from a man of rank, but you ..."

"He is Cerdic, son of Cenred of the Villa, warrior of Deira and heir to his father's estates, he ..." Wallace started to say but was interrupted by Samlen who slapped Wallace with the back of his hand, splitting his lip which now started to bleed heavily.

Wallace was knocked back against some of his men and was stunned into silence.

Samlen looked down at him in disgust and then turned and spat at me.

"Nothing, you are nothing," he roared, his face red with fury. "None of you are anything. You take our land and enslave our people and think you are so mighty. Well, you are wrong. Here, you are filth. Here, you are slaves. Slaves have no rights. A free man and a prince cannot lose face to such as you."

He stomped away towards the door and then turned and looked at the company.

"Your lives mean nothing. I may hang you all; I may sell you as slaves. I don't care. When I come back, I will decide."

He pointed at me and shouted some words to his men, who came forward and pushed Lilla, Wallace and myself out of the door. He then turned back to the rest of the company.

"Enjoy the next day or so in your fine residence," he said gesturing with his hands at the decaying Roman workshop, "it may be your last!"

Then, the door was shut and barred behind us. Samlen and his men marched us out onto the parade ground and over to a gallows large enough to hang ten men. I thought we were going to hang, but Samlen had a longer ordeal planned for us, it seemed. They struck off Wallace's makeshift splint, lashed our hands together and then passed a loop of rope under the knot. The other end of the rope was thrown over the crossbeam of the gallows and was heaved up until we each hung suspended from our wrists, our toes barely touching the ground. Finally it was tied off, around the crossbeam. Wallace by this time had passed out; the pain from his broken arm must have been intolerable.

Samlen now stepped back and addressed us. "I will be back

in the fort soon. My men and I will lay bets on which of you are still alive by then." He squinted up at the skies where gathering storm clouds indicated the warm spring days we had just enjoyed were over, for a while. "Looks like you are going to get wet," he added then laughing, he walked away.

The rope dug into my wrists, cutting the skin so that blood was dripping down my arms, which were already going numb. The tension on my shoulders was unbearable and I was finding it hard to breath. Next to me, Wallace was groaning; I could not begin to imagine his agony. On my other side, Lilla had closed his eyes: perhaps to try and blot out the pain. I shivered. The sun was already low in the sky and soon it started raining.

I groaned in despair. We were fifteen miles from home and inside hostile territory, bound and strung up with no weapons, at the dubious mercy of a madman who might kill us all on a whim, at any moment... and I had absolutely no idea how to escape.

Calcaria Roman Fort

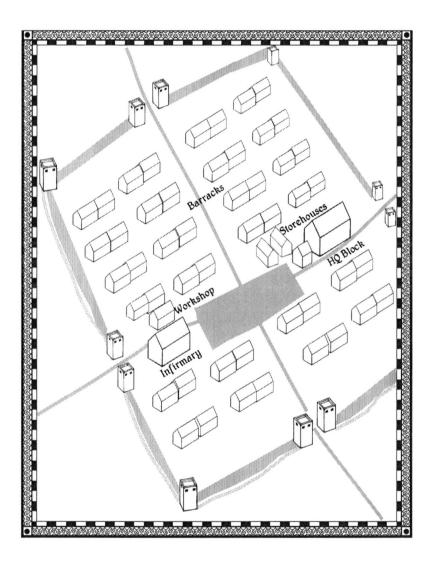

Chapter Ten
The Rescue

It was quite late now and the wind was blowing up a gale so that the rain, having started lightly, was now pelting down. Around us, the Welsh warriors took shelter and waited for the storm to pass. We could not avoid the rain and within minutes were soaked to the skin and it soon felt as if my limbs were frozen solid. Wallace was still groaning as he dangled next to me, but was getting weaker with the passing hours. The weight of his body pulling on his broken arm was obviously causing him agony.

The rain started to lighten after half an hour or so of torrential downpour. Soon afterwards, I noticed that there were groups of the Welsh warriors gathering on the parade ground nearby. Some were observing us with vague interest, but I was sure that it was not only the spectacle of us three Angle warriors that drew them here. More emerged, until at least two hundred of them were standing around in the gathering gloom. All were armed, well equipped and looked ready for the march.

One of them, with a grey cloak wrapped tightly round him, came towards us. He peered at us from a short distance away and then came even closer. As he did, I looked up and now I saw the man's face. For a moment I stared at him, not understanding what I was seeing. For it was not the man I was half expecting to see at any moment: it was not Aedann the traitor, coming over to gloat at us, but to my great surprise the face belonged to the missing red-haired lad, Hussa.

Well, I might not get on with him, but I did not really care who rescued us. I wondered how he had escaped, but then thought I did not care about that, either. All that mattered now was that he was here, disguised as a Welsh warrior, and coming to free us. He stepped closer and our eyes made contact. As they did, my heart sank in despair, for all I could see in them was triumph, contempt and hate. He wasn't going to free us. He had come to gloat.

"So then, you have been caught and will die here," he sneered, "and your father will mourn another son."

"Hussa, try and get a knife and cut us down. Although maybe it's best to wait till the Welsh go away," Lilla said.

Hussa frowned.

"Now, why would I do that, when I can watch you suffer?"

"Hussa, what are you saying?" I asked.

"Dear me, Cerdic, but you are rather dim. Don't you realise I have joined Samlen? Who do you think it was told him about your mother's jewellery and where to find the Villa?"

"You? I thought it was Aedann."

He blinked at that and did not immediately reply. Then he snorted.

"Did it not occur to you that we might be working together?"

Wallace groaned and Hussa glanced over at him, impassively, then back to me.

"Why, Hussa, why?"

"Well, revenge upon you and your family, obviously, but there is more than that. Since my mother died I have nothing in Wicstun, so I have spent less and less time there. I have been travelling a lot and one day, soon after she died, Samlen captured me. I had been out in those woods, beyond the Villa, where we hunted boar. I must have been going further and further west and eventually, I reached the ford on the river and realised I had gone clean through the woods. I was turning to head back, when I was attacked by about a dozen warriors. They took me across the river and brought me in front of Samlen. He was at a camp in that bit of land between the rivers.

"Gods, but he is a monster. I was terrified and tried to get them to let me go, but he just laughed and hit me. He said he wanted to know about Wicstun – how many men were there; what loot there was and so on. He seemed to be planning a raid. I refused to tell them but ..."

Hussa shuddered now and seemed to be reliving something horrific. He did not speak for a couple minutes. Next to me, Wallace was wheezing and then suddenly his chest was wracked by a coughing fit. Finally, Hussa spoke again.

"I don't think I am very brave to be honest. That's another thing your family seem to have over me," he added with a glance in my direction.

Lilla now spoke.

"So, they tortured you and you betrayed us."

Hussa nodded.

"At first I told them tales about there being five hundred warriors at Wicstun and how fierce they were, but they did not believe me. They laughed and then hurt me some more.

"In the end, I told them anything I thought would interest them. Samlen wanted to know about treasure, so I told him about anyone I knew of who had money or precious items. He then let me go. He said he wanted to know more. He said he was coming one day and if I did not keep returning to him with more information, he would kill me. Then, he gave me some money. Not much ... just a little. But I had none myself and what he did give me would feed me for a week. Then, the week was up and I needed more money, so I went and told him about the Fyrd

126

training and who Lord Wallace was and anything I could find. He paid me again and ... I kept on doing it."

He looked me up and down.

"I have good reason to hate you and your family, that's true. So, when I won that tournament on the day of the muster, I was ecstatic. I had triumphed over you, in full view of the people I hated. Not just in full view either, but actually on their land and I had bested their son, as well."

"So that is why you betrayed us?"

"Quiet, Cerdic, let us hear him out," Lilla murmured, wearily.

"In my pride, I thought I could conquer something else. I thought Aidith might succumb to my charms," Hussa went on, with a laugh. I tensed at that and glared at him.

"Did she?" I asked. He shook his head.

"No. Oh, she was happy to spend an hour or two with me, but when I started telling her what I thought about you and your family, she grew angry and in the end went off and left me. I spent a lonely night with just that sword for company."

"Poor chap, my heart bleeds for you," Lilla said, his tongue dripping with sarcasm.

"Quite. Still, I did have the sword and the next day I took every opportunity to brag about it and told everyone how famous a warrior I would be. In the end they got fed up with me and told me if I was so good, why not catch a boar on my own. I said 'I will' and off I went."

"Yes, I know that bit, what then?" I asked.

"Well, I just went and found Samlen and told him about the amber jewellery. Any fool could see it was priceless and I knew that he would be interested. He told me to hide for a while, in order that the company would be delayed returning home, then he could sneak past us. He said that once the raid had begun, to come and find him and I could join his warband and share in its riches."

Lilla hissed.

"You betrayed your country!"

Hussa spat.

"My country! Don't give me that. I've never felt Deira was my country. There I had no past – thanks to Cerdic's family, and certainly no future. Here I can make a new life."

At that point one of the Welshmen called out something and Hussa answered in Welsh.

"Did Aedann teach you that?" I asked him.

He smirked at that question and shook his head.

"Oh, I've picked up a bit of the language these last few months, certainly. One more thing, Cerdic – just to show it has been worthwhile me coming here," and he pulled out a silvery object and twisted it. It caught the moonlight and reflected an amber glow.

"That's part of my mother's earring!"

Hussa nodded.

"There should be enough here to buy a nice house somewhere: slaves and whatever else I want. I would ask you to say thanks to your mother, but you will never see her again, will you?"

"Bastard!"

"Yes, and we know whose, don't we?" He snarled and then turned and walked away over to the other warriors. Samlen One Eye was now amongst them and mounted on a horse. He glanced towards us then he rode across the parade ground and past us, followed by his companies, which now included Hussa. They were marching across the parade ground, not exiting via the southern gate – which we were facing – but going past us towards the west or north gate; I could not tell which.

After they had gone wherever they were going, the warriors who were left behind to hold the fort set a watch on the walls and then most of them retired to their barracks. So, it was the case that after half an hour we were completely alone: three miserable prisoners left out to die in the wind and the rain. I twisted round and looked at my two companions. Wallace was starting to shiver and he seemed to have drifted into an uneasy sleep, disturbed by twitching and sudden moans. He was pale, sweaty and looked truly terrible and I was certain he would not live to see the morning. So, I turned to Lilla.

"We have to escape now: there are not many guards. If we can get free from these bonds, we might stand a chance."

"Not sure I'm going to be much use," the bard mumbled.

"Come on man! We have to try."

Then, I heard the scuffle of feet on the stony ground behind us, felt a cold blade touch the skin of my throat and then someone spoke.

"Evening, Master, what are you hanging about there for?"

I twisted around on the rope, trying to see who it was, although I already recognised the voice. It was the man I had come here to find and to kill. The man who had betrayed us ... or so I had thought. Yet, now it turned out that Hussa was the traitor, but was Aedann his partner as Hussa claimed? If what Hussa had said was true, was Aedann coming to kill me now? Maybe ... or maybe Hussa had betrayed us to Samlen, but Aedann had still taken his chance to escape and join his people. In that case, Aedann might not be in league with him ... or there could be yet another explanation. I needed to know.

"Aedann, that is you, isn't it? I whispered.

"Yes, Master."

"If I'm your master, why is your blade at my throat?"

The blade twitched, the point moving upwards so I could now see it more clearly.

"Let's just say I wanted a little security before we spoke. I saw the look on your face when you were running towards me in that village yesterday – yes I did spot you. You were going to kill me, until that big oaf caught up with you, weren't you?"

I twisted round further, so I could just see the Welshman's eyes and I glared at him. "Damn right, I was – and I tell you what. You promise me right now that you did not betray us, or I will come and kill you after all."

Aedann laughed.

"You're hardly in a state to make such threats and even if you were," Aedann moved nearer and stretched up to whisper close by my ear, "I would like to see you try!"

He raised the blade and I tensed in anticipation of having my throat cut, but it moved away from me and upwards. Aedann had stepped across to stand to my left and was reaching above me, pulling himself up on my shoulder and then sawing at the rope. Suddenly, it gave way and I found that my legs – numb and cold as they were – simply folded away beneath me and I collapsed. With a cry of alarm, Aedann overbalanced and ended up on top of me.

"Get off me!" I hissed and tried to push him away with my hands, but they were as weak as my legs and had no feeling, so it was a feeble effort. Aedann pushed himself up and then suddenly crouched back down.

"What is it?" I asked.

"Hush – guards!" he whispered.

By now it was full dark and the clouds above us blocked the moonlight, so that the visibility was poor. I peered at where Aedann was looking, but at first saw nothing. Then, appearing abruptly out of the gloom, I could see two guards idling towards us, spears rested over their shoulders and shields slung. They were talking to each other and neither looked our way until, when they reached twenty paces away, one of them glanced at us and cried out in alarm. By then, Aedann had leapt like a cat at them and already had buried his blade in the throat of one. The first warrior went down, blood gurgling from his mouth. The other man had a few moments to react and swung his spear off his shoulder to lunge at Aedann. Aedann deftly stepped to the side, let the point pass him and was now inside it, closing in and then stabbing the dagger into the belly of the second man. He gave a scream of agony and then collapsed to the ground, blood spurting out of the wound. Aedann was on top of him now, one hand over the man's mouth to stifle his cries and with the other ... he cut his throat.

My slave, panting hard, wiped the knife on the dead man's cloak and then pulled himself to his feet and scanned the nearby buildings for more enemy warriors. I held my breath, until it was obvious that none were coming and then breathed out, slowly. It had taken barely half a dozen half beats and two men now lay dead, whilst the fort around us slept on: silent and dark.

Aedann turned to me and cocked his head as he looked down at me on the ground.

"Bet you're glad you let me practice with you, now!" he said, then bent down and held out a hand to pull me to my feet. The blood was flowing in my limbs now and I found that with a slight stagger I could walk again. Aedann went to pull his hand away, but I held it fast and asked him the question that was foremost on my mind.

"Aedann, what is going on?"

I had been convinced the slave was the traitor who had told

One Eye of the amber treasure. Yet, would a traitor kill his own kind? Then, there was also Hussa's confession. But, if Aedann was not a traitor why had he run away? I opened my mouth to ask again, but Aedann shook his head.

"Not now, we need to get into shelter and hide. Help me cut the others down," he added in a whisper and moved first to Wallace.

As soon as Wallace's hands were released he slumped down with a moan and Aedann had to support him to prevent him falling to the ground. I stumbled over, legs still weak and helped him as best as I could manage. I could only just feel my arms, but as life returned to them I was able to take over holding the still unconscious Wallace, whilst Aedann went to release Lilla.

"Thunor's balls!" Aedann exclaimed and looking up, I saw that Lilla was standing next to his rope and had clearly freed himself. The bard just shrugged.

"Secrets of the profession," he murmured and winked at me.

"Could you have got free at any time?"

Lilla nodded.

"Then why leave it till now and why tell me you were not much use?"

"I told you, I want a story and that story needs heroes like you two ... besides which, it was an interesting experience," he said, rubbing his wrists.

Intrigued, I wanted to ask more, but I could see he was as tired as I was so, as with Aedann, questions would have to wait.

"Where now?" asked Lilla. I looked at Aedann and raised an eyebrow.

Aedann pointed the dagger to a nearby building where the roof had all but fallen in. It looked dark, cold and abandoned. "There first, I don't think they use it, come on!" Lifting Wallace across his shoulders, he set off at a staggering trot and Lilla and I, both too exhausted to argue, stumbled along behind.

The nearest door in the building, which opened directly onto the parade ground, was blocked with rubble from the roof, but Aedann led us down between the building and the adjacent barracks to a side door. He glanced inside then entered and we followed. This first room was filthy: the roof's timbers were so rotten that some had collapsed opening a hole in the roof, which admitted the damp, miserable weather. However, there was an inner door leading on from it and Aedann walked over and pushed that one open. This second chamber still had an intact roof and so was reasonably dry, although very cold. Wooden frames – maybe from beds or cots – were dotted here and there in the room, although the bedding had long since rotted away. Aedann glanced around the room then lowered his burden gently to the floor.

"This seems to have been used as an infirmary for their sick and wounded," he said. "The Elmetae do not use it, so we should be safe here, for a while."

Wallace was shivering violently now and we needed to get him warm, somehow.

"I think we should start a fire," I said, rubbing the life back into my arms and trying to stop my teeth from chattering.

"If you do, they might know we are hiding here," Lilla pointed out.

I nodded, but then shrugged.

"If we do not, Wallace will die. He is soaked through and very cold. That break to his arm and then the wind and rain was too much for him. We must warm him up, dry his clothes and examine that arm.

"I can treat his arm," Lilla said quietly, "I have studied a little

133

of such things."

"Grettir would be good too, if we could get him. He has been in enough battles to have picked up a thing or two," I mused. "Anyway, let's try and get a small fire going. Maybe over near the door, so the smoke will go that way and it will take a while to show itself. It's dark – with luck the Welsh won't notice it."

Lilla and Aedann gathered wood from the broken bed frames and then Aedann produced a small amount of tinder and a flint, which he started striking to get a spark on the tinder. It took a few minutes to catch, but a small yet cheering fire was soon going and I could feel the warmth gradually creeping back into my cold bones. Wallace had recovered consciousness, but seemed unaware of what was going on. Aedann took off his own cloak and laid it over him and slowly, the Lord of Wicstun stopped shivering quite as violently, although he remained barely aware. We pulled him as close to the fire as we dared then the three of us huddled round the flames, our clothes steaming.

"Now that we are here, we must decide what to do," I said. "But, before we do that, I must know what you are doing here, Aedann. When you left without word, we assumed you'd run away with the Welsh. Then, when we heard Samlen had come looking for my mother's jewellery – the amber treasure as he called it - I thought you must have told him.

Aedann shook his head. "Is that what you now believe?"

"Well, Hussa has admitted to being the traitor, but ... well you tell me. What are you doing here? Go on, Aedann, why did you run?"

"These people are not my people, despite what you say. Oh, we are all Welsh but I am Eboracii – the people of the Kingdom of Eboracum, or Eoforwic as you would call it. Samlen is Elmetae."

134

"So?" I asked. "What's the difference?"

"We are different tribes. Just because we speak the same language and you lump us all together as 'Welsh' does not mean we see ourselves as the same."

"But, you always teased us about Owain and his allies coming to drive us English away."

"Well, the point is you English had me and my family as slaves. I hated that and if Owain came and wiped you out so much the better. But when Samlen came he treated my family just as badly as he did everyone else."

As Aedenn related what had happened, I began to understand: when Samlen raided the Villa, he had taken Gwen and Caerfydd – Aedann's parents – away. Not, as we had believed, to freedom but to yet more slavery. Given the choice of slavery under my father or under Samlen, Aedann had apparently seen my father as the lesser of two evils.

"So, when my parents were taken, I followed," he said. "It was easy enough to find a spear and shield, and in the dark I could pass as an Elmetae warrior. I followed the warband back here and then hid in another of these abandoned buildings. The night before last I located where Samlen was holding the prisoners, but they were too well guarded for me to free them."

"Where are they?" I interrupted, hungry for news of Mildrith.

"Why here, right here in the fort. In one of the other barrack blocks further back, in fact. I was able to find which one and listen to Samlen talking to that Peredur about what they planned for them. Evidently there is a huge slave market in Loidis and in a few days they are to be transferred there and sold."

My spirit had soared at the news that the prisoners were here, but then sank just as quickly when I learned they were to be moved to the Elmet capital. That was a big city, with thousands

135

of inhabitants and once there, I would not be able to find Mildrith. So, we needed to act now: free the company, then the prisoners and get away - and all very quickly.

"So," Aedann continued, "having found them I went away to think what I was going to do. I needed food and so went to barter for some in that village. It was lucky for you that you got stopped and dragged away before you had got to me. No one else saw you hiding in that thicket apart from me, although one young girl insisted she had seen Saxons near the village and they sent word here. After I left the village, I scouted about until I found your warband and was going to talk to you when Peredur jumped you. All I could do was follow at a distance. When I saw the three of you tied up, I realised that now was my best chance," Aedann finished, then he put a hand on my shoulder.

"There is more, Cerdic – and you know this bit already. When I overheard Samlen and Peredur talking, I learnt something. Samlen was bragging about the success of the attack and showing Peredur your mother's jewels and your uncle's sword. Peredur said how lucky Samlen had been to find the jewels, but Samlen said it was not luck; he had already known about them from his tame little Saxon."

"Hussa ..." I hissed.

Aedann nodded.

"So, Hussa lied about you, but the rest is all true then. I wondered at first if he was just ... oh I don't know, making it up to get back at me, perhaps. Right then," I said between gritted teeth, "I'm going to disembowel the bastard!"

Lilla and Aedann looked at each other, but said nothing.

After a moment, Lilla coughed.

"So then," he asked, "how do we escape?"

136

Chapter Eleven
Flight

Wallace moaned and opened his eyes. He looked at us blearily for a moment then spoke.

"Where...?"

"We managed to escape, my Lord. We are hiding in an abandoned part of the fort ..." I started to explain, but by then Wallace had closed his eyes again. However, he was not asleep.

"It's alright ... Cerdic ... I can hear you," he said, "I'm just aching all over and this arm is killing me. I'm not as young as I once was and hanging for hours out there in the rain, it nearly finished me, I can tell you. But, I'm not dead yet, so carry on please. Do you have a plan for escape?"

"Well, I guess the first thing we need to know is where Samlen and his men are," I said, turning to Aedann and then asking him a question. "Have you any idea, Aedann?"

Wallace's eyes shot open.

"Aedann: your slave? I thought he was the traitor?"

I shook my head, took a deep breath and told Wallace about what Aedann was doing here and then about Hussa. When I said that it was in fact Hussa who was the traitor, Wallace frowned.

"Are you sure about this, Cerdic, you aren't ..." he hesitated, perhaps unsure how to phrase his question, "you aren't ... leaping to conclusions, hoping that Hussa really is the culprit?"

I knew what he was thinking: that maybe I would jump at the chance to implicate my half-brother and dirty his name. I shook my head.

"No, my Lord. Oh, I know all about ..." I stopped abruptly

and looked at Lilla and Aedann. How much did they know? Ah well, this was no time to worry about that. "I know all about my father and Hussa's mother," I said. "I know Hussa is my half-brother – my father's bastard son – and I know he blames me for the fact that our father rejected him, albeit at my mother's insistence, when she was carrying me." I stared at Lilla, challenging him to say something, but he kept quiet and just listened, so I went on. "So, I can see why you might think I have a motive to falsely accuse the man, but truly I am not – am I Lilla? Aedann?"

"Lord Wallace, all that Cerdic says is true – I heard it myself from Hussa, not two hours ago," Lilla said and then turned to me. "Don't worry, Cerdic, I won't tell anyone about your father. I make stories and songs: I don't spread gossip. You have my word."

"Mine too ... Master," Aedann agreed.

The fire cracked and popped and we all looked into the flames for a moment.

"Well then, Aedann," Wallace asked at last, "do you know where Samlen went?"

Aedann shrugged.

"When I saw his troops gathering on the parade ground, I decided to find that out if I could, so I tried to sneak out through one of the ruined sections of wall to the west. The stonework has fallen away and the gap filled in with wooden debris," he explained. "It's not hard to pull that away and make a hole. That's how I got in and out during the night the first time and I used it again yesterday to get back in. I thought that I might follow Samlen a little way and see where he was heading, so when I saw them leaving I went back to the gap, but that time there were guards up on the wall nearby and I couldn't get out for fear of being seen."

"So you didn't see which direction they were heading in?" Wallace asked, sounding disappointed.

No, my Lord, I'm sorry," Aedann said, adding as an after-thought, "but they went out the west gate."

"Towards Loidis, maybe," Wallace mused.

"Do we know how strong the garrison is now they have gone?" I asked Aedann.

He nodded at that.

"Well, approximately. Samlen took two hundred men away with him. That leaves fifty or so warriors."

"Fifty? We can manage fifty, Lord," I suggested, "that is, if we can free the company and get our weapons."

Wallace nodded, "Yes, even without weapons, if it comes to it." Then he cocked his head to one side, noticing that Aedann was shaking his head. "What? What is it?"

"I think they also have cavalry here."

"Cavalry?" Wallace asked, his voice tense, "How many?"

"That I don't know, but I saw twenty or so patrolling around the fort yesterday and I don't think any mounted men went with Samlen: none that I saw, in any event."

Wallace looked questioningly at me and then at Lilla, "That puts a different light on it."

We looked at each other and grimaced. Cavalry could be a problem: to us, anyway. Like all Saxon armies we did not use horses in war much at all, other than for our leaders, messengers and lords. Lilla had once told us stories of the Welsh using regiments of cavalry in the past and how terrifying that could be. He looked a little anxious now, but I just shrugged.

"Look, if we need to, we will cope with them ... Lord?" This last word was to Wallace, who was slumped down, head lolling about, looking rather green and I now noticed that he was shivering again.

"Cerdic ... sorry, I can't think. You must come up with something ...," he slurred and then drifted off again. Lilla went across and wrapped his own cloak around Wallace.

Sitting back on his heels the bard shook his head. "Whatever we do, we must do it fast. He won't last long."

I nodded and turned back to Aedann. "Where are our weapons?"

"That, I do know. I saw Peredur have his men stack them all in the cart they had with them when he captured you. The cart was on the corner of the parade ground behind the Headquarters building, but when it started to rain I saw some men move it to a storeroom and wheel it inside."

I tapped my fingers on the ground for a few moments whilst I thought about the problem. To be honest, there were not too many options open to us, so I decided on a plan quickly enough and spelt it out to the other two.

"Aedann and I will go to the storeroom and see about getting the cart. Lilla, you carry Wallace and hide near the building where our company are being held. We release our men, grab up our weapons and Wallace can be loaded on the cart. Then we find and free the townsfolk and get out. Obviously, sooner or later, the alarm will go off and then it could be hard for us, but it sounds as if we have about as many men as the garrison - assuming they have a similar number of cavalry to foot soldiers. If there are more, well ..." I shrugged, "we just have to take our chances."

It was not much of a plan, but the night was drawing to a close and the next couple of hours − the time before dawn − was the best for stealth and surprise.

Outside, it was drizzling gently. That was fine by me, as it was likely to dissuade the Welsh from wandering about. It was also still dark, although over the eastern wall, towards Deira and my home, the sky was beginning to lighten.

Aedann and I left the abandoned infirmary first, keeping to the darkest shadows around the buildings and avoiding the open parade ground. We edged round the square, past the workshop where the company were locked up and across the northern side of the parade ground, until we came to the storeroom. I tried the door and with a horrendous creaking that set my teeth on edge, it opened. I moved inside, but then I stopped after a few paces because I could now see almost nothing in the pitch dark interior. We had no alternative but to swing the doors wide open to let in some of the silvery light from outside.

The light was still pathetically weak, but it was enough to see the cart standing in the middle of a large room, which had work benches along the left side. A few rusting tools hung on the walls above the benches. Edging carefully forward, I reached out with my fingers and gently grabbed the cart handles and tried to pull on them. With the weight of eighty swords, spears and shields upon it, it was extraordinarily heavy and I simply could not budge it. Aedann took the other handle and together, we could now shift it. Hardly daring to breathe, we carefully manoeuvred it towards the door.

We managed to get the cart out of the shed, but it was when I tried to turn it that things went wrong. The heap of weapons and shields were precariously balanced at best. As we turned it the cart gave a lurch to the side and a half dozen spears, a couple of shields and an axe slid off the pile, teetered on the edge and then with an ear splitting crash fell to earth.

We froze as the echoes of the horrendous sound died away. The silence of the night descended once more on the fort. After a moment I let out a breath I had been holding. Aedann shrugged at me - his raised eyebrows showing he was asking the same question as I. Had we got away with it? Then Aedann's face turned into a scowl and I glanced at where he was staring. High up on the side of the fort a light flared in a window as a candle or lamp was lit. Two figures were illuminated by the light - two men peering towards us. A moment later they were gone. Then we heard shouting from inside the fort. It was time to be gone.

"Move now: go!" I hissed at Aedann and we hurtled forward. Across the parade ground we ran, cart bouncing along behind us. Spears and shields clattered up and down and more fell over the side, making a dreadful din as they too crashed to the ground.

"Carry on, don't stop now!" I urged Aedann on, though we were panting under the effort. I could now see our two companions lurking in the darkness next to the building we were heading for. We came to a halt and stood for a moment, catching our breath. Lilla took pity on us and running to the cart, found an axe then ran with it to the workshop door. He removed the bar with one hand and tossed it to the side then he thrust the axe blade into the gap between the doors and gave a mighty wrench one way and then the other, cracking the wood around the lock.

The door was still shut and the lock was holding. Lilla tried again, but the wood was strong and he could not yet break it open.

Over towards the Headquarters building, there was a shout of challenge and a dozen Elmetae armed with swords and shields came running at us.

"Eduard!" I yelled, "Eduard! Can you hear me?"

A muffled response came from inside the workshop.

"You must break the door down: quickly man!"

142

I then turned and rooted about in the cart for a moment, found myself a shield and then I gave a whoop of triumph as underneath the shield I saw the sword I had taken from the Welsh warrior I'd killed at the Villa. I seized it eagerly and went and stood beside Aedann, who was armed with a spear and shield. The cart was on one side of us and the corner of the prison building on the other, which gave us some cover as well as protecting our flanks, at least until the Elmetae could work their way round the other side of the cart. The first two warriors arrived and charged forward, one swinging a battleaxe and the other a sword. I took the blow on my shield and then hacked back with my sword. I connected with the man's shoulder and he fell away, blood spouting. Aedann had been knocked down by his assailant, who was now on my flank. I cut across at him and felt the blade slice into his sword arm. He dropped his sword, staggered backwards and Aedann, scrambling to his feet rammed his shield into the man's face, crushing his nose. As the Elmetae fell to the ground, Aedann picked up the warrior's sword and slashed it across his throat, killing him. There was no time to think about it. To our left, Lilla had found a bow amongst the weapons and was firing over the cart at the group milling around it. Wallace was conscious again, at least for the moment and having located his sword, was standing in the gap beyond the cart, somehow managing to hold back four Welshmen. The man's grit was remarkable, but I caught the look of agony in his eyes and knew he would not long stay on his feet.

Suddenly, the cart moved. Three of the enemy were pulling it away so they could get at us. Lilla seized one handle and heaved it back, towards him. Wallace staggered across from the wall of the building and dropping his sword held onto the other, but we were outmatched and outnumbered and a moment later there was a gap in our defences and half a dozen of them were surging through it.

From behind me, there was a crash and a splintering noise and the doors burst asunder. With a roar, Eduard came out first, swinging a loose plank of wood and leading the company in a charge. Like caged and very angry bears suddenly finding themselves free they fell upon the stunned Elmetae, and it was they who were now outnumbered. The fight did not last long after that. Quickly now, every man armed himself. Cuthbert took his bow back from Lilla and examined it anxiously, like a mother taking her child into her arms. So, we had our weapons back and had freed the company, but now we had to find our captured families and still get away. In the distance I could hear shouts; the remaining garrison was rousing. We had only moments before they were upon us. Wallace, barely conscious, was bundled unceremoniously onto the empty cart and pulling it behind us, we headed towards the barracks where Aedann had said the prisoners were kept, all the while scanning our surroundings in the growing light and waiting for the next attack.

As I headed that way, I felt a hand on my shoulder and I turned to see Grettir, looking grim and unhappy.

"Master Cerdic, you have given that traitorous slave a sword," he said with a jerk of the head at Aedann. I sighed, wearily.

"He took it himself from a man he killed, Grettir. He is on our side."

"But, your father said ..."

"My father is not here!" I shouted and several of the company turned at the noise.

I lowered my voice and whispered to my tutor. "My father is not here: I am. So leave it, Grettir."

"But ..."

"I said leave it!" I shouted.

Grettir recoiled, then just nodded his head curtly and said no more.

I headed away from him, leaving him to brood on his own. I had no time for discussion. The sun was just starting to rise now and casting its early light on a dozen bodies lying on the ancient fort's parade ground. I wondered how many more would be dead before the sun went down.

To the north of the parade ground, beyond the store houses and workshops, there were two rows of long and low barrack buildings: a row of six immediately across our path and then another row between those and the north wall, where there was a gatehouse. Narrow paths passed between each block and the adjacent path linked to another, thus dividing the rows and creating a maze of passageways.

"This way!" shouted Aedann, running down the middle passageway between buildings, which each possessed decaying roofs and rotten doors.

Up ahead, the narrow passage and the one joining it at right angles formed a crossroads.

Suddenly, just as he reached this junction, Aedann gave a cry of alarm and tumbled to the ground. In the space where his head had been a moment before, a spear point was thrust from around the right hand corner. Eduard was just behind Aedann and had to swerve to avoid being impaled. He ran on past the spear head and twisting as he did, grasped the shaft and pulled at it. With a curse, a surprised enemy warrior came hurtling forwards, overbalanced and then, as he tottered forward, he fell to the axe of Sigmund and a swift stab of my sword.

As Aedann scrambled to his feet he followed Eduard, who had carried on around the corner to the right. I, Cuthbert and three others raced after them.

We found a dozen more Elmetae lurking between the back of the barracks and the front of the next row. The space was confined and the numerical advantage of the company pressing up from behind was not going to help. Yelling their challenge, the enemy warriors levelled their spears and advanced towards us. Suddenly, from the rear of the column, I heard Lilla give a shout of surprise. Helped by two other men he had been hauling Wallace along on his cart and had been caught by more warriors coming from Samlen's Headquarters across the parade ground. One of our men was now dead and Lilla was swinging a seax wildly at three warriors, whilst screaming for help. A lad from Wicstun at his side held five more at bay with his spear. Grettir took half a dozen men back to help them and they charged at the Welshmen, drove them back and then retreated, pulling the cart across so that it partially blocked the passageway. More of our men rushed to the rear and with a clattering of wood they linked shields to block the approach. Lilla staggered forward to the crossroads, blood tricking from a wound on his scalp. He leant against the wall of a barracks and took several deep breaths. I trotted over to join him and looked around, trying to work out what to do next.

The fight was now in the tightly confined spaces at the company's rear and along the righthand passageway. That left two routes still open. The passage to the left was blocked by rubble from the adjacent building, the rear wall having collapsed into it making it impassable. The way ahead seemed clear and peering in that direction I could see it led to the palisade at the north wall of the fort – the wall opposite the way we had come in.

"Aedann!" I yelled. He was fighting in the righthand passage. His enemy, a big brute with a bald head and scars all over his arms, was swinging a huge axe two-handed. Aedann watched the weapon come at him, parried it with his shield and then rushed the man, hacking at him with his seax. The man brought back his axe to block the attack and then they were locked in a desperate exchange of blows. Distracted by Aedann, the warrior did not see Eduard's spear thrust until it had impaled him. With the warrior to his front writhing on the ground, Aedann rejoined me.

"Which way are they?" I shouted, above the din.

He pointed further along the passage leading through the next row of barracks.

"That way and then turn left before you reach the outer wall. Be careful to the right though, because the northern gatehouse is there and it will be manned. The prisoners are in a barracks two over with the door facing the north wall."

I looked back down the south passage and saw that Wallace was unconscious again and slumped in his cart. Sigmund was his second in command and I shouted to him.

"What is it lad?" he bellowed and looked my way.

"We have to go this way, Sigmund! Aedann says that is where our people are."

"You sure you trust him?" he asked, looking doubtful as he disengaged from the fight, after being replaced by another man from the village.

I looked at Aedann and hesitated.

"Not before an hour ago," I confessed, "but he freed us and had plenty of opportunity to betray us, besides which, his parents are prisoners of Samlen, as well."

Sigmund nodded and waved several of the men past him up the passageway. Just then, Cuthbert yelled for our attention. He was gesturing, not into the melee that rumbled on in the side

147

passage, but upwards towards the roof of one of the rear barracks. Three Welsh archers were up there and were firing down at us. One missile grazed Cuthbert's shoulder and buried itself into the ground behind me. Another flew high and smashed ineffectively into the wall to the side. The third arrow leapt forth from the bow of its archer, flew straight and true towards us finally smacking, with a sickening noise, into Sigmund's throat.

He stared at me, an expression of utter disbelief on his face, then staggered back against Aedann and slid to the ground, quite dead.

"Bollocks to this!" Cuthbert swore, looking down at Sigmund's body. Then he whirled round and fired two arrows at the enemy. The first shot an archer through the face, killing him instantly. The second hit his comrade in his shoulder, knocking him screaming from the roof. The remaining archer flashed him a look of abject horror and then scuttled back, over the roof top and out of sight.

The closest of our men had seen Sigmund die and many were now looking restless and began to edge back, away from the enemy. If I was honest, I felt like joining them. Wallace was unconscious, Sigmund dead and the man who had fallen at the rear of the company was the oldest headman of the other village contingents. If Cuthwine had been here, he would have been next in line. But, he was not and whatever father said, I was unsure I could fill his shoes. Suddenly, Lilla was at my side, looking sadly down at Sigmund. He then studied my face and I could see that he could detect the doubt in my eyes. Lilla, used to reading an audience, could also feel the panic rising about him. But, he also knew how and when to play a role and did so now.

"Master Cerdic, what are your orders? Should we carry on

down this passageway as Sigmund ordered?"

Well, I might not be as bright as Lilla, but I hope that I am not as hesitant as Aethelric. I could take a hint and gladly took one now.

"Yes ... Yes ... er, Eduard – you and twenty men hold them here. Lilla – go and tell Grettir to start pulling back this way and then try and help Eduard force a path along that eastern passage. We need to get to the east gate and out that way if we are to find the road home. I'll get the prisoners and return here. Go now," I added, as loud as I could; trying to sound confident. Then, turning to the men around me I shouted, "Everyone else: this way, follow me!"

Not waiting to see if anyone did, I ran. It was not much of a speech and I just had to hope they would follow. Aedann told me later that most of the Wicstun Company had looked doubtful, I was only a youth after all, but Lilla, Cuthbert and Eduard bellowed acceptance. Cuthbert and Aedann ran after me and after a moment, the rest of the company followed. I may have been a wet behind the ears greenhorn, but I was still heir to the Villa and that gave me authority. Or else, perhaps the men just wanted someone to make the choices for them. Whatever the reason I did not care and follow me they did.

I now had forty men with me. The other half of the company were fighting under Eduard and Grettir. I reached the end of the passageway and glanced right. There was a gatehouse there just as Aedann had said. Half a dozen Elmetae were on the battlements above the gateway, peering anxiously towards the noise of the fighting. When we emerged, they gave a shout and one of them started firing sling shots at us, though we were at their extreme range and the missiles fell well short. I left Cuthbert and singled out ten of our own slingers to harass them with arrows and sling shots then carried on round to the barracks where the prisoners were.

I thought of Mildrith somewhere within, no doubt terrified by the noise of fighting and having already suffered the gods knew what horrors. I rushed on, eager to free her, Aedann by my side no doubt motivated by the thoughts of his parents, keeping pace with me.

We did not see the two horsemen, until it was almost too late.

"Look out on the right!" one of the men behind yelled and we saw them at the very last moment: two horses galloping straight towards us. Astride them were armoured horsemen, their mail shirts glinting golden in the sunlight. Red cloaks streamed out behind them like tongues of fire and in front, aiming at our hearts, a pair of long lances with bright, sharp points, which now came to claim their victims.

Neither I nor Aedann had spears that might have kept the horses away; instead we each carried a sword. Our only hope was agility. We leapt apart and rolled across the ground. Hooves thundered by an inch from my face, one of them caught my sword and knocked it out of my hand whilst another had caught Aedann a glancing blow in the side of his chest. He now lay, a screwed up ball of agony, by my side. The horsemen galloped past and turned to come again, but by then the rest of our company had caught us up and the enemy, outnumbered as they were, fell back towards the corner of the fort. From there they watched for a chance to dart in again and strike at us.

Rubbing his ribs, Aedann got to his feet and we were off again.

The barracks were unguarded, but had been locked and so one of the woodsmen from Little Compton used a hatchet to hack his way through the door. Once inside, we discovered a scene of utter pandemonium. The villagers and townsfolk were convinced the Welsh were now coming to kill them and so, screaming and panicking, they had backed away into a corner: mothers hiding their children behind them, their faces pale with terror. At first, after we had entered, we were not recognised by the bewildered captives, but one by one the prisoners saw a familiar face and relaxed, cried out and then rushed over to us. I looked about for Mildrith, eager to find her too, but she did not seem to be here. Frantic now, I searched around, yet still I could not find her. Moving through the excited throng, I came upon Aedann. He had located Gwen, his mother, and was standing next to her holding her hands, so I rushed over to them.

"Gwen, where is Mildrith, I can't ..." but, my words caught in my throat as I saw that her eyes were red and filled with tears. I looked down and there I saw Caerfydd lying on a pile of rotten straw, a filthy sack for a blanket laid upon him. His eyes were open, but they looked up at us blankly: he was clearly dead.

"He was injured the evening of the raid, Master," Gwen said with a sob. "They made us march through the night to get here and he had already taken a fever by the next day. I pleaded with them for help, but they just laughed at me. I said I was Welsh, but they hit me then and said I was a traitor to Britain and Eboracum for serving you Angles."

I looked across at Aedann. His eyes were wet as well, but sorrow was already fading to anger, a look of implacable hatred stamped across his features.

"He got weaker and died in the last hour ..." Gwen finished.

I laid my arms about Aedann and Gwen's shoulders. "I'm sorry. If I had been faster maybe ..."

Gwen shook her head. "No Master, he was already dying. Best he died in peace than have to be dragged along in torment."

I nodded, but now had to ask about Mildrith.

Gwen looked at me, suddenly shocked.

"Master, forgive me. I tried to protect her and hide her, but that monster with one eye came looking for her last night. Seemed to know she was here and asked for her. She tried to hide, but he found her and then the brute dragged her screaming outside. I'm sorry ..." her voice trailed away and she broke down and wept.

I was horrified. Samlen had not thought much about Mildrith before last night, then. Not until I had lost control and blurted out her name. It was my fault she was gone and I was afraid I knew what he had in mind for her.

As if reading my thoughts, Gwen said, "He seemed taken by her – she is a beauty and no mistake. He said something about her being a 'tasty morsel' and saving her for the victory celebration ... and then ... then he said she would not have long to wait ..."

I nodded, but I was no longer listening. I had to get away after her; find Samlen and his men and free her. But I knew I could not just run out on the company. I swore under my breath, cursing the gods, and then shouted, perhaps harsher than I needed to, for everyone to move.

Once outside, I looked around at them all. There were thirty of whom only about ten might be able to fight if they needed to. We armed these as best we could then, with my gaze lingering on the pair of horseman still circling off towards the corner of the fort we herded our people along and set off back towards Cuthbert. It appeared that no more guards had joined the half dozen already at the gates, so I left him watching them and started down the narrow passageway.

I had hoped to force a way towards the east gate and get on the shortest road home. However, when I reached the crossroads again, I saw at once that this was not going to be possible. The fight had been escalating whilst I had been away. The south passage was blocked by twenty Elmetae and the cart, which had now had one wheel hacked off it and lay tipped over at an odd angle. Wallace was being helped back to where I was. He looked at me through misty eyes and I could see that he could not yet take command.

To the east, Eduard's predicament was even worse. Thirty or more warriors had formed a solid shield wall at least five men deep. Eduard staggered back to me, blood dripping from a gash above one eye.

"It is no good, Cerdic, we cannot get out that way."

"Right ... damn it! Erm ..."

There was nothing for it but to retreat back to the north side of the fort and go out of the north gate. To do that, I had to capture the gate.

"Hold them here!" I shouted at Eduard and then turned to the rest of the men, shoving the townsfolk out of my way.

"Back, go back. There is no way out this way! Follow me," and I pushed through them to the space between the barracks and the north wall.

There were still only handfuls of Elmetae here and only half a dozen were holding the gatehouse. I sent Aedann and thirty of our men towards the gate to try to force it open. Turning back, I groaned when I spotted that on either side of where the company was fighting were other passageways running from the centre of the fort to the north gate. The two western ones I was not concerned with; many of the buildings over there seemed to have collapsed and blocked the access. The eastern passages were different, however, because the Welsh might try to bring men through them to outflank and surround our men still fighting in that maze. I took Cuthbert and the few archers and slings-men we had and stationed them near the passageways to fire on any sign of movement.

Meanwhile, I went back and found Grettir. He had now retreated to the junction and was holding well there. Eduard could not progress, but was holding his own.

It was a tricky manoeuvre, but they had now to pull back both of their groups into the northern passageway. It had to be at the same time and we needed to be able to form up a shield wall again once we had done it.

Eduard glanced across at Grettir, who nodded and they both shouted, "Run lads!" Both of them at the same time hacked wildly about them to hold back the Welsh. Their men ran towards me, where I stood in the northern passage with half a dozen more men. We let them pass and then shouted to Eduard and Grettir. They turned and ran. Arrows spat at them and spears thrust forwards, but the Welsh were impeded by being bunched up and with Eduard grinning wildly and Grettir panting hard, they both passed me and we closed the gap.

I left Grettir and Eduard to command the rear guard and ran back to the gate. The cavalry force had grown. Four more had joined the the first two through a gap in the west wall, but six were not enough to worry us too much. I was more anxious that groups of the Welsh would appear through the other passage-ways, so I knew we must quickly take the gate.

Rushing to the north gate, I saw that it was still shut and barred. An archer and a slinger on the battlements above the gate were keeping us away with intermittent but accurate fire. At least one missile had found its mark, for I now spotted a youth from the village lying on the ground. His face screwed up in agony he was clutching at his arm, which looked broken. One of the other men was examining it and trying to strap it up.

Cuthbert had joined us when he saw the problem and was exchanging shots with the gatehouse guards. However, he had now started to run out of arrows and was gathering up those fired from the battlements, using them against their former owners. Others joined him and soon they gave a huge cheer as the Welsh archer fell screaming, an arrow through his lungs. The slingshot man hunkered down and kept out of view.

I picked up an abandoned shield, pushed through the company to the front and found Aedann. His face was grim, but when he caught me looking at him, he looked away. Time for talking later, his face said, and he was right. Lilla appeared and I sent him to fetch Grettir and Eduard and their men.

"Right then, we need that gate open. Come on!" and I ran forward screaming. Leadership seemed to be mostly about running towards the enemy and hoping to the gods that the other bastards followed you. Today they did. With a huge roar, the company surged forward and reached the gates. More Welshmen had climbed up to the battlements above us and were pelting us with whatever they could find. Others knelt and thrust spears down at us. We held our shields over our heads and I heard a din as something hard bounced off mine.

A moment's effort had the bar on the gate removed and the gates pulled back, towards us. I stepped to the side and let the company pass and the townsfolk follow. I then looked back towards the passageway, waiting for Eduard and Grettir's group to emerge. At first, no one came, but then at last I saw them backing out of the passage. Over towards the corner of the fort, the cavalrymen saw them as well and sensing an easier target, moved towards them.

"Eduard!" I bellowed trying to draw my friend's attention to his danger, but he was too far away to hear me call.

"Cuthbert!" I shouted, now needing archers, but when Cuthbert arrived with his bow he had no arrows left.

I looked desperately towards Eduard and Grettir, and the dozen men with them. The horses walked forward; the lances dipped and as the riders dug in their heels, the horses started to trot and then canter.

"Eduard!" I screamed, knowing it was in vain: my friends and the other men were doomed.

Then, the horsemen spurred into a gallop and charged.

Chapter Twelve
The Army

I watched helplessly as the galloping horses pounded across the ground towards Eduard. He finally heard them coming and turned to see death closing in on him, mounted on iron-shod hooves. Desperately he dragged two men round and together they levelled their spears to try to deflect or impale the horses.

It would not have been anywhere near enough to stop the charge and the armoured cavalry would have cut down our men like a scythe in a field of barley. Ironically, it was the Welsh themselves who saved my friends. What I had feared earlier – that more Welsh would emerge through the eastern passageways and surround us – now happened. A dozen Elmetae warriors had been pulled away from those following up Eduard and Grettir and had run down the adjacent passage. Emerging on the open ground, they swung round to cut off our men. In so doing, they saved Eduard and his companions' lives.

For now, as the cavalry charged forward they saw with alarm that their countrymen were suddenly running in front of them and in desperation, they heaved on the reins and turned away, aborting their attack. They then circled off to the west to regroup. I knew that this was our only chance to get away and I took it.

"Aedann, a score of you come with me. Charge!" I ordered and off we went, crashing into the rear of the newly arrived Elmetae, who were surging around Eduard's beleaguered band. Our attack took them by surprise and we cut down half a dozen before they reacted. The momentum took us right through them to join up with Eduard.

Now united, our desperation giving us the strength of madmen, we slew the Welsh surrounding us.

"Right, that's it. Pull back!" I shouted and as a tightly huddled mass of thirty or so warriors, we retreated towards the gate. Shields overlapped shields; spears projected in all directions. The Welsh pouring out of the passageway harried us all the way, but they had suffered many losses and once we joined the others at the gateway, we had over eighty warriors and thirty townsfolk and were far too strong for them. Even so, I did not feel we were strong enough to force our way back through the fort to the east gate, for although we now outnumbered our foe, there was also an unknown quantity of horsemen to worry about. Had the Welsh been even a little more organised, they might have stopped us in our tracks, but their attack was not coordinated.

Outside the gatehouse the track led northwards. I had hoped to pass round the outside of the fort and reach the eastern road home to Deira, but I saw now that this was impossible. The ground dropped away steeply towards the river and at the bottom of the slope it was marshy and boggy. Half a dozen men might make it, but well over one hundred, including injured men and townsfolk, would not.

So, I turned my gaze north to the track exiting the gate: where did that go? Ah, I said to myself, Wallace's map - that was the answer. I rushed over to where he was resting, supported by two men from Wicstun. Inside the fort, the Welsh were gathering and the horsemen were hovering fifty paces away. Still, there were only forty or so Welsh in all − too few to attack us, for the present. More may soon come though and I was anxious about how many horsemen they had in total. I had to decide what to do and quickly.

"My Lord" I said. There was no response.

"My Lord," I said again and he at last opened his eyes and looked at me, but without recognition.

"Lord, it's Cerdic ... Cerdic, son of Cenred from the Villa."

Finally his eyes widened slightly and he focussed on me.

"Cerdic? Where are we?"

"Still in Calcaria. We are trying to escape, but I need your map, quickly!"

He nodded, but then coughed violently for several moments and I glanced anxiously at the gathering enemy, every second seeming an eternity. When he finally recovered, he reached inside his tunic and pulled out the oilskin-wrapped parchment and handed it to me.

"Cerdic ... I'm sorry," he said.

I shook my head.

"Not your fault, Lord: just rest and we will get you home."

His head had slumped again and I feared I was lying to him. As it was, he was not likely to make it home. Then again, were any of us? I rolled open the map and stared blankly at the markings and symbols. I recognised the lines representing the rivers: Derwent, just west of the Villa and the Ouse. There was also the fort of Calcaria - if that was the fort I was looking at - then the track, which looked like it was once a Roman road, curved north to pass over a tributary river that joined the Ouse further east. I followed the line beyond the crossing and saw that it reached a large town or city. There were letters next to it, but like most Angles I had never learned to read.

"Lilla!" I shouted. The poet jogged over to me. I showed him the map and asked him what the city was.

"Eoforwic, Cerdic: it's Eoforwic, beyond the River Wharfe."

"That's only ten or twenty miles away, if I'm right," I mused.

Lilla nodded.

"That is where we are going then." I raised my voice to get everyone's attention.

"We go this way. It's about two miles to the river," I jabbed a finger at the map, "and another ten to Eoforwic. Then we will be safe. Grettir and Eduard will lead with half the men. Then the townsfolk will follow them and finally Aedann and I will bring up the rear, with the other half of the company. Lilla, you come with me too. Everyone, keep your eyes open for more horsemen. Stay together and we will make it. Let's go!"

So, off we went. The path sloped gently downhill. To our right the ground fell away steeply, but to our left it was all flat and open fields. Some distance away on the other side of the fields there was more woodland. All was clear in that direction. As I ran, I kept looking anxiously behind me at the Welsh. They let us leave, but most of them followed us at a distance of a few hundred paces, hoping perhaps that the column would begin to drift apart and there would be stragglers to attack. I was worried about that too and I did not let Eduard set a pace that was too quick for the women and children to keep up.

So, for an hour, we moved along the track at little more than a crawl and like wolves, the Welsh kept pace with us. A group of them even started to overtake us to our left, moving parallel with the road, but far out of bow range. I could do nothing to stop them, so I let them be. One relief at least was that there were no cavalry in sight. Lilla pointed that out.

"Those damned horses are not following," he muttered.

"Thanks be to Woden for that then!" Cuthbert replied.

"You fool; it's worse not knowing where they are than being able to see them," Aedann grumbled and I glanced towards him. He was walking with his mother, supporting her as she stum-

160

bled along in his arms. I had misjudged him gravely and he had risen above that to - well, to all intents and purposes – to save us. Yet, where was I taking him? Back to slavery again under his old masters. Life must seem pretty grim for him.

"You had to say it, didn't you? Tempted fate you did!" Cuthbert replied. Then I saw why. The cavalry had not left us: now they were back.

Out in the fields towards the woods, maybe half a mile distant, we could glimpse them moving from copse to copse and between small hamlets and farmsteads. There were a lot more of them now. They had not pursued us at once, as it seemed they had wanted to gather their whole strength. There was silence in the company as we walked along, each of us counting their numbers.

"Forty, I think," Lilla said, squinting.

Cuthbert shook his head.

"No, I count nearer fifty."

I believed Cuthbert, whose sight, like his archery, was acute and accurate. So then, there were fifty horsemen keeping pace with us and moving ahead and perhaps forty spearmen following on foot. We still outnumbered them, but not with warriors: we had many wounded and sick with us, as well as women and children who would not or could not fight. Our only hope was to reach the ford over the River Wharfe before they caught us up. I ran ahead to the front of the column. Eduard and Grettir had seen the horsemen too and were, despite my earlier orders to keep it slow, pushing the pace as fast as they could.

I looked ahead to see if I could see the river. At first I could not, due to the trees and hedgerows blocking the view, but we then passed over the crest of a small hill and there, half a mile away amongst marshes and woodlands the river lay like a dark green ribbon. I looked over to the horsemen and thought we might manage to reach it ahead of them.

"Master Cerdic, look that way," Grettir urged me. He was pointing towards the horsemen.

Irritated, I snapped back at him, "Yes, I see them Grettir, I'm not blind!"

"No, look the other side of them!"

I looked beyond the horsemen. The small hill we were on gave us the advantage to see a long way and the woods had now become sparser and given way to open meadows, so we could see many miles to the west. It was hazy, but I could pick out the road: a long brown-black scar on the landscape, coming out of the fort and heading west, joining, it seemed, another road that ran straight as an arrow from north to south. A Roman road: there was no doubting that.

What Grettir had seen, though, was not just those roads, but smoke. Close to that junction smoke was rising from fifty or more fires: camp fires from an army, which this early in the morning would be cooking food and preparing for the march. An army of maybe five hundred men – all invisible at this distance, but betrayed by the many smoke plumes.

Samlen had marched that way the night before with two hundred men. Now what had happened? Had he been joined by others? Had Ceredig of Elmet finally consented to go to war? Was this the army of Elmet, paid for by my mother's jewellery: One Eye's amber treasure? Was poor Mildrith there amongst the enemy? Had Samlen touched her yet, or was he really planning to use her for his pleasure on the night they won the battle with us? Was Hussa there too, gloating about his triumph and enjoying his half-sister's anguish? I closed my eyes and swore.

"King Aelle needs to be told, come on," I said grimly and

pushed the pace even faster.

We dropped down the slope and the army was lost from sight. The horsemen, though, were not. They were now well ahead of us and starting to move back across the fields, trying to cut us off from the ford ahead of us. Looking that way, I felt hope rise, as it seemed they would not be able to reach us. The road was dipping down to a marshy plain that ran alongside the river. On the right side of the road the ground was now level with us, but on the left – where the horsemen were coming from – it fell suddenly away and I could see that ahead of us, the road followed the edge of a cliff. It was only fifty or so feet high, but quite impassable to cavalry.

Further ahead still, the cliff and the road dropped down to the level of the river, but it looked to me as if the marsh came right up to this point, effectively blocking off any access from the fields on our left up on to the road. As we got closer, however, my hope turned to fear as I now could see that I was wrong. There was in fact the narrowest of gaps between the end of the cliff and the boggy ground. The marsh appeared to be full of deep pools that would prevent the horsemen crossing. The cliff blocked them also, but there was a path of bare earth and clay running between them, no more than five feet wide. Five feet: enough for two horses to pass abreast. That was where the horses were heading: that was where the danger lay.

"Keep up the pace!" I shouted to Eduard and then ran back to the rear of the company. As I ran past them, I could see from the wild eyes and pale faces of the women, that many had seen the horses and knew that our chances of escape were small. When I reached the back of the column and looked at the Welsh warriors pursuing us, I grimaced, for I could see that our chances had just got even smaller.

163

The Elmetae following us on foot were now jogging along and were less than fifty paces behind us. They were close enough now for me to see the faces of the men who chased us: close enough to see the hungry expressions and in particular the smug, expectant smiles. The Welsh had not simply come hurtling after us, no indeed: they had been clever. Their leaders had known their land. They knew how the terrain lay up this road and with the forces available to them had laid a trap for us. Soon, we would be smashed between a hammer and an anvil: the hammer of their cavalry and the anvil of their shield wall. I flung a silent curse at Loki. The god was playing his tricks again: permitting us to escape and letting us feel we were safe, before finally allowing us be caught, a mere quarter of a mile from the river, the border with Deira and safety.

Unless ... unless we could reach the river first: then there was still a chance of escape. Well then, there was no time for hesitation: every second counted now.

"Run!" I bellowed. "Run like all the demons in the world are after you!"

Run we did. Eduard, making light of his wounded shoulder lifted Wallace onto his back and ran as fast as any of us, despite the burden. Even little Gwen dragged along by her son, picked up her heels and scampered along. If we could keep the pace up, we might yet manage to escape.

Then Loki laughed again and I saw we were doomed.

On the road ahead of us, the Welsh cavalry now stood. The hammer had arrived and we were still a hundred paces from the river. A hundred paces: that was all, but it might as well have been a mile. We stopped running and gasping for breath, awaited our fate.

But, one of us did not stop running. Aedann let go of his

mother's hand and carried on towards the horses. Twisting his head round, he shouted back to us.

"Come on, keep running. They are not all here yet. Keep running, you English bastards!"

Cuthbert pushed his way to the front and pointed.

"He's right, there are only three of them on the road: scouts ahead of the main squadron, I figure."

I could see it now and I glanced behind. The Welsh were less than fifty paces away, but in front, the hammer was not quite the threat I had thought. The other horses were coming, but were still a hundred paces away, moving into a narrow column to pass between the cliff and the marsh. Aedann was right: there was still a chance.

"Run!" I shouted and again we were off. Lungs and throats burning, the company and the townsfolk ran straight at the three cavalry. Horsemen are a threat to infantry and we fear them above all other enemies, but not just three against over a hundred. They knew it too and as we closed on them they spurred their mounts and veered away onto the fields to the east.

Meanwhile, Aedann was no longer running down the road. He had turned and headed into the little path between bog and cliff. There, he swung his shield round, drew his sword and braced himself in the gap. The horsemen would have to ride him down to get to the column. Eduard and Grettir saw what he was doing and ran to join him. They had spears as well as shields and stood either side of him, overlapping his shield and dropping the spear points towards the coming horsemen. Three more of the company joined them and formed a rear rank. Cuthbert had managed to scavenge half a dozen arrows and notching one of them on the string, stood behind and to the side of them.

The first of the company had reached the ford. I stopped them there and we let the townsfolk start to cross. The Welsh were closing in, seemingly keen on revenge and the rest of the company were milling about. I knew that I had only seconds to play with.

"Shield wall: form a shield wall now!" I shouted the order. It was the first time we had done this together since we had practised at the Villa just a few days before and they were all clumsy finding their places, but gradually our shield wall took shape. I started the wall just at the end of the cliff, so as to protect our men on the path and then slanted it across the road onto the bog beyond, angled to protect us from the three horsemen, who were circling about over there and still posed a threat if they chose the right moment to attack. The Welsh foot soldiers had stopped running and with a clattering of shields and spears, were also forming up opposite us.

Now, we finally had the advantage. There were more of us and we held a good position. The Elmetae hammered weapons on shields and screamed abuse at us, goading us into attacking them. Some of the company moved forward, but I hauled them back.

"Don't be bloody idiots – they want us to attack. Stay still and let them come to us."

I was not going to be a fool that way, but I was worried about the one weakness we did have. If the Welsh cavalry could break through the tiny group on the muddy path, they would be round behind our main shield wall and would unleash a horror upon us. All now depended on Aedann and his five comrades. The pounding of iron hooves on clay told me that the moment of decision had come: the horsemen had arrived!

The leading one spurred his mount and shouted an incomprehensible war cry as, without hesitation, he charged towards

166

Eduard. His lance was long and sharp and he targeted Eduard's throat. Eduard pulled up his shield and the lance struck it hard, just above the centre. The blow knocked Eduard back, so that he ended up lying on top of the man behind.

There was a cry of triumph and the Welshman spurred on to ride them down. Aedann took one step forward and stabbed his sword hard straight up into the man's belly. The triumph now turned to horror and then to agony. With a scream, he fell backwards. His horse, dragged over by the weight, reared up onto its hind legs. Eduard, clambering back to his feet, brought up his spear and plunged it into the beast's groin.

There was a gut-wrenching squeal of agony from the animal as it fell with a crash, back onto its rider, crushing him under it. It then lay on the ground, thrashing and writhing, as its life poured out into the marsh beside the path. One hoof caught Aedann on the knee and he screamed as his leg gave way. The next horseman arrived and made to jump over the still twitching body of the first horse, looking to land on Eduard.

As it left the ground, there was a twang, followed by another and two arrows caught the rider in the throat. He fell off the horse and landed in a deep pool of muddy water in the bog. The weight of his armour pulled him down under the surface, where he choked on his own blood and drowned in the filthy water. His horse spun round and headed back the way it had come, crashing into the column behind. In the resulting chaos, two more horses slid into the bog. Twang-twang-twang and three more arrows followed, all finding their marks, so four dead and dying horses blocked the narrow path. At last, the horsemen reined in and hung back. Cuthbert had one last arrow loaded, but he did not fire, instead he stood, aiming at the horses and waiting for them to come again.

The Welsh shield wall had fallen silent. They had been expecting the cavalry to break through. Now that had failed, I could see their leader studying us and counting our numbers. Was he going to try and attack, hoping that the horses would find a gap to break through after all?

Out in the field, the three scouts moved over to talk to him and I could see that they were pointing across the river. I bent my neck to look that way, but at first I saw nothing. Then, there was movement: twenty, no thirty spearmen, moving down the road towards the ford from the other side. I had an anxious moment as I thought of that army we had seen earlier. Was this a part of it, already in Deira and coming to cut us off?

Then I saw that with the spearmen were some of the townsfolk from Wicstun. They were coming towards us and leading what I could now plainly see were fellow Deiran warriors. With a splash, they were across the river behind us. My knees trembling with relief I stumbled over to their leader: a severe looking bald-headed man, who looked at me sceptically as I approached.

"Where is your lord?" he asked.

"There he is," I pointed at Wallace, who was sitting on the road, looking exhausted and only just conscious, "but he has been injured. His lieutenant was killed at Calcaria so ..."

"So, the lad took over. Did it bloody marvellously actually – saved us all ..." Wallace said weakly and then, struggling to his feet, he staggered over to us.

"But you have saved us all now, Lord ... erm ...?" I hesitated, not knowing who the man was.

"Earl Harald, of Eoforwic," he answered. "But, it looks like the danger is over," he added, nodding his head towards the Welsh, who were backing off down the road. In the fields to the west, the cavalry were also retreating leaving half a dozen men dead on the path and in the marsh.

I blew out a long breath: the enemy finally knew they could not beat us today, so we were safe. I went and helped Wallace and together we led the company across the river and back into Deira.

When we reached the far side, I turned back to see Aedann limping across, surrounded by men from the company who were clapping him on the back.

"For a Welsh bastard, you were pretty good there!" Eduard said to him and with a wink at me, he carried on down the road after the company. Grettir hung back and stood looking at Aedann, not saying anything. Suddenly, he nodded his head at the lad: the closest that the gruff old teacher ever got to saying he had been wrong about a man. Aedann had proven his worth, the nod said. He glanced at me and tilted his head for a moment, acknowledging that I had been right. Then he turned away. In a moment, I was left alone with Aedann.

"Well then, I went to Elmet to find and probably kill you, but you saved us all. I thank you for that. For a slave, you sure know how to fight," I added.

Aedann looked pained now, reminded that here, on this side of the river, that was all he was − a slave. He tossed the sword down onto the road.

"You had better take that. You know what your father says about slaves having weapons."

I reached down and picked up the sword, then studied him for a moment. Finally, I made up my mind. I turned the weapon round and handed him the hilt.

"You're no slave. Take it, you've earned it," I said.

"But, your father ..."

"Take it," I repeated and this time he did.

"I will deal with my father," I added.

He grinned at me and together we walked down the road.

Chapter Thirteen
Council of Aelle

Earl Harald led us along the road to Eoforwic, then halted in the first settlement we came to: a tiny village with just a couple of dozen hovels clustered around the headman's hut. One doubled as a rundown alehouse. Here, he allowed us to rest, get a meal, dress our wounds and in many cases grab a few hours' sleep.

A little later in the day, he came and found Wallace and me in the corner of the ale house. Lilla and Grettir were examining his arm, afraid the traumas of our ordeal had increased the risk of infection - or worse. If it had turned black and begun to rot away there was nothing they could do and Wallace was as good as dead.

When it was unwrapped we could all see the arm was badly swollen and almost black, but that was bruising, for whilst agonisingly stiff it did not smell infected. Relieved, they strapped it up again and Wallace sat back on the bench, leant against the wall and took a long draught of his ale. After some broth and a tankard of beer, Wallace was more alert than he had been since his brutal attack from Samlen.

"How's the arm, Wallace?" Harald's face was dark when he sat down opposite Wallace.

"Hurts like buggery, but I'll live; for now any way," Wallace said and took another sup at his mug.

"Glad to hear it. Right then, I came to tell you that after Cerdic here told me about that army you had seen in Elmet, I sent out scouts and they confirmed that there is indeed a force of over four hundred spears. They are camped just the other side of the border close to the Roman road."

"I wonder what he is planning," Wallace mused as he wiped the bowl with bread, chewed on it and then swilled it down with more ale. He frowned and looked up at Harald. "Is there any news about Owain and where he is?"

Harald shook his head. "Last I heard, he was still in Rheged, but his army is getting bigger each day, all the rumours say, so it can't be long now."

"But where ... where will they attack?"

"I have no idea," Harald shrugged, "but the King might. That is the other thing I came to tell you, he must know of Samlen One Eye's army as quickly as possible. I was about to head off anyway. Just yesterday, I received a summons to Godnundingham: Aelle is calling a great council. Everyone expects he will call out the Fyrd and then it will be war."

"We are already at war, Harald," Wallace said.

Harald grunted and then nodded. He finished off his own tankard and got up to leave.

"Get your men ready, Wallace," he said. Then, raising his voice so that everyone in the tavern could hear, he added, "We will march within the hour to the King's hall."

There was some groaning at the thought of setting out again, from more than one of the company, but a scowl from Wallace silenced them and the men went back to their meals, or muttered curses into their ale.

As a young man, Aelle had conquered the Welsh kingdom of Eboracum including the prize, their capital: the city he would call Eoforwic. Eoforwic was a rich city and probably the most important city in the North. However, Aelle did not rule from there. He held court not far from Wicstun in his halls at Godnundingham. It was to this stronghold that we now marched.

Our road went northeast to Eoforwic and as we marched along it I grew excited with the anticipation of seeing the city at last. I was to be disappointed: before we reached it, Harald led us down a branching road heading east. We would save ten miles and several hours this way, he explained, as it cut off a big loop and saved us going north of the city and back southeast to Godnundingham. I swallowed my disappointment: the King's summons had been urgent and Harald had no time to permit my sightseeing.

It took the balance of that day and most of the next to reach Wicstun. Harald allowed us to stop there overnight and let the townsfolk go home. As we came close to the town, a shriek of joy rang out from the tannery, which was a couple of hundred yards to the north. Two auburn-hairedgirls of about my own age or younger, rushed out to us and over to their mother and threw themselves at her, hugging her tightly to them. The tanner, himself limping from a wound he had taken defending his family from the raid, joined them and we passed them by and left them to their joy. Then, as if this was an alarm signal to rouse the town, suddenly the road ahead was full of people. They came out of their houses and workshops and walked towards the company, searching the faces of those we brought with us, some expectant, some not daring to hope until they had seen the ones they looked for. Soon enough, the tears of joy and sorrow started. Joy for those we had saved, sorrow for those we had left behind in a foreign land.

Sorrow aside, for the most part, the people of Wicstun wanted to hold a great feast to welcome their families – and us – home. But then, when they were told that the fighting was not yet over and indeed that the war was probably only just beginning, their exuberance subsided, for a while. In the end though, it was if everyone decided to take what happiness they could today, uncertain of what the approaching weeks would bring and soon the ale houses were full and the beer flowing.

Eduard, Cuthbert and I were drinking ale and eating bread in the 'Wolves Head' tavern, whilst we waited for the orders to resume our march, when my father found me. Wallace had sent a message to him about the royal summons.

He rushed over and embraced me. It had been four days since I last saw him: he was moving about much more easily now and although his scars were still ugly, they were beginning to fade. He sat down and asked the question that I had been dreading.

"Mildrith ...?" he asked.

I shook my head and saw the blood drain from his face.

"She's alive, Father, but Samlen has taken her with him to his army. I tried to find her but ... she was gone, when I got there."

He stared at me, his mouth moving but no words coming. At last he spoke, "Is she ... I mean, did he touch her?"

I shook my head. "No ... that is, I don't think so - and I don't think he will either, not yet at least," and I told him about Samlen's boast.

"I'll find her, Father. I promise."

He looked into my eyes then nodded, reached out and put his hand on mine, giving it a squeeze. "We both will," he said.

Suddenly his eyes widened in anger and he pushed past me with a roar. The tavern noise ceased in an instant and all eyes turned at the cause of the commotion. Aedann had come into the room, and on seeing him, Father had burst across it and in an instant he had the lad by the neck pinned up against the far wall. Tightening his grip, he reached for his hunting knife and placed the blade against Aedann's throat.

174

"Master please ..." Aedann croaked.

"Treacherous snake, I'll slit your throat and feed you to the ravens."

"Father, I ..."

My father turned a face that was red with fury towards me.

"What are you doing, Cerdic? Sitting on your arse drinking ale, while this piece of horse shit is walking around?" Then he saw that Aedann was wearing a sword and his face grew redder, "Walking about with a sword! Have you lost your senses? This turd betrayed us. Woden's balls but I am going to rip out his guts, he's the reason Mildrith is gone."

I leapt across, grasped his wrist and forced the knife away from Aedann's throat.

"No, Father, he's not!" I said, as calmly as I could.

"What crap is this?"

My father's face was now almost purple and his eyes bulging. I knew how terrible his anger could get and my heart was pounding like the galloping hoofs of the Elmetae cavalry, but I had to try to explain.

"It's not crap, it's the truth. Aedann did not betray us, it was ..." I hesitated now, thinking to mention Hussa, but then feeling that this was not the best time. "... it was not Aedann, anyway. No, he left the Villa to find his parents. He rescued us in Elmet. If it was not for him, I would be dead now. That is why I gave him a sword. He earned it."

"Earned it, are you mad? He's a slave."

"No, Father, he's not. I freed him."

At that my father actually let go of Aedann and turned to stare at me.

"You're making free with my property, boy," he finally said, with a deep growl, "Cuthwine has not been dead a week and now you go on as if I am dead too."

I shook my head. I was scared of the old man. He had a ferocious temper, particularly if he felt disrespected. I'd rarely stood up to him before – but I would today.

"No, Father, it's not like that. Aedann rescued us, he fought with us and helped us free the prisoners and then was a hero when we got away, risking his own life to save ours. He took that sword off a man he killed and it's his by right. I will obey you in anything you say but," I gritted my teeth, "... but Aedann remains free."

He stared at me for a full minute and around me I could hear men shuffling their feet awkwardly. Glancing at them, though, I saw that none of them was looking away and indeed they all were staring at us, fascinated by this exchange. This was the Wicstun Company and I had led them for a day and brought them home. But, I was still a lad and they wanted to know what guts I really had.

"If I agree, if I free him, what will he do? Where will his loyalty be?" Father said, now looking at Aedann.

Aedann said nothing although he seemed to be thinking about the question, but I answered first.

"If you are asking for loyalty, then that is a question for after you free him, not before. Loyalty and fealty can only come from a free man."

Father thought about that then nodded. "Good answer, I suppose," he admitted, with grudging respect. "So, you're a hero, are you, Aedann?"

Aedann shrugged. "Too bloody right I am, my Lord. But what I want is ... I just want to kill that one-eyed bastard. My father is dead because of him and I want revenge."

"On Samlen?"

Aedann nodded.

"That's a good answer too," Father mused rubbing his cheek. "Very well then, Aedann son of Caerfydd the Welshman, I release you from slavery. You're a free man, as these men will witness."

Aedann nodded and smiled. He then drew his sword and I felt my father tense, expecting a blow. Aedann looked straight into my father's eyes and then, suddenly, he knelt in front of him and offered up the hilt of his sword.

"I, Aedann son of Caerfydd, swear loyalty to your house and your heirs and offer my sword in your service. I will go where you will ... but I ask to go with Master Cerdic and to go to war."

Then, he stood up.

"That's all we need, a bloody Welshman in the army," Eduard said into his ale, but loud enough for us all to hear. Aedann smiled and suddenly the tavern was full of laughter again.

Harald let the men sleep late the following day but by early afternoon, we set off again, led by Harald and Wallace. Wallace's arm was still in a sling and he was sitting on his horse a little stiffly, but he was alert and looking better than he had just two days before. Northeast we went, with Father walking with us this time. We spoke of Mother and Sunniva and how worried they were now all the family had left. Father's voice faltered whenever he mentioned Cuthwine or Mildrith and despite the bright spring day, I too grew mournful and maudlin. I was not sure how to tell him about Hussa's part in the raid, but I just had to. I took a deep breath.

"Father, you know I told you that Aedann was not the traitor and that it was not him that told Samlen about Mother's jewellery?"

He looked across at me, as we continued to walk, side by side.

"Yes."

"Well, I've not told you who did betray us, have I?"

He frowned and then shook his head.

"Well ... I did not mention this in front of the men in the tavern, but we know who betrayed us."

He stopped walking and put a hand on my shoulder.

"Go on, tell me. Who was it, then?"

"Hussa," I replied.

He recoiled at the name of his son then he just stared at me, shaking his head.

"No!" he said at last, unable to accept what he was being told.

"Hussa, Father: it was Hussa."

So, as we resumed the march, I now gave an account of all that occurred in Calcaria. When I had finished, he was silent for many minutes, staring away from me at the fields we passed.

"Very well," he said at last. "Leave Hussa to me – I will deal with him. He's my responsibility."

"We will deal with him together, Father," I replied.

We arrived at the King's hall just as it became fully dark. To reach the hall, we passed through a gap in a high rampart and the external ditch that surrounded it, and entered a courtyard beyond. Here there were pens for livestock, a well, numerous outhouses and craftsmen's workshops. The gateway through the rampart was built from massive logs, reinforced with iron bars and guarded by fierce looking warriors, who questioned Lord Wallace and Earl Harald before permitting us entry.

We could now see the hall itself. Granted it was a Saxon hall and as such made from wood and not built of stone. It was, however, a vast building: rectangular in shape with a tall sloping roof, from the centre of which a swirl of smoke emerged from some fire within. The walls were supported by huge upright posts, perhaps a yard apart, and additional buttresses lay up against the wall. The hall's vast double doors were, like the main gate, braced inside and out by iron bands: this was a building most definitely built for defence. A couple of hundred men could hold the ramparts for many weeks, if need be. Any assault on this place would be costly in the lives of the attackers.

Wallace halted the company outside the great hall and went within for a few moments. He then emerged and ordered us to go inside and find some food and drink, for the King was inviting all warriors to his tables tonight. The council itself would be tomorrow.

Entering the smoky hall, I was struck by the size of the cavernous interior. Two long tables stretched the length of each wall. At both of these, scores of men were sitting on benches, eating and drinking. Dozens of slaves were busy refilling ale tankards or bringing in more food from doors that exited at the far end, into the kitchens. A roaring fire burnt in a pit in the centre of the hall, its smoke finding escape through a hole in the roof directly above. Opposite the entrance, a third table stood at right angles to the others joining them at the far end. Here again, warriors sat on either side, but these were clearly men of importance, rank and wealth. Earl Harald was taken up to the King's table, whilst we were waved to spare benches on the side tables, but not before bowing towards the King.

Wallace sat between my father, and Lilla and I opposite them. The rest of the company, Cuthbert and Eduard included, found places where they could. Wallace picked up a chicken leg, bit into it and then used it to point towards the high table.

"That is King Aelle, Cerdic," he said, indicating a man in his sixties sitting in the exact centre, on a raised chair. He appeared rather frail, which surprised me after all the tales I had heard. I said this to my father and Wallace.

"Ah boy, but fate grants us all a span of years. You should have seen him leading our armies almost twenty years ago into Eoforwic. He was tall and strong then. If he appears weak now, remember all that he achieved in taking command of a few scattered settlements when he was just a youth, barely older than you, and forging Deira from them. That was forty years ago now, when I was just a child," Wallace said looking admiringly at the older man.

Wallace went on to point out other men of worth, including those who would no doubt command the companies of our army, if war was really to come.

"Him you know, of course," he said, pointing to the overweight and unimpressive man sitting to the right of the King. "Prince Aethelric, the King's eldest son, at least of those that live. Did you know that Firebrand's real name was Aethelric also?"

I had not known that. So Aethelric had been the name of Firebrand of Bernicia — the old king and father to their current king, Aethelfrith. It seemed odd that Bernicia and Deira should have princes and kings of the same name. I mentioned this.

"Not really, Cerdic, Ric is a common name and Aethel is, of course, a noble title. It means nobly born — the nobly born Ric if you like," Wallace explained, amiably.

Next to him, Wallace told me, sat Herecic, Aethelric's son, who was perhaps ten years old. One place further along, I could see a boy who was about the same age, or perhaps slightly older.

"That is Prince Edwin. He is Aelle's youngest son and from what I have heard as strong-willed a lad as you would want to meet. Coming on well in his studies of fighting too," Wallace added. I looked at Edwin for a moment and then away. I suppose when you consider how long he and I were to spend together in just a few years, fate should have given me a sign that he would be of importance to me and indeed all of Northumbria. However, it did not and instead I found myself gazing at an attractive, dark-haired and finely dressed lady of about eighteen years, who was pouring wine into Aelle's goblet.

"Yes, she is pretty eh, Cerdic?" said Wallace slyly. Cuthbert and Eduard heard this and sniggered and my father grinned at me.

"I see you are growing up, boy," he said, "but such ladies are not for farmers' sons. Tell the boy who she is, Wallace."

"That is the Princess Acha, Aelle's only daughter, Cerdic, and well beyond your hopes. Mind you, I approve of your tastes."

"Who is the man to the left of the King?" I asked, mainly to change the subject. I pointed at a tall, broad-shouldered man, whose once blond hair was touched by silver and grey. He was looking around the room with a serious, even critical expression, as if the King's warriors were treating life a bit too lightly.

"Earl Sabert. He has lands east along the coasts and brings two companies from the Wolds and Moors," Wallace frowned, "be careful round him, Cerdic, he does not suffer fools gladly and has little tolerance for youth."

I shrugged and drank some more ale. I didn't see that I had any reason to have dealings with the Earl of the Eastern Marches.

We ate and drank into the early hours and then found a corner of the hall to sleep in. After the horrors of the last few days, the drink and warmth allowed me to drift into a pleasant sleep.

The following morning, I woke with a horrendous pain in my head and a sour taste in my mouth. Around me, groans and curses suggested that not a few others felt as I did. I dragged myself to my feet, pulled on my tunic, boots and cloak and went out into the cold dawn to breathe some fresh air and to have a piss.

Soon others stirred and we began to gather in small groups and talk of war and, in the case of many from the Wicstun Company, revenge on Elmet. A little later that morning, the warriors still inside the great hall were evicted and the lords gathered to discuss the situation. My father and Wallace attended, but the rest of us from Wicstun along with most of the other warriors who had been there when we had arrived last night, were left outside.

Grettir decided that we might as well practice with our arms and indeed, with companies from elsewhere in Deira present to drill with, we were able to assemble for the first time as a larger army. We practised moving in a close formation of three hundred or more men in three ranks. Those boys like Cuthbert, who had proven more adept with bow or sling, were selected for this role in battle and they would try running forward, hitting mock targets and then scuttling back to shelter behind us.

Towards noon, Lilla came and found me.

"Gods, but you look a mess," Lilla said.

"Thanks: so do you," I lied. Lilla always looked immaculate, even after a battle.

"Come on," he said, holding out a clean tunic then tussling a hand through my hair and dragging it into some shape. "Put this on; the King wants to see you."

I froze in the act of straightening my clothes.

"What?"

"You heard me, seems he wants to hear from the hero of Calcaria," Lilla said, biting into an apple.

"Why does he think I'm a hero?"

"Oh, that would be because I told him," he mumbled, around a mouthful of apple.

I stared at the bard, but he just held up his hands.

"It's what I do, Cerdic ... you know, tell stories. That's why I came to Elmet – I did tell you."

"Huh! Very well, but what does he want to know?"

"What you know about One Eye, Elmet's army, that kind of thing."

So there I was – summoned into the council of Aelle. The hall had been cleared of the debris of the previous night's feast. All the tables had been moved to the sides of the hall and chairs brought out for the lords to sit on, in two lines down each side. They stared at me as I walked in, so I searched the room for friendly faces. There was Lord Harald nodding at me in recognition and Lord Wallace, looking alert and attentive. Next to him sat my father. There were thirty other lords or masters of lands, both large and small. Some wore chain armour as if they had already decided that war was coming. Sabert was an exception. He did not wear armour, but sat with a dull, dark green cloak wrapped round him. He studied me with a sceptical expression as I approached the King.

I looked now towards the other end of the hall. Aelle was there, sitting in a high-backed chair and to his right stood Aethelric, his head bent as he whispered in his father's ear. When he saw me he gave that vague smile that a man gives when he feels he ought to recognise someone, but can't quite recall where they met. He said something to his father and now Aelle looked up at me. His body was indeed frail, but in his eyes was an intensity like the glow from a blacksmith's forge. I could well imagine how he had once inspired a nation. One day soon, alas, the fire would die, but having seen him in his dotage I felt somehow sad that I had not known him when he was young.

Lilla and I stopped in front of him and we both bowed.

"Sire, this is Cerdic, son of Cenred of the Villa," Lilla introduced me.

Aelle nodded.

"I knew your uncle, lad. He was a fine man and maybe the bravest warrior I ever knew ..." he said and as his voice trailed off, the light in his eyes dimmed for a moment and he seemed to be looking somewhere else – to another time perhaps, when he had been younger. Suddenly, they snapped back into focus and he continued to speak. "So then, Cerdic, Lilla has already sung your praises."

I coloured at that and glanced at the bard.

"But now, please tell me in your own words what you saw in Elmet."

So I did. I told of going to Elmet and of the capture of the company. I told of meeting One Eye, the treachery of Hussa – but without mentioning he was my brother - and the courage of Aedann; of how I had felt despair about Mildrith and finally, I described the army I had seen from afar.

They all listened to me in silence, but all the while I spoke, Aelle kept those burning eyes on me, not commenting and not giving any indication if he approved or disapproved. After I had finished he nodded once, then at last he spoke.

"It is a pity you did not kill that Hussa when you saw him."

"I could not, Sire: but I will the next time."

I noticed my father's expression as I said these words. He was uncomfortable. Was he thinking about Hussa's mother? Was he realising that one of his sons might soon have to fight – and kill - the other one?

I was dismissed at that point, but as I walked towards the door, I paid close attention to what was said next.

"I ... I think it is a trap," stuttered Aethelric. "Samlen's army is a trick. He is trying to draw us away north. We should march on Loidis, like we planned to."

"Catraeth, my son, you are forgetting Catraeth. Every indication is that Samlen is going there. That is where the danger is."

Now, a new voice spoke, dripping with scepticism.

"Sire, you place a lot on the words of a mere boy. Dare we commit our army on some wild goose chase on the back of what this youth might have seen?"

I turned at the doorway and glanced towards the voice. The speaker was Earl Sabert. He was facing the King but his arm was stretched out and pointing at me. Then, the doors slammed shut leaving me standing outside, feeling angry and ridiculed. More than that, it left me wondering where and what Catraeth was.

At midday, a meal of bread and dried meat was provided and then, in the afternoon, we held a wrestling competition. Cuthbert was beaten in the first round, but Eduard and I were able to win several bouts. In the end, a great brute from the Wolds, named Alfred, defeated Eduard and won.

Finally, as dusk approached, the news came that a decision to call out the Fyrd had been reached. All the men were called to order and instructed to be ready to march at dawn. Little detail was given beyond that. Wallace and my father were still inside the hall, but Lilla found me and told me that my father and he, along with a dozen other men, were being sent out east on fast horses to call in the Fyrd from the outlying settlements along the Humber and up in moors. That came as a shock. I had assumed that I would be travelling with them both, but now we were going our separate ways.

That night, the food was simpler and less ale was served. I saw my father briefly as he came to get his weapons and equipment. He looked anxious, but he would not at first speak of why, saying only that he had to leave at once. He clasped me to him, wished me luck and turned away, but then stopped and glanced back at me.

"Cerdic, I am going away tonight with Lilla, to the East."

"I know, Father – to call in the Fyrd."

He shook his head. "No – well, at least we will do that on the way."

"The way where?"

"To the coast son, we are to get to Scearburgh by dawn and find a fast ship. Then, we are to sail north, to Bernicia. I hope to reach it tomorrow night."

"Bernicia, that means ... Aethelfrith?"

He nodded.

"The King told me I was injured and could not fight, but could serve him best by persuading Aethelfrith to come to our aid."

Confused now, I frowned at that news.

"You're not to tell anyone, but the rumour that Owain is assembling a vast army is true. The biggest in a lifetime: two thousand spears at least."

I gasped and Eduard, sitting at a fire nearby, looked over at me anxiously.

"Two thousand: but that's impossible!" I whispered.

"Aelle does not think so. His spies tell him this army is huge and it is coming, Cerdic. It is coming within a few days and Deira cannot beat it alone. I have to persuade Aethelfrith that we Angles must unite or die separately."

I nodded.

"Be careful, Father."

"I will. Besides – I have Lilla. He knows Aethelfrith and will help. Probably bore me with tales of Cerdic the hero, as well."

I smiled at that, but then noticed my father was still looking worried.

"There is another thing. Aelle is too old to lead the army. He is giving command to Aethelric."

My heart sank at that news. Hesitant, vague, forgetful Aethelric was in charge of the army!

"Aethelric!" I hissed the word and saw men turning to look at me, suspiciously. I turned away from them and whispered, "Aethelric? Are you sure?"

"I'm afraid so, Cerdic. I'm anxious that even if I can persuade Aethelfrith to march, it will still take us a few days to come. What worries me is that the Prince will," now he also whispered, but even softer than me, "... lose his nerve. If he considers a retreat, you must try to help Wallace persuade him to stay on. I will come, Cerdic. I WILL COME. Do you understand? Aethelric must wait for me and keep the army at Catraeth."

Catraeth: there was that word again. Where was it? Was it in Elmet? I was not sure of that. Although of course I had seen Samlen's five hundred men there. Was that part of the army heading to Catraeth? Why was it so damned important? I opened my mouth to ask my father, but just then, Lilla came across riding one horse and leading another.

My father mounted it and glanced down at me.

"I'm coming back, son: be careful!"

Then, he spurred his horse and they were away, galloping even before they left the gate and riding out into the dark.

I yawned and went and found a place beside Eduard. He offered me his jug of ale and I took a swig and passed it back. The flames in the camp fire drew my gaze and I was struck at how bright they were. Like the fire within Aelle. The old King saw something, knew something and as a result we were marching in the morning to Catraeth.

187

What was Catraeth? What would we find there? I had headed to Elmet expecting to find Mildrith, to confront a traitor and kill Samlen, to take back the amber treasure and my uncle's sword. I had achieved none of that. Mildrith was gone with Samlen, who had my uncle's sword and the traitor was with them still. Not Aedann, as I had thought, but Hussa: Hussa who carried some of the amber treasure as reward for the betrayal of his country.

So, in the morning, were we heading back to Elmet? I wondered if perhaps I would find them all there. Would there be one huge battle to decide the future of the North? Would the Welsh or the Angles triumph? Would my people be swept into the sea?

Would I find Mildrith, Samlen, Hussa, the treasure and the sword at the same place ...

... at a place called Catraeth.?

Chapter Fourteen
North

T he next day we were woken half an hour before a cold grey dawn, one on which the sun was concealed by deep banks of fog rolling down from the moors. The mist filled me with a sense of foreboding and it seemed that I was not the only one. For, as we gathered around the camp fires, broke our fast and organised our equipment, we all spoke in hushed whispers, each sensing the same tension in the men about us that made us jump in alarm when the noise of a dropped pan or a pair of shields clattering together rang out through the gloom.

It was with a sense of relief that we finally marched out, heading north and west back along the Roman road towards the city of Eoforwic. Prince Aethelric would join us on the road, we were told, but for now Harald was leading us to his city. At last, I was going to get my wish and I would visit the city I had been desperate to go and see throughout my childhood. As we approached and we could see the vastness of it – far bigger than any of the places I had visited before – I could not help but smile, which made me laugh at my childish excitement. I was marching off to war after all – indeed I might die in the battle – and yet, here I was getting excited over seeing a few shops and taverns! Then, we entered the gates and I decided to just enjoy the moment.

A city of many thousands, Eoforwic was the greatest trading hub in the North. A settlement had been here before the Romans, but it was they who made it their northern capital and the base for one of their legions. After they had gone, it was the focus of Welsh resistance to my ancestors' invasion. The great

King, Coel Hen, had made it his city. In many ways it was still Welsh, despite almost twenty years of occupation by Deira, for the Romans had taught the Welsh about living and trading in cities and they had not lost that entirely yet, whereas we Saxons still preferred our villages and market towns.

The road we followed took us along the north bank of the River Ouse and through the stone walls that enclosed the Roman legion fortress on that side of the river. Earl Harald and his warriors ignored the garrison buildings. So too had the Anglo-Saxon traders who had come to make a living in the city. We Deirans, not comfortable with the eerie, tomb-like barracks, had abandoned them to the Eboracii tribesmen to live in; apparently they did not mind them as much as we did.

We passed the command building, which was three stories high; its courtyard lined with stone pillars the width of tree trunks and the height of the tallest oaks. Then we halted at the foot of the stone bridge that crossed the Ouse. Here, Harald let us fall out and rest while we waited for the mustering of his two companies from the city.

Wallace, who seemed to have recovered fully from his ordeal, though his arm was still in a sling, gave us freedom to cross the river and explore. "Just be back here in two hours and don't get drunk, or I'll hang you from one of those pillars!" he threatened.

On the far side of the river was the civilian city. That was how the Romans had built it: garrison on the one side and city on the other. Here was row upon row and street upon street of houses, little estates and a vast trading centre, market and workshop district. The scale was overwhelming, but just as we had done in Samlen's stronghold in the old Roman fort of Calcaria, we could not miss the decay around us. There was hardly a building where the tiles had not fallen off the roof, or where the walls were not cracked. Indeed, there was hardly a street without a house abandoned due to the scale of damage from the storms and winds of two hundred winters or the destruction Aelle's army had caused seventeen years before. Yet, the Welsh lived on in whatever shelter they could find, whilst the Saxons built new houses of wood in the gaps between the stone buildings or on the land outside the walls. A sudden thought came to me that we were like children playing in our parents' house whilst they were away: making a bit of a mess, but assuming that they would sort it all out in the end. But, of course, the parents of this city would never come home.

Aedann, Cuthbert, Eduard and I strolled through the maze, taking in the bewildering variety of stalls and trade houses of all kinds. The smell was unbelievable – a heady mix of urine from the tanneries, human waste tossed in the street or down open privy pits, exotic spices traded from across the North Sea and from as far away as the fabled cities of Byzantium and Rome, smoke rising from five hundred fires and forges, the alluring scent of roasting pig or lamb and a thousand other smells I could not place. Our ears were assaulted by a clamour of sounds ranging from the cries of animals being slaughtered, the clanging of hammer on sword, spear, nail and chain in a score of forges; children screaming and crying in unseen alleyways and houses; the call of hawkers and salesman and the constant rumble of human conversation in English and Welsh.

It was still, as I have said, mainly a Welsh city – although ruled by us Deirans – and I became aware as we walked about that we were being watched. Small groups of dark-haired youths followed us as we walked along, or gathered on corners and stared at us with ill-disguised loathing. They whispered to each other in the Welsh tongue, but fell silent if we got close. Nevertheless,

Aedann had heard what they were saying.

"They have heard some rumours that Owain's army has left Rheged and he is to join with Samlen, but they did not say where," Aedann muttered to me.

Aedann might not know, but I had a pretty shrewd idea of the name of the place.

"What do they think about that, then?"

Aedann shrugged.

"Most of them have grown up, like me, knowing that once our people ruled his city like most of this land and now we are slaves, or at best second class free men. You Angles rule the city and own the land. Now, they hear that Owain is coming to kill you and drive you into the sea. How do you think they feel?"

I nodded, looking at the nearest group of young men who were now laughing as they looked at us, as if we were sheep soon to the slaughter and they knew who was wielding the knife.

"What about you, Aedann? How do you feel about it?" I asked, with a sidelong glance at my former slave. He looked at the youths and shrugged.

"I made my promise, Master Cerdic; I'm serving your father."

"But, that takes you to war against your own people."

He nodded. "Ironic, is it not, that my enemy, Samlen is Welsh so to kill him I must fight with the conquerors of my people."

Wallace came and found me with Cuthbert and Eduard appraising a bow on a fletcher's stall. He waved at me and I went over to him. Eduard and Cuthbert stayed at the stall and began haggling for the bow, whilst Aedann wandered off towards one of the groups of Welsh lads. He seemed to be making an effort so that they did not think he was with us and I watched him, wondering what he was doing, until Wallace started talking.

"Ah, Cerdic, I have been meaning to have a word. I have to

say that I was impressed – more than impressed in fact – by your conduct in Elmet. You are just a lad and to have done what you did – taking command of my company like that ..."

"I did not intend to, my Lord ... but after Sigmund died..."

He held up his good hand. "There was no one else and you felt like you had to do it. Well done, anyway," he said, with a nod. "Yes, you did well, but be aware that others might not believe you are up to the task ahead. If anything happens to me, do not be afraid to speak your mind."

I frowned at that. What did he mean? He seemed to see my confusion.

"Cerdic, I know what your father's task is. The King spoke to me and said I must ensure that the army stays at Catraeth long enough for Aethelfrith to arrive. If I can't then you must."

"Me?" I was startled. "What can I do?"

"Just do not be afraid to say what you believe. There are some here who will try and shout you down and use your youth against you. Ignore them ... the future of our whole people could depend on it."

I nodded, not sure what to say, the sudden responsibility heavy on my shoulders. Then I wanted to ask about Catraeth, but Wallace glanced at the height of the sun, which was passing midday, and he gathered up Cuthbert and Eduard and led us back to where the men were collecting. Aedann turned up a few minutes later and I was going to ask him where he had been, but he went over to his kit, busied himself cleaning his sword and did not talk to me.

I was expecting us to march across the bridge and southwest towards Elmet, back down the road we had traversed only a few days before – then onwards to the war. But after we had crossed the river, we instead left the fortress by the North Gate and up onto Dere Street: the road that went all the way to the Roman Wall and then on even further. I looked back at the smoke over the city, feeling as if each step we took northwards was taking me away from Mildrith, Samlen and my uncle's sword.

We stopped for the night at a small hamlet, a few miles north of the city and I went to ask Wallace what he knew about where we were going. I found him leaving the camp and riding further up the road.

"My Lord," I said. He turned to look at me.

"Ah, Cerdic, your feet got blisters, eh?"

"Er, yes a few, my Lord, but ..."

"Not now, Cerdic, I am off to scout ahead. I will be back tomorrow."

"But, my Lord, why are we going this way. Elmet is that way," I said pointing to the south. "Where are we going?"

"We are not going to Elmet, Cerdic. We are going north: north to Catraeth," and with that, he galloped away.

Suddenly, instead of the gloom of a week before, or the excitement and desire for revenge of the last few days, I felt nothing but fury and confusion. What in the name of Woden were we doing marching north up this blasted road?

In a whirl of frustration, I turned back to our camp to tell the others. Most of them just told me to calm down and that we would be told in time where we were going. But none of them could calm me and I stomped off to find a place to be alone and sulk.

I was still in a foul mood the following morning when we broke camp and got back on to Dere Street. Our little army must now have been about four hundred men strong. The companies from Eoforwic and the Wolds led the way whilst we trailed along behind. The men in most of these companies were five years and more older than us youngsters and at first they ignored us or treated us as callow children, but Grettir must have spoken to them about the raid into Elmet, as later that day they began to talk to us and discuss the battles they had fought and to listen to our tales.

As we halted for a meal at noon, my spirits lifted a bit when Cuthbert told a poetic version of the gallant fight of the three young heroes, who defeated the hordes of the Welsh to rescue the defenceless women and children. The older men chortled and teased, but they enjoyed the tale and treated us better afterwards. As we set off again, I walked near Cuthbert and asked him where he had learnt to tell a tale that way.

"Oh, from Lilla the bard, Cerdic. I often dreamed of travelling as a wandering poet. You know, going from village to village and learning the tales and stories of the folks along the way. Lilla says there are many things a man can learn by travelling. He has visited the palaces of kings and even gone to Elmet and Rheged."

Cuthbert's mention of Elmet darkened my mood again.

"Did Lilla tell you why we would be marching to this Catraeth place, rather than attacking Elmet?" I asked with a sour voice, "I mean, what is so important about this town anyway?"

"I thought I taught you better than that, Master Cerdic," came the reproachful voice of Grettir from a few ranks behind. "It is not for us to consider or guess why we go thither or what we are asked to do when we are there. King Aelle is our lord and it is enough that he has a purpose in mind."

"What a load of tripe," I thought to myself and I fell into another silent sulk, until we broke off the march that night and made camp. I decided that enough was enough. Wallace had said I was second in command of the company. So I was going to ask someone about where we were going, and by chance, Aethelric, Earl Harald and Earl Sabert walked past our part of the camp and wandered over to our fire to warm their hands.

"Sire, can you tell me why we are going to this Catraeth place and not Elmet?"

The company fell silent and all eyes turned to me. Most were curious – all men want to know where they are going. Grettir hissed and told me that I would be told all I needed to know.

"Well spoken, loyal yeoman but ... but the men should know something of why we are going to this Catraeth place, don't you think?" said Aethelric.

"My Lord," started Grettir, "there is no need ..."

"Quite right too! Sire," Sabert said, his eyebrows bristling. "I said before, he is just a youth. He needs to keep silent and learn that princes do not need to explain what they do."

Aethelric nodded, but then seeing my downcast expression, seemed to change his mind again.

"Perhaps ... but, there are some advantages to being a prince and the son of the King, and since it was he who gave me orders to command this little force, I am in the position of knowing why we are going north."

"Our captain has gone on ahead, my Lord: the boy is my responsibility. I'm sure he will make a fine warrior and leader one day, but he can be a bit outspoken," Grettir apologised, glowering in my direction.

"Oh, I already know master, erm ... what did you say your name was?" he turned to me, but Grettir answered.

"He is Cerdic, son of Cenred of the Villa, Sire."

The Prince looked at me more closely and raised his eyebrows. My cheeks flushed red and I said a quiet prayer to Thunor to help me control my speech in the future.

Aethelric nodded, seemed about to speak, but then looked blank and turned to Earl Harald. "Erm ... Harald, can you explain it to the lad?" He spoke vaguely, adding, "You are better at that kind of thing."

"And possibly he can remember it, as well," Eduard muttered under his breath, although a few of the company must have heard and seeing the grins on their faces, I thought that more than a few agreed with him. Sabert seemed to hear it as well and looking sharply towards me and Eduard, seemed about to say something, but just then Harald nodded at the Prince and waved at me to come forward.

"Come here, young Cerdic, you seem keen to understand our plans and policies. Let's see how well you do."

I nodded and shuffled forward. The company was very quick to move out of the way, I noticed.

Harald pointed at a low hillock just outside the camp, beside the road. "Stand up there and look westward then tell me what you can see," he ordered.

I did as I was told. To my front I saw fairly flat fields, empty this early in the season. Here and there were scattered copses, but mostly it was open countryside. Beyond the fields I could see the dark shapes of the Pennines forming a barrier from far to the south to way beyond my sight to the north. I commented on this.

"Now then, turn and look behind you," Harald ordered.

I did as instructed and faced east. A river ran from north to south not far from the road and beyond this were more fields. I could see beyond the fields, dim and distant, the bulky forms of the moors. Not as high as the mountains to the west, but still prominent over the low ground where I stood.

"Finally, look north and tell me what you see there."

"The countryside is less open," I said, observing that the scattered copses were denser and the flat fields gave way to rising ground as it climbed towards the numerous hills I could see running east to the moors and west to the Pennines. The river snaked from the northwest towards the southeast on the far side of the road: the flat, straight Roman road.

I described all this, and Harald nodded at me.

"Up ahead in those hills and copses is Catraeth. It sits on this road on either side of a stone bridge that crosses the river as it comes down from the mountains. Beyond the river – not far beyond mind you – the road divides. Dere Street continues to the North, through the valley of the River Tees and up towards Bernicia. The branch runs west through the Pennines to Rheged. Between the branches a few miles away from here – in the angle as it were – stands an old earthen fort, what we call Stanwick Camp," he paused and then he raised his eyebrows, "Have you heard of it?"

I shook my head.

"I have, my Lord, but I have never been there," Grettir said behind me.

"Splendid, well done," piped in Aethelric, evidently eager to be involved.

Grettir bowed to the Prince, who apparently had nothing further to add, as he then nodded at Harald to go on. Sabert tapped his foot impatiently.

"Sire, we need to leave this nonsense and get on with our counsel. We are wasting our time," the earl moaned.

"I don't think so," said Harald. "The lad wants to understand and I think that is fine. Anyway," he said, ignoring Sabert's affronted grunt and continuing, "this was of old a garrison to defend the pathways and has again been turned into such. All the land ahead of us was Welsh – the Kingdom of the Pennines. During the last wars a few years ago, we took advantage of the weakness of the Welsh and their inability to respond and captured this land, just as we did with Eoforwic."

He walked up to join me at the top of the small mound and put his hand on my shoulder.

"We have heard from our spies and agents that the Welsh have recovered from their defeats under Bernicia. Their strength has grown and they are determined to strike back at us. You have all heard rumours of armies training, equipping and gathering. Their great kings make talk of war. Their bards Taliesin and Aneirin sing of heroes of the past and urge their warriors onto greater deeds. And ... we hear mention of a word."

He took his hand away from my shoulder and pointed north, "The word is 'Catraeth'. You see Cerdic, Catraeth lies in a very important location. It sits on the main road from Deira to Bernicia through this valley between the mountains and the moors. It also sits on the main road from Rheged to what was once the Kingdom of the Pennines. Whoever holds Catraeth, dominates this region. If the Welsh of Elmet, Srathclyde, Rheged and Manau Goddodin can take it, they would divide Bernicia from Deira again. Once more, they would become the most powerful lords in the North and they would be a threat to us. We would not be safe in our land: not with our fertile plains and our valleys full of grain to tempt them south, to reclaim what they believe is theirs."

"But, my Lord, what of Elmet?" I asked.

"Ah yes, what of Elmet? Of course, that is the only Welsh land east of the mountains now. It is also a threat, as you know only too well." He looked at me and gave a smile of acknowledgement. And it seemed to me that he was aware of the common man's difficulties as well as moving in the counsels of kings. What a king he could have made, had he been prince and not Aethelric.

He went on, "Elmet has kept within its borders until recently. But now they attack us without warning and with a fairly small force: one hundred men or so. A heavy raid no doubt, but hardly a threat. Surely they know we would attack them in return. But, that is the point. We think it was a mistake. We think that Samlen raided the Villa and Wicstun because of greed and without the blessing of Ceredig"

My eyes widened and in my mind I saw my mother's jewellery and a picture of Hussa taunting me with that earring. Harald seemed to read my thoughts.

"Yes Cerdic, Elmet is part of the northern Welsh alliance. No doubt Elmet has been promised lands in Deira in return for its part in the war. Samlen was already assembling the army and was kicking his heels at Calcaria, itching to attack us. It did not take much of an excuse: just the tales of a traitor babbling about 'amber treasure,' to save his own skin or line his own pockets. Just that and he was over that border in a flash."

Harald paused and looked at the Prince, as if to see if he wanted to add anything, but Aethelric was smiling and nodding inanely, so he turned back to me.

"Actually this Hussa has done us a favour you know, Cerdic," then seeing my frown, he held up his hand. "Oh, I don't mean I approve. It's just that had it not been for the raid and as a result Wallace taking this company into Elmet, we would not have seen that army heading north. We would not have known to send scouts to follow it. Therefore, we would not have realised it was heading towards Catraeth. That knowledge confirms to us all the suspicions we already had. Hussa, in effect, has tipped the Welsh hand."

Then he frowned. "Still, it will be a hard battle," and dropping his voice added, "I hope your father will succeed in his mission ...." Again addressing all the company, he added; "Now we must press on. The Prince and I await Wallace's return to plan the battle. The battle may have already begun and it will be desperate. Tomorrow, we march to Catraeth!"

I watched him walk away with Aethelric and Sabert towards the Prince's tent. I then turned to look at the company and saw that some important facts were sinking in. We were not just attacking Elmet and facing its five hundred men, but a much larger force. The company did not know it was two thousand strong, but they were not stupid and knew the task ahead was going to be hard. Some of them glared at me, perhaps wishing they could have been left in ignorance a few hours longer.

"You had to ask, didn't you?" said Eduard, as I moved down the mound and came to stand beside him. Cuthbert, ashen-faced, said nothing but just swallowed hard.

The following day we continued on our way. Grettir had told us earlier what Harald had repeated: that we were now beyond the borders of what, before a few years ago was Deira and within the old Kingdom of Pennine. The local folk kept away from us, but those I saw had the dark hair of the Welsh. Wallace galloped into the camp that night and went straight in to see Harald, Sabert and Aethelric.

I wished I could eavesdrop on that conversation, perhaps overhear some words of comfort to share with everyone, but Cuthbert and I were given guard duty on the road a few hundred yards from the camp. Just before midnight, he pointed out to me a small patrol of warriors, armed with bows and spears, standing on a hill half a mile from us. They observed the camp for a few moments and then disappeared into the gloom.

I stayed at the hill, but I told Cuthbert to run to Harald and report what we had seen. While he was gone it grew darker and sounds of the animals of the night came to me across the fields. I felt exposed and very alone. The trees and bushes grew shadows and their shapes distorted and became in my mind sentinels of Samlen's army lurking out there, waiting to attack and drag me away to him. It was a relief when a few minutes later, Cuthbert, Harald, Aethelric and Wallace joined me. I pointed out where the warriors had been observing us. As I did, we noticed that two of of them had returned. Making no attempt to hide themselves they came towards us and as they got closer we saw they were each leading a horse. These then were not the warriors we thought we had seen. They walked down the hill, holding their hands away from their sides to show they were no threat.

"They're ours," Harald muttered and motioned them forward.

When they came up, we saw they were indeed Angles, who then bowed in respect to Aethelric. One of them then spoke.

"My Prince, I come from Stanwick Camp. I am asked to urge you to hurry on as quickly as you can. Our enemy has come with many men and my Lord believes that an assault on his fortress is imminent. Indeed, I fear it may already have fallen."

"How long ago did you leave the fortress?" Wallace asked.

"We left when the sun was sinking in the sky, perhaps three hours ago. We have ridden hard without stopping," said the messenger.

"Then even at a fast march it will take us the best part of a day to reach the camp," Wallace calculated.

"My Lord begs you to come fast," urged the messenger once more.

Aethelric looked at the messenger and then back to our camp. "I … I don't know. I … think the men need to sleep."

He looked at Harald and seemed to be pleading for advice.

Harald thought for a moment. "I suggest, Sire, that we wake the army just before dawn, in about four hours. We will march straight away thereafter. If we push on without rest we can reach Stanwick camp by some time in the afternoon."

Aethelric nodded.

"That sounds fair to me."

Harald bit his lip. He seemed to be struggling not to shout at the Prince to be more decisive, but instead he turned to me. Cuthbert and I were sent to get some rest and Eduard and Aedann were woken and went off grumbling, to watch the road. I found it difficult to sleep at first. Images of Samlen One Eye wielding my uncle's sword, or holding the amber treasure or … caressing Mildrith came into my mind and tormented me. But, sleep I did and I felt oddly refreshed when Cuthbert shook my shoulder. It was still dark, but in the east there was a faint red glow: the dawn was coming. Just as before, I wondered if I or any of us would see the sun set at Calcaria this day.

Then, our company rose and each man drank a little ale or water. Some chewed on salted meat or smoked cheese. I ate an apple I had picked from an orchard we had passed the previous day. Soon we assembled on the road and Aethelric, now mounted again, waved us on north.

We marched on, while the sun rose to our right over the dark moors, reached its zenith then rolled slowly round to our rear.

After we had crossed the narrow stone bridge at Catraeth, our guides led us along the road a little further until it branched. We turned northwest, towards the mountains. After a mile or two, we left the Roman road and veered off it to the right. Eventually the track we were following climbed a gentle slope and levelled out. Harald halted the army a little way down the slope and the captains of the company, along with their seconds, went up to take a look.

It was then that I got my first sight of Stanwick Camp. The ancient fortress was indeed huge. It was surrounded by a deep ditch. The earth from the ditch had been thrown up to create a bank perhaps eight feet tall. On top of the bank, a wooden palisade had been built to shelter the defenders. The outer perimeter was lozenge-shaped and ran for some five miles around. It was a good mile across from bank to bank and surrounded – for its entire perimeter – by a continuous wall, which had sturdy gates to block entry via the roads if the defenders so desired to deny it. Beyond the gates, the smoke from a least fifty cook fires was rising from as many huts. In the centre was a very large lords' hall. Milling around inside the fortress we could just make out scores of men and women. The walls were manned by several hundred warriors, their battle standards fluttering in the early summer breeze.

Impressive though the camp might be, the spectacle to the west of it was even more magnificent. For, lined up about one hundred paces west of the embankment was a large body of men. There appeared to be six companies of spear-armed foot soldiers from Rheged and a couple from Strathclyde beyond them. In all, they had about eight hundred warriors formed up in a formation facing east, towards Stanwick Camp, with yet more companies in reserve. Scattered here and there, a little ahead of the main body, there were groups of skirmishers armed with bows or slings for the most part, although I could see at least ten men with a handful of short javelins and one fellow with a curious wooden device I had never seen before but I later heard was called a crossbow.

I then spotted more Welsh, this time immediately in front of us and only a few hundred paces distant. There were about five hundred of them and they were lined up, facing away from us, towards the southern walls of the camp. Even though they faced away from us, there was no mistaking their nationality from their dress and the banners that flapped about above their heads: these were Elmetae. Right there, a long bow shot away, was Samlen's army: the army I had come to find.

I searched back and forth amongst the enemy for a sight of One Eye, Hussa or Mildrith, but could see none of them. Were they here? If so: where?

The Welsh had arrived at Catraeth and were about to launch their attack. In Stanwick Camp, there were perhaps five hundred English warriors at most. In a few minutes the enemy assault would hit the embankment and with numbers in their favour, the Welsh would win.

Our army was back down the slope, to keep it out of view of the enemy. Then, Aethelric sent for the captains and Wallace took me along. Immediately our captains began to argue. One of them, who commanded a company from the moors, was all for marching east to come at the camp from the eastern side and reinforce it. Wallace and Harald were in favour of attacking now, straight into the back of the Elmetae and taking them by surprise.

"That's lunacy and suicide. In fact, this whole battle is. I say we pull back and hold the bridge at Catraeth," Sabert said.

"No, we must attack," I responded vehemently. Sabert spun round and glared at me.

"Silence boy!" he hissed.

"I will not be quiet," I replied and Wallace smiled behind

Sabert's back, encouraging me to carry on. "We have to buy time for my father and Aethelfrith to come."

"Aethelfrith is not coming. He's no fool. He knows the stories of this army's size. There is no help on the way – we must pull back and defend the bridge."

While the arguments and advice flowed, I glanced west towards the mountains and then north beyond the Welsh companies. I was surprised to see a glint of sunlight glancing off metal some miles away. I looked again, thinking I may have imagined the sight. But again I saw it. Beyond the open ground there were some woods. I was now certain that troops were hiding there. I was just about to try and get someone's attention, when Harald barked out some orders and Aethelric nodded helplessly.

Harald and Wallace had got their way. Sabert threw a dark look at me and stomped back to his men. Wallace gave me a pat on the shoulder and then he and I went jogging back towards the company.

"Ready lads!" he shouted. "Here we go!"

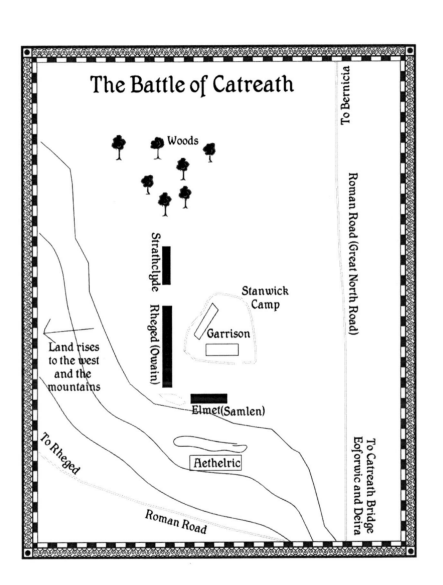

The Battle of Catreath

Woods

To Bernicia

Roman Road (Great North Road)

Strathclyde

Rheged (Owain)

Stanwick Camp

Garrison

Land rises
to the west
and the
mountains

Elmet(Samlen)

To Rheged

Aethelric

To Catreath Bridge
Eoforwic and Deira

Roman Road

Chapter Fifteen
The Battle of Catraeth

Wallace organised our company into a battle formation of three lines. Veteran warriors, like Grettir, stood in a line at the rear to bolster the men in front and to give advice and encouragement during the fight. In front of them was a line of young warriors, for whom this was their first battle. Eduard, Cuthbert and I were here with the other youths we had trained with over the last few years. Although we had fought a few skirmishes, including the desperate, confused fight at Calcaria, I would soon learn that a full battle is a different story. In the front rank were the twenty- and thirty-year-old men. These were more experienced than us, as well as being fitter and stronger than the veterans, who were interspersed in the middle ranks with us youths, to keep us steady.

Dotted along the front line, a small group of these warriors was formed up into a triangular formation pointing away from the main shield wall. These wedges were made up of the strongest and fiercest fighters. Their job was to try to cut like teeth into the enemy shield wall and break it asunder. Nearest the enemy, fifty yards in front of us towards the crest of the hill, Cuthbert and other skirmish troops were positioned. I noticed that my friend was hopping about nervously, but at least he already had his bow in his hand. Cuth was always calmer when he held a bow. Behind our battle line stood our captains, their house warriors gathered around their battle standards. I was just in front and to the right of Wallace's standard. It was a white wolf on a background of green. When the wind caught it and it unfurled, it seemed as if the wolf was charging across the plains towards its prey.

Harald now walked along the whole army and inspected us. Aethelric himself did not seem to be sure what to do and did not object when the Earl organised the six companies so they now formed a continuous line, three or four men deep and perhaps one hundred men wide. Our company was second from the left.

Wallace had told us that we were going to attack the rear of the Elmetae force. On hearing this news there were many smiles amongst the Wicstun Company, as men saw a chance for revenge on those who had attacked our homes or a chance to even a few scores. However, some of the older men grumbled and looked surprised. We might indeed, they said, be able to gain an advantage over Samlen's men, but what if we did not surprise them? Overall, the Welsh had more men than us and things could turn against us very quickly.

Nevertheless, we prepared ourselves for what was to come. Most men had a mouthful or more of beer that they had carried from Eoforwic. Several uttered prayers to Woden or the Valkyries I did neither, for I realised that I was finally going to fight in a battle. Here, my childhood dreams had come true and as this fact dawned upon me, my mouth suddenly felt very dry and my throat tightened. I had fought before, of course, during the raids on the Villa and the escape from Calcaria, but in both cases it came on so quickly, that I scarcely had time to think.

Today was quite different. We took some minutes preparing ourselves and a man has a chance to think in that time. Visions of home come to you. I thought of my mother and Sunniva, my sister, staring after me as I left. Images of happier times flashed in my mind: feasting in the great barn, laughter and games in the firelight, obscure riddles by the bard Lilla; a glimpse of Aidith looking beautiful and alluring in the half light ... and the memory of a kiss.

On the brink of battle, a man is afraid. You fear injury for the pain it might bring. You fear death for the uncertainty of it. You fear failure for the shame it would carry with it. Out in the open, Cuthbert looked like a hunted hare. His eyes were wild and his head was jerking left and right, as if searching for a way out. Perhaps, like me, he could not quite take it all in. But then he blinked, shook his head and started stringing his bow.

Eduard, standing next to me, appeared keen and excited. There was never much space for thought in my friend's mind. Right now, I was certain that only the songs of poets were in it. Looking at him, I experienced a moment of perfect clarity and two thoughts came to me. Firstly, this place is where Eduard belonged. If he survived, it would be in battle that his life would have meaning. Just as clearly, I realised that this was not true of me. Ironic, given that I would spend much of my life on one battlefield or another, but all I wanted at that moment was to find Mildrith and go home.

In front of us, Aethelric, Harald, Sabert and the other lords were apparently satisfied that we were ready and waved us forward, but signalled for us to move as quietly as we could in order to increase our chances of catching the enemy by surprise.

When we were just below the crest line, Aethelric did not hesitate, but marched briskly off in front of us towards the enemy. He may be indecisive and vague, but he did not lack for courage, I will give him that. He would surely get cut to pieces by the enemy before we could reach then. Harald saw this too, for he intercepted the Prince and escorted him to a safer place behind Wallace. Then, Harald waved his arm and pointed his sword over the crest of the rise in front of us. The captains ordered us forward and we were off to attack the foe. Overhead, the sun was descending in the western sky, but the day was still warm, the skies clear and blue. Birds swooped and soared, enjoying this perfect summer's evening. Meanwhile below, the killing was about to start: the battle of Catraeth had begun.

Form up, form up!" hissed Wallace. The call was taken up by some of the older men, who passed it on in hushed voices. We moved closer together and then turned, angling our bodies so our left side was facing the Welsh, bringing our shields to bear. We overlapped our shields with the men on either side, trying to maximise the protection these boards of wood offered. Only a few of the men, along with lords like Aethelric, Sabert, Harald and Wallace, wore armour made of interlinked chains of metal, strong enough to deflect sword blows. The rest of us trusted in our shields, the whims of fate and the courage of our fellows. I was lucky in at least having a helmet, which was made of bone and wood. It felt loose and I pushed it down onto my head.

"Spears, overhead!" ordered our captain. We took our spears and held them halfway along the length in our right hands as we had been taught. Our elbows were bent so the spears were held at the level of our shoulders where, for the moment, we rested them.

Across the small space of a few hundred yards, our enemy had still not noticed us, intent as they were upon the assault on the camp, although a few heads twisted this way and that, perhaps seeking the source of some new noise they had heard. The Welsh though were clashing their spears against shields, trying to frighten our men in the fort. Unlike us, they made no attempt to minimise the racket and this noise pretty much drowned out our own.

Once we had passed over the crest line, I could now see an

exchange of arrows between the Welsh attackers and our fellow Deirans in the fortress. Here and there they were hitting home and the first deaths of the day were occurring, but most of the arrows bounced harmlessly off shields and were wasted.

We advanced another twenty paces, with Harald leading our companies so as to hit the rear of the enemy line. For a few heartbeats it seemed as if we would achieve total surprise. Then one of the Welshmen turned, moved away from his army and started fiddling with his britches, looking for a place to relieve himself. He glanced up and his mouth opened as he saw four hundred warriors heading straight for him. For an instant, he just stared at us in shock, but then he let out a cry of alarm. More faces turned and suddenly the Elmetae were all bellowing and pointing, the game was up: we had been seen!

A moment later, there was a shout from a small hillock not far from the Elmetae and upon which the Welsh lords stood, and I could see one of them gesturing our way. I felt an icy chill shoot down my spine as I recognised the scarred, ugly face. There he was: there was Samlen and he was standing next to three or four other princes and kings directing the battle. One of the kings wore a shining gold-coloured breast plate of solid metal and his arms and legs were also sheathed in mail, but not the sort that our lords wore, made of rings of iron. This appeared to be more like the scales of a fish, each scale overlapping the one below it. Such a rare and precious suit could not be worn by anyone else: this had to be Owain.

Owain turned to a warrior standing behind him and the man ran towards the back of the Welsh army where they had a few reserve companies following up the leading troops. He soon had them angling out towards us and in their urgency they moved so quickly that it now became obvious we would not reach the

Elmetae before these other companies reached us. With a roar, Harald halted us and prepared to defend against the attack. The Welsh were closer now and I could make out their faces and pick out individuals: some of them strong, experienced veterans, some like Aedann, Eduard, Cuthbert and me, in their first battle. For how many of us would it be our last, I wondered fleetingly.

More Welsh companies came towards us. They had, for the moment, abandoned their attack upon the fortress. Leaving only two companies to watch the walls, the rest were coming our way.

Without anyone noticing him go, Aethelric had moved to a small rise in the ground so that he could easily be seen by all present. He was frankly hopeless as a commander. He had no grasp of tactics, could not make a decision and tried too hard to please everyone. But there was one thing he could do: he could make a bloody good speech.

"Warriors of Deira, today I call on you to fight bravely. This is not a fight we wished for. We have lived in peace, happy to farm and to trade and to remain secure within our borders these last fifteen and more years. Now, a threat has come to our pastures. The Welsh would drive us from the lands our fathers fought for and won."

He did not mention that it had been our race who had originally taken the lands from the Welsh, but that was not a thought for today. Today, Aethelric stirred up our hatred with his simple message.

"Their raiders have burnt our land, slain our warriors and raped our women. If they are not stopped they will come back and try again." He paused, while some among us shouted, "Never!" and, "Let them try!"

He then continued, "Some of you might wonder why you came here, so far away from your homes. Is this your war? Some of you may wish to be elsewhere. But I say this to you: unless we join together and be rid of this menace, none of us will ever be safe. The Welsh are united in an alliance to drive us away. This place is where they intend to start and it is at this place that they will be stopped."

We crashed our spears against our shields and shouted out oaths that we would destroy the Welsh enemy or die trying. The enemy were close now and the Prince moved back to stand near Harald. Then, we waited for the attack to come.

The Welsh halted some fifty paces away and to our surprise, they began singing in their strange tongue.

"They are calling to their God to defeat us," Grettir said, "I have heard them sing like this before." Not far away, Aethelric heard his words and turned to us all.

"Call to Woden, men of Deira!" bellowed the Prince.

Grettir and the other veterans began pounding their own shields with their spears. Soon, our entire company took up the beat, followed by the companies from Eoforwic. Then, we began chanting, "Woden! Woden!"

Woden was worshiped at the temple at Godnundingham, as well as at shrines in many villages and most of our people trusted in him.

The chanting went on, becoming louder and louder. It did battle now with Christian hymns sung by the Welsh to our fore. Whether Pagan or Christian, the purpose was the same: to put courage into our souls. To set the hearts pounding and to make us believe we could not lose – that we could not die. Indeed to fire us up to fever pitch.

Then, the slaughter would begin.

Suddenly, there was a great shout from the enemy and as one they moved towards us. A handful of archers and slingers ran ahead of them, trying to weaken our line by killing or wounding as many as they could, so that when the shield wall arrived the wedges could bite into the weak spots and cut us apart. Cuthbert and a couple of dozen of our skirmishers exchanged shots with the enemy archers and also fired at the mass of men bearing down upon us. In the scale of this battle it would make little difference, I thought, until a moment later when a sling stone missing the front row, glanced off my shield and ricocheted away from my helmet. I was stunned by the blow and staggered backwards into Grettir who caught me and held me up, until my head stopped spinning. When my vision did clear, the first thing I saw was an arrow taking the warrior in front of me, in the neck. He collapsed back onto my shield and slid gurgling and choking onto the ground where, after what seemed like an eternity of thrashing and twitching, he finally died. The warrior to his left looked down at him, shrugged and then picked him up by his tunic, heaving him forward to form an obstacle to the attack.

"Close up, close up," came the cry from the rear and the warrior was forgotten as the front rank moved together.

The Welsh were closer now, so that I could make out their features as they advanced. A rugged, scar-faced old veteran scowled at us in rage, whilst next to him a gangly-limbed youth of no more than fourteen years quivered and shook in fear as he tried to hold a shield that was too heavy for him. All men are just human in the end and their army had its fair share of anger, rage and fear − just the same as ours. Yet the simple truth was that they had more men than we did and they were all coming right at us.

Our archers moved out of the way to the flanks as the main body of the enemy closed upon us. Over on the right wing, I heard Earl Sabert order his companies to angle backwards, so as to try and deny the more numerous enemy access to our flanks.

They were closer now: only twenty yards away and both sides started to hurl small javelins and throwing axes. Eduard groaned as an axe bounced off his shield and gashed across his right shoulder, already weakened by his previous injury. Another warrior in the front rank fell, with a javelin impaled through his arm and he was dragged back, screaming, to the rear. The ranks closed up to fill the gap. Our missiles found targets as well and the scarred old veteran was hit in the leg, tripped and fell, then the youth stumbled over him leaving them both in a heap on the ground, but still their army came on. They were five yards away now. I straightened my arm and brought my spear up so as to be ready to strike down over an enemy shield.

Suddenly, I saw Hussa. There he was, in the Elmetae shield wall, towards the rear. He had a helmet too, as well as a shirt of mail armour, so I figured that some of the worth of my mother's earring had perhaps already been spent. He was not far from me now, maybe just thirty yards away and I wondered if I could work my way over to him, but as soon as I had the thought, he was gone from sight as the warrior in front of him lifted his shield higher. Then, all thoughts of Hussa were banished as the Welsh charged at us.

A huge, red-headed warrior with a battleaxe came screaming towards us, followed by four others, just ahead of their main shield wall. He leapt at our front rank and brought the great blade down upon a warrior from the village. The poor fellow was lucky to die at once, cut almost in two by the blow. This was the wedge tactic at work: the enemy were trying to cut their way into our shield wall, to make a breach and pour through the gap.

A moment later, the armies collided as spears splintered against shields. The force of the blow knocked some men right

216

off their feet and the enemy fell upon these warriors and hewed at them.

Eduard lunged forward with his spear and skewered a man through the neck. He roared in triumph as the victim crashed back through the ranks. My spear, however, smashed against a shield boss and to my alarm the spearhead snapped right off. Now, in the crush of bodies, I struggled to find my sword. Eventually my fingers folded around the hilt and I pulled it free of the baldric and brought it up high.

The world was now filled with the pleas of the dying, the screams of the living, the clatter of shields and the ring of blades as the two bodies of men pushed against each other. To me it seemed that any strategy had been abandoned. Victory and defeat depended simply on who would tire first and who would give way.

There was a sudden shout of alarm from my right. Looking that way, helped by our position on rising ground, I saw that one of the companies from Eoforwic was beginning to fall back, pushed by the Welsh to the front and also threatened on their flank by a score of enemy warriors that were overlapping that wing of our army. Once they broke, the enemy would be able to get round behind us. I was not alone in spotting this: I could feel panic rising along the whole army. The enemy sensed this too, for they pushed forward eager for the kill.

Then, horns sounded from Stanwick camp and I could now see that the gates had opened and out from the fortress charged the companies of Deirans that had held it. They ran out with no thought for formation. Their leaders had grasped that speed was essential and like a river in flood they surged down upon the left and rear of the Welsh, just where the pressure of their attack had almost led to disaster for us. The tide of battle now swung back our way again. Soon, we had united with our fellow companies from the fortress and were pushing the Welsh west and north, so we had swung round and the camp was now to our rear. The Welsh counter attacked and brought in, as fresh reinforcements, the redundant companies who had been watching the fortress.

For an instant, the situation again hung in the balance. Then, our counter attack began to lose impetus.

At that moment a sole trumpet sounded, bright and loud, away to the north. It was soon joined by others. They swelled into a fanfare and seconds later out of the woods to the north, cavalry emerged. The Welsh leaders had prepared a surprise that they now expected would win them the battle.

Of that charge, poems and songs have been written. The most moving was penned by the Welsh poet Aneirin, who was present amongst their ranks. Years later it was popular in the court of King Cadfan of Gwynedd, which is where I heard it. What a race the Welsh are for song: songs of joy, songs of beauty and songs of war.

How does it go?

Warriors went to Catraeth, embattled, with a cry;
A host of horsemen in dark blue armour, charging nigh;
Spear shafts held aloft, of sharp steel pointed;
And shining swords which the Angles, with death anointed.

Well, I have never been much of a poet, but I agree with Aneirin's theme. The charge of the Goddodin was indeed magnificent. They were three hundred strong. Every one rode a fine steed and wore a mail shirt, which in the late afternoon sun had a blue tinge to it. Each carried a shield, painted blue with an eagle design in the centre. Forward they charged with lance and blade. Forward came the Goddodin, allies of Strathclyde and Rheged; charging to bring death and defeat to us English. I had seen how frightening just a few dozen cavalry were in Elmet. Three hundred was, frankly, terrifying.

They started under the trees and moved forward a little way onto the open fields. They halted there a moment to form up. Then, the captain raised his sword aloft and brought it down to point at the flank of our army. There was a second fanfare and the cavalry began walking forward. Then they were trotting and finally, galloping. Faster and faster the horses came, urged on by their riders. Now, as they closed, the lances were brought down to point at the enemy: to point at us!

My fellow Angles to our right had seen their doom. Men in their rear ranks – those immediately at risk – began to pull back or turned at least to face the threat. Others threw down spears and shields and started to run. But, it was already too late for them. A moment later, the Goddodin reached their foe. There was a loud crash and then the slaughter began.

Cavalry, such as the Welsh used of old, was effective in three ways. Firstly, the men themselves carried spear or sword to pierce, slash and cut at the enemy. Secondly, the speed and weight of the mounts was sufficient to kill or maim by itself. Finally, the sight and noise of several hundred armoured cavalry thundering towards a body of men would cause terror and panic. This alone might be sufficient to break the will to fight of even the bravest warriors. One moment there was an orderly fighting force, the next a fleeing mass of humanity – ripe for the slaughter.

Such was what occurred over on the Deiran right wing that day. The flank collapsed and several hundred warriors broke and began to run in all directions. The Goddodin cavalry was amongst them in a flash. Scores of our men died in a moment, falling under the steel and hooves of the enemy.

The effect of the charge on the morale of the rest of the Welsh army was instantaneous. Where, five minutes ago their shield wall had been about to crack open, they now pushed back with fresh impetus, so soon we were giving ground all over, while to the north, the Goddodin cavalry was cutting its way further into our army.

As I was in the second rank, it was difficult to do much other than push forward. Then, a man to my front was felled by a red-headed Welshman and went down with a scream. The enemy brute, sensing the change in the fortune of the battle, leapt into the space created and hewed to left and right, cutting down our men on both sides and widening the gap in our front rank. Suddenly, I was face to face with a Welsh veteran. Grinning, his yellow teeth dripping with spittle, he swung his axe back preparing to bring it down upon me. On either side, his companions advanced − pushing their wedge deeper into our line.

Grettir, standing behind me, lunged with his spear towards the red-headed warrior, who dodged to his side and then shattered it with a blow from his weapon. However, in doing so he had opened himself up and I jumped forward and rammed my shield against him, cracking some of his ribs and causing him to cry out in agony. My victory was short-lived, however, as the pain just seemed to intensify his fury, so that he now roared at me, seized my shield and heaved it downwards and then swung back his axe preparing to hack at my neck.

In desperation, my feet slipping and sliding on blood and gore, I swung my sword over the top of my shield, bringing it down hard upon his left arm, cutting deep into the muscle and opening an artery, which now spurted forth blood. He shouted an oath at that and his face screwed up in rage but, before he could hew at me, Eduard, having impaled his own opponent on his spear, followed up by advancing a step, then seized the warrior's weapon arm. Whilst he was thus distracted, I hacked at him again and this time my blow landed higher up his arm, on his shoulder. As he went down on one knee, I plunged my blade into his chest and a great gush of blood drenched my hand then, with a final cry of pain, he was dead.

Eduard picked up the man's axe and swung it wildly at the Welsh behind him who, taken aback by the death of the great fighter they were following, held back a moment. I slashed at the man to my right and cut his throat open. For a few heartbeats, the pressure was off and gasping for breath, we fell back and reformed our shield wall.

Along the left wing, where I was fighting, the Deiran force was holding well, but it was at the other end of our line where the enemy was directing his wrath. The cavalry were now behind our right wing and the slaughter went on and on, so that it could not be long before we broke and all was lost. That moment came all too soon: for now, the rout began.

Firstly, twenty men at the rear, close to where the monsters on horseback were attacking us, threw down their spears and turning away, ran east towards the camp. Another twenty joined them, then fifty more until, in a heartbeat, the whole army turned and ran. Harald shouted at them, he bellowed and cursed as the men ran past him.

"Stand firm, you bastards! Come back you cowards!"

But, it was no use. Once an army is running it takes a miracle to stop it and that day there was to be no miracle. There was just blood, death and steel and the horror of three hundred mounted warriors cutting and hacking at us as we ran. The Welsh shouted in triumph and – close by now – I could see Owain come forward with Samlen by his side, both laughing in glee. Then, with a huge wave of his arm which encompassed all his army, he ordered the pursuit.

Suddenly, Aedann pushed past me and moved out of the shield wall. He shouted something in Welsh and both Samlen and Owain stared at him. Aedann drew his sword and moved forward towards them. He was going to challenge Samlen – right here in the middle of the rout. But, I didn't let him. I seized the collar of his tunic with my hand and dragged him back behind the shields.

"Let me go, Cerdic."

"No, don't be a fool. You dying now won't help."

"But I want to kill him."

"So do we all, but let's live today and see about that tomorrow, eh son?" Eduard said. Aedann slammed his sword against his shield in frustration but then, after directing another glare full of hatred back towards Samlen, he relented.

By now, we had all moved back a few hundred paces and the right wing was pinned against Stanwick camp. Its outer ditch and palisades, which had been built to protect our army, now prevented the escape of the very men who were here to defend it. The Goddodin rode on and hacked their way into dense masses of panicstricken, unarmed warriors who had abandoned their weapons when they started to run.

I was now close to Wallace, Harald and the Prince. The Prince's house troops were standing firm and Wallace was shouting at the Wicstun Company to join them.

Gradually, some sanity returned and in tens and twenties, men started to huddle around the Prince's company and those of us with shields attempted to reform our shield wall.

The Welsh warriors began to lap around our left wing, just as the cavalry were pushing us from the right. I said there was no miracle that day, but there was just a glimmer of hope: for the battle had raged some hours now and the sun was sinking fast in the west.

It would be dark soon and escape is certainly easier in the dark. There was one other hope – one other chance. We had been retreating now for several hundred yards along the southern edge of Stanwick camp and I suddenly became aware that the gates to the fortress were open and only a hundred yards away. If we could just get inside ....

"My Lord," I shouted at Wallace, he didn't hear me: I tried again.

"My Lord," I bellowed and this time he turned, so I pointed towards the open gates. He now also understood the chance for escape and he turned to shout over to Earl Harald. Harald frowned at him for a moment and then he nodded and roared out an order to the whole army.

"Fall back, but keep it orderly. Fall back, but keep together!" Harald yelled and we did.

With only fifty yards now to go, I felt that we might just make it. Just those very few paces and we could close the gates and take refuge from the army that wanted to destroy us. Just forty-five paces now ... but then, I saw that it was no use.

A hundred of the Goddodin cavalry, having finished the slaughter west of the camp, had circled behind their own army and were now passing to the south of us. As they curved around us, their commander saw the open gates of Stanwick Camp.

He saw us withdrawing in stages, slowly moving towards the fortress and safety. In an instant, he too realised what we were trying to do and digging in their heels, the enemy horsemen charged again.

If they reached the gate first ... we were dead!

Chapter Sixteen
The Prince Makes a Decision

Suddenly, Wallace was next to me. "Cerdic, I have to do something fast. If I don't make it to the camp, get the Prince inside and then stay there till your father arrives. Don't let Sabert persuade Aethelric to leave."

"What ...?"

"No time to explain," he shouted back over his shoulder. Then he ran out into the open space between the cavalry and the gate. Seeing his example, twenty of the Prince's guards, as well as a dozen warriors from Wicstun joined him. More started to go, including Eduard, but I held him back because I now knew what Wallace was doing. He was sacrificing himself to save his Prince, his army and maybe, his country.

"Harald, we must go now!" I yelled. The Earl of Eoforwic twisted his head round and nodded at me then, pointing at the gates, ordered the rest of the army to get inside as quickly as they could. Meanwhile, Wallace and his men had formed a small shield wall, with Wallace at its centre, his broken arm strapped to the inside of his shield. His standard bearer was next to him and the running wolf fluttered in the breeze.

The Goddodin charged and their lances smashed and shattered into Wallace's shields. Half of the shield wall was knocked over in that first charge and the cavalry milled around and wheeled this way and that, whilst hacking down with swords or jabbing with lances. Still the banner stood and I could see Wallace swinging a sword with his one good hand and cutting off a cavalryman's head.

"Keep pulling back! Keep it together!" shouted Harald. I took up the call and heard it echoed from further along our line. I glanced over and saw Sabert there with at least some of his men still alive.

Twenty yards to go now and fifty of the Goddodin swerved around the fight surrounding Wallace and started to move towards us. Owain had seen what we were trying to do and was frantically yelling at them to charge the gates and stop us. His men were pushing forward now, trying to catch us, trying to slow us down for just a few moments so the horses could seal our doom.

Ten yards to go and the horses were very close: too close in fact and I could now see that we were going to be beaten: the horses would reach the gates first. With a whoop, they surged forward and blocked our escape and then turned to charge into our rear. Just then, as I thought we were caught and dead, there was a volley of arrows and a dozen horses fell screaming and kicking. The arrows were coming from the battlements behind us. Cuthbert and the skirmishers had reached the camp before the horses and were firing down at them to drive them away. Five more Goddodin warriors tumbled from their saddles and the rest swerved away, out of range.

Now, at last, we were passing through the gates. Seeing this, the cavalry came back again and dared the arrow fire to crash into our shields. Six of our men were knocked down and three killed outright, but Eduard stepped forward, stabbed up with his spear into the belly of a horse, rammed the edge of his shield down hard to crush the throat of another Goddodin, who was floundering on the ground, then pulled one of our men inside by his tunic.

Now we were inside the fortress and the gates were already

closing.

"Push men, push," shouted Harald and together we pushed against the gates first to close them, then to hold them shut whilst the gate bar was dropped into its slot. Barrels, carts and logs were now piled up against the inside. I ran up the steps to the battlements and looked down at the Welsh army milling about outside. Our archers continued to fire down upon them, killing or injuring many at the gate. Finally, after one last attempt to force the entrance, they pulled back and gave up trying to get in − for the moment at least.

It was almost too dark to see more than a few dozen yards. But just at the edge of the gloom, I saw the Wolf's head banner was still standing. Wallace and his last few men were surrounded out there, yet they were only about sixty yards from the gates. I turned to Harald.

"My Lord, let me take fifty men and rescue Wallace," I offered. Eduard stepped up to my side at once and nodded his agreement. But Harald shook his head.

"Sorry, Cerdic, but I cannot spare fifty men."

"But my Lord ..."

Harald turned to me.

"No, Cerdic. I'm sorry. I know he is your father's friend, but if we open the gates we will be overrun. Wallace knew this. He chose to do this to save the army ... for today at least," he added gloomily and we all looked out with a sense of frustration and impotence towards the wolf banner and its defenders.

There were now five hundred Welshmen swarming all around Wallace's small company. For a moment, I hoped that he might hold them at bay and perhaps slowly retreat to the fortress. Then, the enemy charged as one and I felt a lump in my throat as I saw the banner fall to the ground and not come up again. It was finally over: after all that he had been through, Lord Wallace was dead. On the battlements, Harald squeezed my shoulder and, without a word, left to find Aethelric. Eduard placed a hand on my arm as well and tried to comfort me.

"Sorry Cerdic. I know Wallace was a friend of your family as well as of your father. If it helps at all, that was a bloody brave thing he just did. Think about that," he said and then went to find Cuthbert. So finally I stood alone, looking towards the fallen Wolf banner and the bodies of our men. I was suddenly over-whelmed by all that had occurred today. Just a few hours ago, the Prince had spoken of us slaughtering these Welsh invaders, but now those words seemed foolish and naive. Half our army had died and it was the Welsh who were triumphant: who now believed they had won the battle of Catraeth.

The truth was – they probably had.

I turned my back on the battlefield and in a daze, stumbled along the walkway to the steps leading down from the battle-ments. Wallace's last words came to me then and with the hor-ror of what had just happened still gnawing at me, I went to prevent a prince from running away.

At the top of the steps I stopped and looked around the inte-rior of the fortress. Fires had been started by the men to warm themselves on this cool night and also to cook on. I realised that I had eaten nothing since that apple before dawn. Gods, but how long ago was that? Yet, I did not feel I could eat. The horrors of the day, Wallace's death and the vision of his wolfshead banner falling, churned my stomach and I felt hollow inside.

From where I was standing, I could get some idea of the state of the army and at once could see that we were in terrible trou-ble. The original garrison at Stanwick camp had been about five hundred and we had brought four hundred more spears that morning. We had started the battle, then, with just less than a thousand spears. Owain, Samlen and their allies had over two thousand men on the field. Both sides had suffered losses but we had fared far worse. I looked around the camp and wondered how many men we actually had left.

Walking down the steps and wandering from fire to fire, I glanced at the dirty, drawn faces that stared despondently into the flames or back at me without any expression. How many had lost friends today? I figured most of them ... most of us. I might have said that Wallace's company had come out of the day better than most, save that Wallace himself was dead and the company had lost its standard. Along with Wallace, a dozen of his household and most of the veterans had perished. Still, that gave us around sixty men out of eighty-five alive at the end of the day, including my friends and, mercifully, Grettir. Of course, being alive is one thing, but it's what state you are in that counts. Some had been wounded and I passed men screaming as they were held down to have arrow heads pulled out of them. Others grimaced and bit on leather straps as wounds were stitched or bones set. Then, of course, there were the wounds to the soul. Men had seen friends cut down and choke on their own blood and vomit and had been unable to do anything to help them. Each time it happened they had left part of themselves behind, out on the battlefield.

In Harald's companies from Eoforwic, as well as the ones from the moors, the situation was far worse. Two hundred men had marched with us from the city. They had shared a camp with us and had listened and laughed, just as we had, to Cuthbert's tales of our valour. Of them, no more than one man in three sat around those fires.

The garrison of Stanwick camp had been just as badly mauled

by the Goddodin. Sabert's two companies from the coast and Wolds were probably in the best condition of all, save mine, but even they had lost thirty men each.

In all, I estimated our losses at around four hundred men. I could not believe that Owain had lost as many as that, but even if he had, that meant that he now had fifteen hundred spears to our mere five hundred: three men for every one of ours. I walked towards the hall knowing, even before I entered, that Sabert would be in an uncompromising mood.

The hall at Stanwick camp was a single-roomed structure, built in the previous year when the dangers of Rheged's growing strength threatened war one day. War had come and today it was the scene for a council of war. Aethelric sat despondently in the single tall-backed chair, which resembled his father's throne and which occupied the end of the hall. Harald, Sabert and half a dozen lesser nobles from the other companies, were slumped in scattered chairs and on benches. Harald was eating a roast chicken leg and drinking mead, as I entered. He glanced up and rolled his eyes at me then gestured with his thumb in the direction of Sabert. It was Earl Sabert who was speaking now.

"We should leave and leave soon, your Highness, under cover of darkness. The battle is lost and our only hope is flight ...," the old lord was saying. He stopped when he saw me and tilted his head.

"Ah, the young farmer. Well, it seems that your father did not come, after all. I was certain this campaign was futile," he said again addressing the Prince. "We should leave and go back to the bridge at Catraeth."

Harald belched loudly.

"You have a comment to add perhaps, Lord Harald," Sabert asked acidly.

Harald pushed his stool back and turned to face him.

"Indeed I do. You say leave. I say... how? How could we leave? Owain is out there with two men or more for each of ours. You expect him to just let us go?"

Sabert laughed at that.

"I expect him to be pissed about now: on mead and ale from our supplies, or having his pleasure with a dozen local girls. They think they have won the battle and they are damn well right: they have. In an hour or two, in the dead of night we go out – east. Even if they have a guard or two the main army is off to the west – you can see the fires. We take down the palisade and go out over the ditch, make for the road, then south to Catraeth."

I looked at Aethelric and damn me if he was not nodding. I had to change his mind and quickly.

"Then what?" Harald was asking.

"We hold the bridge. The waters are high with the spring rain and also due to the snow melting in the mountains. Owain can only cross at Catraeth – unless he goes out east, through the moors – and that is a very long way. We have more companies mustering in the moors if," and again he looked at me, "Cenred has managed to get that right."

"So, we hold them at Catraeth. We wait for more men and we break them there," Sabert concluded firmly and the Prince was still nodding.

"That won't work," I said loudly. Everyone turned to look at me.

"Please tell me, farm boy, why it won't work?" Sabert said, his voice dripping with sarcasm. "I'm dying to know what your great experience has taught you."

I shook my head, "I don't have much of that ... but I do have a

Welshman in my company. Can I bring him in here?"

Aethelric's head snapped up at that.

"A ... Welsh ...man, here. Why do you want him?"

"Well, I am sure we would all like to lynch one and it is easier than going all the way to Owain's camp after all," Sabert said and despite myself, even I laughed at that.

"He has pledged fealty to my father and me. He was talking to the Welsh in Eoforwic and I think you need to know something of what he heard," I explained when the jeers had died down.

Aethelric nodded and I turned and told one of the Prince's guards to go and fetch Aedann. While we waited, Harald brought me a cup of mead. I thanked him and in my thirst drank it quickly then immediately regretted my action, as on an empty stomach the mead went straight to my head.

"How sure are you of your father persuading Aethelfrith?" Harald asked me quietly, so no one else could hear.

I shrugged. "How sure are we of anything in life? We hope for the best, prepare for the worse and give thanks to the gods if we live another day. Fate takes care of the rest. But you can be sure that he will do his best. He can be ... very determined, when he wants to be," I replied.

Harald nodded. "Good enough for me."

Aedann walked into the hall and seemingly not intimidated in the slightest by the stares of the assembled lords, strode right up to the Prince and bowed.

"You wanted to speak to me, your Highness?"

Aethelric's expression suggested he had no intention of doing anything of the sort. He pointed vaguely at me, and Aedann turned to ask me what I wanted.

"Aedann, I need you to tell the Prince what you found out by talking to the Welsh in Eoforwic. What were they hoping for?"

The Welshman nodded and paused to collect his thoughts then turned back to the Prince.

"There exists a sizeable proportion of the population of Eoforwic who are far from happy at being ruled by your father, your Highness."

Sabert snorted at that. "You don't tell us anything we don't already know."

"Wait, I have not finished," Aedann said cooly. "Most of the population have heard the growing rumours of Owain's coming and stories are going around that you will be slaughtered by him here. Those stories have found a very favourable audience."

"Again, this is not exactly news to us, Welshman. Your Highness, he has nothing to tell us that we don't know," Sabert said.

"Give him a chance ... my Lord!" I said brusquely.

"Aye, let's hear the boy out," Harald agreed.

Aedann studied us all for a long time, remaining silent whilst he appeared to be weighing up what next to say.

"Well, are you going to say anything?" Sabert said at last, tapping his foot in irritation.

"Will you still tell me you already knew what I was about to say, if I tell you that right now five hundred young Welshmen are armed and in hiding in Eoforwic? All they wait for is news that the battle here is lost. Then they will rise up, kill the garrison you left there and seize the city for Owain."

I stared at Aedann: this was news even to me.

Sabert's eyes snapped over to fix me with an outraged glare. "You did not think it was worth telling us this before now?" he snarled.

I shrugged, to hide my own ignorance. "Would you have believed the words of a Welshman, or a farmer?" I challenged him in return.

"Are ... are you ... sure?" Aethelric asked, addressing the dark-haired youth.

"Yes, Highness, my people are passing knives and swords around. They are arming and they are waiting. They await one thing: they await news of a victory here and then they will act," Aedann repeated.

Fuming, Sabert stomped over to the fire and stood by it, warming his hands and glowering with contempt at my former slave. Aethelric and Harald were silent, apparently just as shocked and unsure what now to do. I knew I had to act quickly to take advantage of the moment, to make sure that Aethelric now made the right choice. I moved forward to address the Prince.

"So, Highness, if we retreat to the bridge, as Sabert suggests, Eoforwic will hear of it and the Eboracii will rise up. Our line of retreat and supply will have gone. Do you dare risk that?"

Aethelric looked confused now. Sabert was shaking his head, but had no immediate argument to counter my own.

Before he could say anything, Harald, spoke grimly, "It's worse than that, Highness."

Aethelric groaned then slumped back in his chair and put his hands over his head, unhappy to be receiving so much bad news. A moment later he looked up and nodded at Harald to go on.

"Well, my Prince, the whole land from here to Eoforwic was – not long ago – Welsh, occupied by either the tribes of the Eboracii or the Pennines. There are still many Welsh living here. If Eoforwic falls we could have an uprising on a huge scale. We could find a thousand swords and spears marching up Dere Street and attacking us from behind, at the bridge. That would be that, I think."

He said this and then glanced round the room his raised eyebrows challenging anyone to gainsay him. Even Sabert pursed his lips at the thought and nodded reluctantly. Then the older lord's eyes narrowed and he raised a hand and pointed it at Aedann.

"All this supposes that this Welshman is not a spy. He refers to the Welsh in Eoforwic as his people. Is that not a giveaway? I say he was planted here to sow discontent and create disunity. I say let us torture him to get the truth."

At that, I drew my sword and stood in front of Aedann.

"This man is pledged to me. I will not allow any harm to come to him!" I glared at Sabert.

"Do not draw your sword in the Prince's hall!" Sabert hissed.

Harald put his hand on my arm. "Your argument is made, Cerdic, but put the blade down."

I did and bowed at Aethelric. "Apologies, Highness, but the point remains. I will take an oath that this man does not lie."

Aethelric looked even more confused, but eventually rallied to ask a question. "If what he says is true, what must we do, Cerdic?"

I pointed at the reeds that covered the hard-packed earth of the hall's floor.

"Stay here: right here. We hold a fortress and we still have five hundred men. Supplies are plentiful and there are fresh water springs and a well. We stay and we hold, until my father comes with Aethelfrith."

I looked at the lords around me. Some were nodding and others looking anxiously at each other. The door to the hall opened at this moment and Cuthbert came in and talked to a guard, who glanced at me. I nodded at him to permit my friend to enter.

Sabert slapped his thigh in frustration.

"Supplies are not an issue: numbers are. Even with five hundred men we will be hard pressed to hold Owain out of here, even for a day. Unless your father comes tomorrow, all will be lost."

Cuthbert arrived at my side and bent to whisper in my ear. I smiled and then winked at him.

"If we only had some idea if he was coming and how soon," the Prince was muttering to himself.

"Maybe we do, Highness. Cuthbert, repeat what you just told me."

Cuthbert looked terrified at having to do that and I could see his hands were shaking.

"I ... I," he stammered.

"It's alright Cuth, just say it: it's important."

He took a deep breath then cleared his throat. "Highness, there are fires to the north."

All eyes now turned to him.

"A f ... fire? Where?" the Prince stuttered fearfully.

"Not just one fire, I said fires, Sire: scores of them. It's an army out there, it cannot be anything else."

Harald stepped forward.

"How far boy, how far?"

Cuthbert screwed up his eyes like he did when estimating a range for his bow. He nodded his head after a moment.

"Perhaps ten miles, maybe more, but the low clouds reflect the glow."

"It has to be Aethelfrith!" I said.

"It could be," Sabert conceded, "or your Welshman's word might already be true. It could be an uprising gathering to come here, rallying to Owain's call. Sire, we can't take the risk. We must leave now!"

"Sire," I interrupted desperately, "if it is my father and Aethelfrith then we have to stay. It's our only hope. We must stay and occupy Owain's army long enough for Aethelfrith to come and then, together, we can defeat him."

Harald took less than a second to agree.

"I say stay!" He slammed his tankard down on the table.

Suddenly, there was pandemonium as all the lords began talking at once.

Cuthbert took us all by surprise, not least me, by shouting at them to be quiet. They all stared at him in outrage. He spoke and this time his voice was steady, determined and even noble.

"It's like one of Lilla's sagas. Remember when Urien was attacking Lindisfarne and Firebrand stood on the causeway ...?" His eyes grew distant as he thought back several years to the evenings when as boys we had listened to the bard's tales.

"*Come no nearer viper. I tire of retreat. I will die here or I will prevail here and his bondsmen struck spear on shield and roared their defiance.*"

I was impressed; Cuth had Lilla's tone and voice down very well.

Sabert snorted. "This is not a tale, lad. This is real life. We are all going to die if we stay."

But Sabert had not noticed the Prince. Aethelric knew his own limitations: how poor a leader and how clueless in battle he was. But he had been listening to Cuthbert and would know Lilla's words well, for it was one of the bard's most popular sagas. Something in it inspired Aethelric. As he stared at Cuthbert, colour came back into his pale face. The main task or role of a king, prince or lord was to make decisions. This Prince's decision, this night, would be critical to the outcome of this battle and thus to the survival of an Anglo-Saxon kingdom in the North - and possibly even to the future of the English race. He opened his mouth and made that decision.

"We will stay," he said, "and we will fight and pray to the gods that Aethelfrith comes in time."

Sabert's face was dark for a moment, but then he bowed.

"So be it. It seems that all our fates depend on the eyesight of this man," he said. Then, still looking at Cuthbert, added, "In which case, may I suggest that your Highness sends this scout to go and find Aethelfrith for us and bring him here."

"Eh?" mumbled Cuthbert followed by a hasty, "my Lord."

Sabert was grinning nastily now.

"Your vision seems sharp and there is no doubting your agility and speed. Aethelfrith must know that we need aid quickly, so you can carry that news to him."

"Yes ... that seems fair," muttered the Prince, back to his customary vagueness. "I suggest, Harald, you look to setting our defences and then, everyone, get some sleep."

I left the hall with Aedann and Cuthbert in tow, but as soon as I was outside I spun round and faced the Welshman.

"Why did you not tell me about the uprising in Eoforwic, before now?"

Those dark green eyes stared at me for a moment, before he answered.

"When I arrived in Eoforwic, I had ideas I was returning to my own people ..."

"Like you said, just now?"

He nodded then shrugged.

"Yes, they are Eboracii. They are Welsh and I do speak their language, so I felt some bond there. When I heard them talking, I cannot deny I was excited. For an hour or two when we left the city my mind was full of dreams of a kingdom of Eboracum reborn – maybe even your people as slaves for a change."

His eyes grew distant. Was he seeing images of my father toiling in the fields while he sat back and drank mead? If so, he was a fool, for my father worked as hard as anyone.

"If that's the case, why then speak now? Your words swayed the Prince's decision; you must have known they would?"

"Well, I said I thought these things for an hour or two. Then, I began realising that I have more in common with you all," and at this he waved a hand towards me and Cuthbert.

" Don't get me wrong, I'm very proud to come from the race I do and their past and history belong to me. However, my present and future belongs with you. Do not forget also that One Eye is Welsh too, as are his people, and then look at the things he has done. In the end, a man is more than his people's past. It's his friends and companions, his family and his deeds today, that matter."

I nodded and then glanced across at Cuthbert, who I saw had not been listening. He was looking anxious and I realised he was preoccupied with his mission out into the dark.

"You'll be fine, Cuth. Sabert might be an ornery so and so, but he spotted that you are a natural hunter and scout. No one will see you and you will find my father, I'm sure of it."

Cuthbert nodded, looking a little brighter.

"Just don't take too long about it!" Aedann grunted.

Cuthbert and I found him a dark cloak to wear, fresh arrows and bow strings, food and drink. Then, we went to the northeast corner of the fortress and climbed up to the palisade. We had one sentry up there keeping watch and I asked him if he had seen any enemy activity.

"No, my Lord," he answered and I dismissed him back to his duty.

The slope beyond the palisade was acute and the ditch at its base deep. Seeing that, I abandoned a brief idea that I had entertained, of giving Cuthbert a horse. There was no way he would get it down there and the main gate was blocked and too well watched by Owain's men to go out that way. In any event, he was a poor horseman at best and was far better on two legs.

We removed one of the upright posts in the palisade, creating a narrow gap just wide enough for my friend to squeeze through. He poked his head out and looked around and then turned back to me, to say goodbye. I placed my hands on his shoulders and looked him in the eye, "Be careful, but be quick," I said simply.

He nodded. "Stay safe, Cerdic, I will be back."

With that he slid quietly down the slope, climbed the far side pulling himself up by the tree roots and, with a last glance at me, was gone between the trees and into the night.

It was now about two or three in the morning and it would be dawn in less than five hours. Returning to the fires, I saw that they had burnt low. The men had taken shelter in whatever hut or building they could find or else, wrapped up in their cloaks, were huddled near the fires. Harald came past and waved me over to him.

"Right then, the guard is set. Nothing more to do for a few hours: let's both get some sleep. We will be glad of it come the morrow."

I nodded and realised just how shattered I felt. I could not be bothered to find anywhere to sleep, so I rolled up in my cloak next to a fire and closed my eyes. In an instant, I was asleep.

When Harald woke me, it was still dark, but a faint glow of light on the eastern horizon told me it would be day soon.

We roused the men who, groaning, coughing and complaining, hunched around fires to warm themselves, splashed water on their faces and toasted some stale bread over the flames, or ate whatever else they could find. There wasn't much.

Eduard stumbled over to me, eating what looked like bacon. I smiled to myself; he always managed to scavenge something to eat. He looked at me and his face wore an unusually anxious expression.

"Aedann told me, that you sent Cuth to go and find Aethelfrith."

I nodded.

"You think that was wise?"

"Can you think of anyone better?" I replied.

He thought about it a moment.

"Well no, but still, it's Cuth."

"I know, I'm worried too, but he will be fine. It's us I'm more concerned about right now. Give me some of that bacon: I'm starving."

My breakfast was interrupted, though, as horns now sounded from outside the gates. Our sentries on the walls waved at us. Eduard and I exchanged glances. Was that Aethelfrith already? I scuttled up to the battlement, joined by Sabert, Harald and eventually, a yawning, very sleepy, Aethelric.

I took in the view from the battlements for the first time in the daylight. Owain's army had camped in scattered spots on the battlefield, avoiding the bodies of the fallen where they could. I saw that a few of the slain were piled up in heaps, whilst their weapons and shields had been collected and stacked together, but other than that, no attempt had yet been made to clear the field and it looked truly appalling. Ravens and crows as well as the occasional fox, were busy with their grisly habit of picking over the bodies of the fallen. What yesterday had been a thousand young fit men was now just food and bloody offal for the animals. Occasionally, some of Owain's men would throw stones at them to clear them away, but soon they would be back. I tried not to think whether a bird would be picking morsels from my dead flesh later in the day.

Owain's army would have been as exhausted as ours and had just found spots away from the dead, lit fires and slept. Now, a small deputation was approaching the gates. Twenty or so warriors accompanied the lords and carried banners. Under them stood Owain and Samlen, along with other Welsh kings I did not recognise. I saw, with a scowl, that Hussa accompanied them. He carried a banner as well, but he was dragging it across the ground in apparent contempt. Anger seethed in me as I realised it was the wolfshead banner of our company.

The deputation halted outside the gates and looked up at us.

Owain, resplendent in his golden armour, stepped out to the front. Hussa moved forward with him. Owain shouted something in Welsh; Hussa then repeated it in English. So, Hussa was now moving in the circles of kings, acting as a translator.

"Who has authority to negotiate for you?" Hussa said.

"I do!" Aethelric shouted back, his voice full of defiance and nobility. I had to admit that although he was not much use for anything else, when we needed a speech giving, he was your man.

Hussa whispered something to Owain who replied.

"Prince Aethelric of Deira?"

Aethelric turned to me and said in undertone, "Is that not the boy who bested you in that tournament? I gave him his sword, didn't I?"

"Yes, Lord, it's Hussa!"

"You know who I am, traitor!" Aethelric shouted down.

Owain continued talking and Hussa translating.

"The Lords of Rheged, Elmet, Strathclyde and Manau Goddodin are here and I speak for them. YOU are defeated. We claim this land for the Kingdom of the Pennines and demand you lay down your arms to prevent further loss of life."

Aethelric did not hesitate. "Traitor, tell your new masters that this fort and this land are ours and we will fight to defend them."

Owain laughed and replied.

"With what?" Hussa said with a sneer. "You have what – four hundred or so men? We have three times your number. You'll be slaughtered."

"I offer you a chance," Aethelric said, ignoring Hussa, "leave now and we will let you depart with weapons and banners and what spoils you have taken."

I glanced at him sharply. Did that include Mildrith?

Owain laughed again and he turned and said something to Samlen who nodded.

From behind him, his men dragged out three young women, all dressed in fine clothes and wearing my mother's jewels. The sunlight caught the amber and it glowed. I almost cried out as I noticed that one of them was Mildrith. She appeared to be unhurt, but was clearly terrified. She looked up and saw me on the battlements.

"Cerdic!" she shouted, "help me!"

Samlen looked up at me smugly and shouted in English.

"Our friend told us you were here. Is it spoils like these you will let us take? Pretty aren't they?" he added, stroking Mildrith's face. She shied away, shuddering at his touch.

"Samlen, if you have harmed her ..." I shouted, unable to contain myself.

"Oh, not yet: not quite yet. I am saving that pleasure," he emphasised the last word with a leer at his men, who laughed, "for tonight, when you are dead. Then, my men are looking forward to it as well. I'm a good lord and share the spoils round."

"Bastard!" I shouted.

Owain now spoke again and Hussa repeated his words in a taunting voice.

"So then, I think we can dispense with your offer and come to ours."

"What is that?" Aethelric asked.

"Oh, I believe we can be just as generous. We will let you march away with all your weapons in full honour of war. As you can see, our army is scattered and not ready to fight you. You can safely go south to the bridge at Catraeth. You will leave this land and we will let you survive ..." Hussa stopped for a moment and checked he had some words right "... and King Owain will even allow you to take these spoils with you." He waved at Mildrith – his half-sister.

Samlen scowled at that and I was grimacing at the offer, as well. Would they really let us go, give us back Mildrith and permit us to march away unharmed? But, if they did, all we had feared would come to pass. Eoforwic would rise up, we would get caught and killed at the bridge and we would not be here when father arrived. When father arrived .... The realisation hit me like a sledgehammer: of course, that is what was behind it all.

"Reject the offer!" I hissed at Aethelric.

"What are you saying lad, he will let us go and you will get your sister back. Don't you love her?" Sabert asked, severely.

"I don't think he will keep his word. It's just a trick to make us leave this place and get us out into the open," I now looked at the scattered camps of Welsh and quickly counted numbers. I could see perhaps five hundred men. That meant a thousand were out of sight, somewhere. My gaze fell on the edge of the battlefield where the land dipped away down the southern slope: the same slope where we had hidden, out of sight of the Welsh, only the day before.

"I'm sure of it. They have the bulk of their men ready to ambush us."

Behind me Grettir had been standing, keeping silent, but now the veteran spoke.

"Master Cerdic is correct. I count no more than four hundred men out there."

"Why, what is he doing?" Sabert asked.

I knew, or thought I did.

"Aethelfrith: Owain knows he is coming and wants us dead quickly so he can defeat him in turn. Then, nothing can stop him."

"Very well then," Aethelric said, lifting his voice and shouting down to Owain and his lords. "I must reject your offer. We will not surrender, viper, we die here or prevail here!"

I smiled and wished Cuthbert had been around to hear that. I glanced at Harald and he winked at me. "You will have to tell your friend," he whispered, "our Prince is not as weak as he thought." Then his face looked serious again and I knew what he was thinking: we had first to survive the day, of course.

"Very well," Hussa shouted out Owain's reply. "You have sealed your fate. No prisoners will be taken this day!"

Now, Owain's horns sounded again, but with a different tone. Suddenly, we saw their missing thousand men. They came over the rise as we had done the previous noon, darkening the southern horizon with their numbers and marched in formation towards us. The men around the camp fires quickly assembled and I saw that most already had their weapons at hand. They were already prepared and well organised and I knew that I had been right. Owain had heard about Aethelfrith and was determined to finish us and then turn and destroy him.

Harald yelled an order and our own horns sounded and suddenly our men were arming and assembling on the battlements. I glanced northwards over the far palisade as I tried and hoped to see an army coming. But, there was nothing moving out there. Turning away and slapping my own helmet on, I drew my sword and prepared for battle.

Towards us, fifteen hundred men marched and far away, Loki laughed and rolled his dice.

Chapter Seventeen
Aethelfrith

A man has five senses and each and every one of them gets used in a battle. That morning of the second day of the Battle of Catraeth, my senses were overwhelmed. You see with a terrifying clarity the approaching army; perceive the fear mingled equally with hate in the eyes of the enemy as well as the terrified pleading expressions of those you have struck down. You feel your heart pounding and later, in the terrible crush of battle, the indescribable sensations of your blade cutting flesh and bone, the searing pain of injury and the air burning in your lungs. Your mouth tastes of blood and you can smell – gods, the smell – sweat, shit and piss and the appalling stench of viscera as men's entrails spill steaming from their guts, and always the smoke of burning buildings catching in your throat and making your eyes stream.

Above and beyond all of that, however, is the sense of hearing: it is the sounds you will recall more than anything else when you think of battles you have been in. At least, that is how it is for me. That morning it was the horns and drums of Owain's army echoing up at us in daunting clamour that I hear in my nightmares still, and that even today, years later, wake me in sweat-soaked terror. Then I hear again the screams; the crashing of spears on shields and the taunting war cries the enemy shouted at us. Finally, the voice of Owain, Samlen and a score of other kings, princes and lords, calling them forward.

And forward, they came.

There was urgency in that charge and a kind of heroic recklessness, which confirmed to me that Owain was keen to have this business done and done quickly; so then he could turn to the real task of this day. Almost all of his fifteen hundred men charged at once. There was no reserve, apart from a hundred or so Goddodin cavalry. There was no formation, save one large mass. There was little strategy except one: get inside Stanwick camp and kill us all, as soon as they could.

We had but a few archers and slingers left – maybe fifty – but these pelted the enemy with arrow and stone. That brought some screams, as perhaps a dozen men caught a missile in some unprotected part and fell beneath the feet of their countrymen to be crushed. However, little that we did could disrupt their shield wall or diminish their numbers and on they still came.

"Throw anything you can at them!" Harald bellowed.

Grettir and Eduard took a dozen men and returned with stones and bricks, burnt logs, axes and even the remains of a roasted boar. Other companies did the same and brought back anything that might make a missile. All went over the wall as the enemy closed on us and more of them fell, killed or injured. Not enough though ... nowhere near enough.

The Welsh army had reached the outer ditch. Some of them, led by Owain, were lucky and had come up against the gate where there was no ditch. They threw themselves against it, trying by brute force to smash their way in. Glancing that way, to my left, I saw that Harald's men were on my side of the gate and Sabert's company, beyond it. Harald had the remnants of the Stanwick garrison in reserve behind the gate. I turned to look to my front again across the southern ditch at the enemy army.

Most of them had to traverse the ten-foot deep ditch, which ran around the camp at the foot of the palisade. A few hours before, the agile Cuthbert had passed across the same ditch, carefully and slowly by himself, but this army just fell down into it. A good number fell too fast and too far and smashed ankles or landed on elbow joints which snapped on impact. Their peril was made worse when dozens more of their comrades tumbled down on top of them, crushing them. And then still more fell upon these men. Soon, the ditch was full of a writhing mass of warriors, trying to make headway across the bloody debris below them.

Others though ... too many others, slid down the outer ditch wall or held on to the spear shafts of their fellow warriors and dropped down more carefully. These were better placed to come across to the near side of the ditch. We pelted them with stones and rubble to little effect. I heaved up a large blackened stone, retrieved from the nearby camp fire, and tossed it downwards. As I did, one youth, no older than I, looked straight up at me and saw – too late – the stone coming for him. It smashed into his face and with a blood-curdling cry he fell back, dead. A moment later, a sling stone fired from the far side of the ditch ricocheted off my helmet and I tumbled backwards myself, my head now spinning.

I felt strong arms heave me up and as my sight returned, saw the anxious face of Grettir staring at me. His lips were moving and for a moment the ringing in my ears prevented me hearing his words. I remember thinking that the terrible din of the battle was gone and maybe that I was dying. Then, with a rapidity that made me dizzy, the noise was back and I could hear the old retainer speaking.

"...you hear me, Master? Can you see me? ... it's Grettir."

I nodded and put my hand on my head, then took it away and inspected it. I had expected to see blood, but my helmet had saved me. I looked around for it and saw that Grettir was holding it out to me.

"I ... I am fine, Grettir, just a bit stunned," I said, climbing unsteadily to my feet and shaking my head to clear it. Grettir nodded and handed me the helmet, before stepping back into the line at the wall.

I stood for a moment to regain my senses and looked at the battle below. Owain was leading repeated charges at the gate, but as yet the sturdy oak structure was holding and Sabert's men from one side and Harald's from the other were causing great injury to any Welshman that approached. Beyond the gate still more of Sabert's men were pelting the right wing of the Welsh as they tried to climb the wall there. In front of us, the enemy had reached the ditch below our section of the palisade and were trying to clamber up it.

Eduard was yelling foul abuse at the warriors beneath him and – standing beside him – Aedann seemed to be repeating his words in Welsh. Below, I could hear furious replies. I smiled for a moment at some of Eduard's juicer words and wondered how well they translated; then I stepped forward next to Eduard and looked down.

My smile dropped.

Immediately underneath us, scores of the enemy had come up to only a few feet below the palisade. We kept on throwing what we could at them, but our supplies of effective missiles had all but run out and unhindered now, the enemy were climbing up each other, or using knives thrust into the packed earth as hand holds to pull themselves up. So, at last, when fifty or so had reached the palisade, one of their chieftains gave a loud bellow and they made a surge at it.

The top of a head popped up over the palisade and I cracked it open like a nut with my sword and the warrior fell back down.

To my side, Eduard gave a roar and using an axe he had found, was hacking mercilessly left and right. Dozens died as they tried to come over the top, but still more came on and suddenly, with a cry, the lad next to me was impaled on a spear and fell screaming down into the camp behind. A pair of huge warriors leapt over the wall and in an instant the enemy were amongst us. One of them, with a ragged black beard, still had his shield and rammed it into my stomach so that I doubled over in agony. Eduard stepped back and cut at him, slicing his shoulder open, but in doing so, left the wall for a moment and so another pair of Welshmen were over in a flash.

I scrambled to my feet, protecting myself with my shield and swung wildly left and right with my sword. Eduard was doing the same and I now saw that Aedann had also been forced back from the wall. All three of us were teetering on the inside edge of the fighting platform that ran around the camp, with no place to go backwards except a sharp fall onto the hard-packed earth below, where a number of our men were already lying groaning or dead.

Grettir was the other side of the pair of warriors who had come over first. He shouted something at them and as the nearest one turned, hacked at his neck. The man fell to his knees, blood gushing from an artery, then his eyes rolled upwards and he lay still. That left the one with the black beard, whom Eduard had injured, and as he turned to cut at Grettir, I slashed at his legs and cut them from under him. Grettir stepped forward and finished him with a stab to the throat.

Beyond Grettir, the Welsh had not managed to reach the wall, but to my right I saw that we were losing the battle. On the far side of Aedann, fifty enemy warriors were now massing on the battlements and had killed our men there or pushed them over the edge. Now they had an opening and none of our army stood the other side of them. All they needed to do was push along the battlements, down the steps and they could come behind us wherever they wished or – more likely – fall on the men at the gate and open it. More Welsh were poised to come up and over the wall: we had to act fast.

"Shield wall, Wicstun Company, shield wall!" I shouted and locked shields with Grettir and Eduard.

"Form a column, three wide. Shields locked!" I ordered and hesitating, the men started to turn towards me.

"Quickly men!" Grettir backed me up and soon the men were shuffling into a long column facing along the battlements towards us, three men wide and with shields locked behind each other.

"Now!" I shouted at Eduard and Grettir and we pushed forward as a few more Welshmen came over the wall. Surprised by us, they were unbalanced and fell back, screaming, into the ditch behind taking two more with them.

"Turn!" I shouted and we wheeled round to the right. The rest of the company came up behind us and now we were a long column of steel and iron: a battering ram with one purpose – to clear the battlements.

We pushed along the battlements up to the first Welshmen, who now turned to face us. They were not formed up, however, and we were and as we cut and hacked and pushed, they fell to our blades and spears. We stepped forward and I had Grettir angle his shield left to protect us from men trying to come over the wall, or from missile fire from beyond the ditch, whilst Eduard and I kept ours facing along the wall. Gradually, though, the enemy realised the danger and a huge brute of a warrior chieftain dragged and kicked his men into line and with a rattling and banging of wood on wood, they dragged their shields together and formed a wall.

Now, it was down to brute force: our will against their will. They were desperate to finish us fast and to be ready for their next battle. We were desperate to hold on for just another hour or so. When it comes to brute force and a trial of strength, there are few men stronger than Eduard and I was glad to have him at my side.

I have no idea how long that struggle lasted, but it seemed an age. Muscles ached and sinews popped under the effort. Knives, spears and blades stabbed back and forth over the shields. Gradually as men fell on both sides we edged along, inch by inch and yard by yard until I felt I could stand the effort no longer. Then, with shocking suddenness, the shield wall ahead of us just gave way. The enemy started to pull back, then a few started to run and in an instant the sixty or so of them were hurtling away from us along the battlements. We advanced and cut several more down and then there were no more left. I shouted in triumph, but then the cry caught in my throat, as I saw that the danger was not yet over.

The giant leading the Welsh had held us long enough to plan his action. Now I could see that he was leading his men down from the battlements and swinging round to the gateway. I looked that way expecting that Harald would lead a counter attack with the hundred men he had held in reserve at the gate. Then I saw that there was no reserve company. Over on the other side of the battle Sabert's men had been swept off the battlements and down to the camp, so Harald had committed the reserve to repel the enemy back over the wall. This meant that as the chieftain led his fifty men towards the gate, there were just ten of our warriors there, struggling to hold the gates shut as

Owain forced his way in.

The men at the gate never saw the danger until it was too late. With a vicious cry, the giant chieftain hacked two down with the same swing of his huge blade and in an instant his men had killed the others. They were busy clearing the rubble we had piled against the gates. Soon, the gates would be opened and if that happened ...

"Wicstun Company, follow me!" I shouted and without looking to see if they followed, I ran along the battlements to the steps. Now, as I tumbled down them, I did glance back and saw that almost the whole company was following me, save half a dozen men Grettir had ordered to stay with him and try to guard the wall.

It was a risk. Whilst we abandoned the wall the enemy might bring more men across, but the gates were critical. If they opened, then all was lost. At the gates, the last of the rubble had been cleared and now the bar was being lifted. I had no time to form up into any formation.

"Charge!" was all I could find the breath to yell, as we crashed into the rear of the Welsh and a confused swirling melee began. Now again, all the senses were bombarded and overwhelmed and in the end, ignored. All that was left was an almost blind madness, as you lay about you at anything that moved and hoped to the gods it was an enemy and not a friend. We fought with fury and abandon, as we strove to reach the gates and prevent them opening.

But we failed.

With a thud, the bar was dropped to the ground and the chieftain himself reached out both arms and pulled the gates open. Twenty yards away, Owain was standing surrounded by hundreds of warriors, rallying them after the latest charge at the gates had failed. Scores had died trying to force their way in. Now, they gave a huge shout of triumph and came on again.

The chieftain had turned and saw me advancing on him. He laughed and swung his monstrous sword round in a huge arc, aiming to cut me in two. The sword never reached me. Eduard, with his shield in front of him, just charged straight at the man. They both fell in a heap, but it was Eduard who got up. The chieftain was writhing on the ground, a dagger in his belly. He spat at Eduard and then died.

We had killed the Welsh who had opened the gate and now Eduard, Aedann and I stood in the opening with the twenty men that were all that were left from our company. Outside the gates, five hundred enemy warriors charged towards us.

Owain reached us first, his armour shining in the sunlight giving him the appearance of a bronze statue or a warrior god in his full glory. His huge house troops, all wearing chain armour and carrying vicious looking two-handed swords, charged with him. There was no time for terror now, just cut and thrust, the ramming of shields, wheeling round, dodging blows, staggering backwards then recovering and advancing again.

All the time, we were being pushed back into the camp and at that moment, I was certain we were doomed. Harald and Sabert were leading their men down from the battlements to join us, but I could sense it was futile. Aethelric himself was now beside me and swung wildly with his blade at Owain, but the smile on the King of Rheged's face told me that he knew it was all but over.

That just got me angry, boiling mad in fact, at the stupidity of everything. After all our efforts we would die here and Deira would fall. My family would mourn me and as for little Mildrith, Samlen would celebrate his victory. That made me wonder where Samlen was. No doubt somewhere in the battle, but not where I could get to him and stop him from touching my sister. Unless...

Unless, I could kill Owain.

Blind rage and fury gave me strength and careless of my life, I came back at the golden king, hacking recklessly at his armour, ignoring the pain as his guards smashed swords against my shield or took slices out of my arms and legs. My fury took him by surprise and he stumbled over the chieftain's body, slipped in his guts and then, with a cry, he fell...

I was on him in an instant and plunged my sword into his throat.

His eyes met mine and in them was shock and denial. His plans and dreams of glory bled away with his lifeblood into the soil of Catraeth field and then his eyes glazed and he was dead.

Suddenly, there was a moment of silence as all on both sides looked on in stunned disbelief, weapons stilled. Into that silence came the other sound I remember from Catraeth, as I sit in sweat-soaked terror recovering from my nightmares. The clear sounds of more horns. Not horns from Elmet, Strathcyde, Rheged or even the Goddodin, but English horns heralding an English army: Bernician horns.

Aethelfrith had come.

There was another great fanfare off to the northwest. This came from out beyond the enemy's left wing. For a moment, I stared that way, but could see nothing because of the palisades. Then, Grettir shouted from the battlements.

"Woden's buttocks! It's the Bernicians. Aethelfrith is here: they have come to the battle."

In front of me, the enemy's confidence waned and fear came upon their faces. A few backed away, more joined them and with a clattering of dropped weapons and shields, they started to run.

I ran too, but up to the battlements joined by Aethelric, Sabert and Harald and we stared out onto to the battlefield, to see if the Bernicians had come, after all. And indeed they had: one thousand spears had marched south from Bernicia and crossed the Tees. Like a shadow rolling across the fields, they came onwards, moving relentlessly to fall on the fleeing enemy.

A murmur ran amongst our men who were crowding the battlements and I looked to see what had caused it. Then, for the first time, I saw the man who would have such an effect on my early years. He walked forward between two companies, surrounded by a half dozen cruel looking house guards, yet he was taller than any of them, by several inches. He wore a pair of leather britches and a tunic of tough brown cloth, over which he had a shirt of metal rings. By his side a great sword hung from a shoulder strap. His grey cloak, billowed around by the wind, served to exaggerate his size. Crowning all was a helm of iron with metal bands and strips that were extended to form nose and cheek guards. He was still young: perhaps twenty-five years or so, although a light brown beard gave him the appearance of being a few years older.

This then was the man who had fought under his father in the siege on Lindisfarne and helped him to take advantage of the chaos following Urien's death. After Firebrand's death, Aethelfrith had unified the scattered Bernicians and finally secured a kingdom on the Tweed. That was not enough, for he had fought battles further afield to weaken his enemies and now he strode forward to confront the last chance those enemies had to defeat him.

This was Aethelfrith.

When the Bernicians joined the battle; it was over in minutes.

They cut into the rear of the enemy, obliterating the brave God-dodin cavalry and rolling up the Welsh army.

Increasingly outflanked, the Welsh from north of the wall were dying. The Goddodin had perished. The pressure there mounted until suddenly, the morale of the entire enemy army cracked like an acorn under a shoe and they were running like a flood westwards towards the pass. The Bernicians pursued them and with a shout of joy we Deirans ran after them, eager for revenge. In the release of fear that followed, a blood-mad-ness overcame us. We took no prisoners and without pity slew all we could catch.

The attempt to restore the Welsh Kingdom of the Pennines had failed. The finest, best equipped and noblest of the warriors of the old North were dead, captured or fleeing, scattered and leaderless. Never again would the Welsh field an army of such quality and size: an echo of the armies of Rome. We halted our pursuit at the pass to Rheged and turned back, exhausted and triumphant.

After that, the armies moved towards the enemy camps and the looting began. The dead and the wounded were searched: for gold, for fine swords, for beads, for anything of value. Such has ever been the reward of victory.

Suddenly, a cold terror gripped my heart. Somewhere on one of these camps was Mildrith. No doubt somewhere also here, if he had survived the slaughter, was Samlen, with my uncle's sword and the amber treasure. But all that I counted as naught if I could just find Mildrith. I glared around me at Deiran and Ber-nician alike: friends who now became enemies if they reached my sister first. With their blood burning for loot, would they ignore other lusts if they found her?

"Mildrith! I shouted. Near me, Aedann and Eduard heard me

and the expressions on their faces, showed me they too realised my fear.

"Mildrith!" we all shouted and started running across the battlefield.

Chapter Eighteen
Mildrith

I stopped running after a few moments, realising it was futile to just go on dashing like a headless chicken around the battlefield. I needed to think. I had seen no sign of Owain's main camp when we pursued the Welsh across the southern half of the battlefield and it certainly had not been down the slope that ran to the Rheged road.

"Think, Cerdic, think," I urged myself.

Owain's army had come across the mountains down that road, but the road slanted southeast, towards Catraeth, whilst Stanwick camp was due east of the pass. So, Owain would have swung off the road towards the fortress. Then, with night approaching soon, he would have set up an encampment somewhere along the way.

Aethelfrith's charge coming from the north had forced the fleeing Welsh to take a more southerly route at first, so their rout and our pursuit had not taken us through their camp. Nor, at any time, had we seen Samlen, Mildrith or Hussa. I wondered if perhaps Samlen had spotted the disaster earlier than most on the battlefield and knew that all was lost. What would he do? Or come to think of it, what would Hussa do?

What, on this entire battlefield, was worth the entire value of almost everything else on it? That was an easy question with an easy answer: the amber treasure; the treasure Samlen had paraded on his captured girls. Certainly he would take no chances with that. He would send it back to camp, escorted with a man he could trust: Hussa, of course.

Now the battle was lost that was where they would be.

"Quick lads, this way and pray to the gods that we are the first there."

Gasping for breath as we ran, we headed north towards where I estimated Owain's men had been marching from when we had first seen them. As we ran we passed heaps of bodies from the previous day's battle, many mauled horrendously, ghastly pale in appearance, covered in dried blood and pecked at by birds. Here and there we saw groups of two or three Welsh warriors, who had tried to hide but having then been caught were being made to suffer through their agonising final moments by vengeful Deirans or Bernicians. Many of our army had lost friends on this battlefield and they made the captives pay for it.

A scream broke out close by to us as a doomed youth was held down by a dozen Deiran warriors, whilst another of the victors approached with a burning log and moved it towards his skin. I looked away, suddenly sickened by the sight, but I could not avoid hearing the terrible screeching pleas for mercy nor the nauseating stench of burning flesh.

We ran on past a few larger groups of Welshmen who were fighting desperate last ditch stands: twenty here or thirty there, but surrounded now by many score of Angles. One group of proud looking veterans clustered together around the tattered remains of their once proud banner. A dozen of them locked shields and slowly retreated towards the mountains. Around them, the battlefield was full of English warriors baying and yelling for their blood. Fresh corpses littering the ground around the enemy showed that these men were making us pay for each of their lives. Yet, as I glanced back at them, I saw our men rush once more at them and, like Wallace's standard last night, their banner finally fell.

Up ahead was a copse of oak trees, which we entered and passed through. Beyond it was an empty field with a slope running away to the north, but still no camp visible.

"There!" Eduard said, pointing; off to the west we saw a cloud of smoke that must have come from many fires. It was at least half a mile away and feeling exhausted, I groaned. Beside me, Eduard and Aedann looked set to collapse. Still, full of fear as I was about Mildrith's fate, I found enough strength to push us on again until we came to a little hillock, beyond which we could see the smoke rising. Reaching the top, with our lungs burning and limbs stiff, we paused now to catch our breath and I could see that at last we had found what we were searching for. The Welsh camp lay in the small valley beneath us, on either side of a narrow steam which had come down from the mountains.

A dozen tents were surrounded by at least a hundred camp fires – most long since burnt out. Three of the tents were already on fire and – with dismay – I saw that we were not, in fact, the first to arrive. Indeed, we were far from the first. A hundred or so Angles – mostly Bernicians – were here before us and were moving around the fires, looking into any sacks or bundles they found for coins or any items of worth. Then they pressed on towards the tents, which promised yet more loot. Was Mildrith in one of them?

I launched myself down the slope followed by Eduard and Aedann, who came hurtling after me, our spears, shields and swords clattering against each other as we slid and stumbled towards the camp. Several Bernicians turned their heads at the sound and seeing us rushing towards them, hurried to pick up their weapons and moved in our direction, snarling at us. Before they reached me, I slid to a halt, lifted up my arms and shouted.

"Wait there: we are Deiran, not Welsh!"

261

Aedann wisely kept silent, at this point.

"Yeh, mate, well, so what? We rescued your hides, so we get first pickings here. Piss off!" An ugly looking brute speaking strangely accented English, growled at us. Several other Bernicians gathered round him and glared at us, daring us to start a fight.

"Relax friends; you can have anything you find except ..."

"Except what, you're keeping the good stuff from us, then?"

"No − I'm looking for a girl."

They all burst out laughing. "Look, friend, we all want one of those, you know what I mean?"

"This one is his sister, arsehole, and if any of you have touched her, you will have me to answer to!" Eduard shouted. The Bernicians took one look at my huge friend and his axe, still glistening with blood and then it was they who now held out their hands.

"Hey now, we are all friends: no need to get angry. But honestly lads, there are no girls here. You might try the tents," their leader said and pointed that way keen now, it seemed, to be rid of us.

We ran that way, splitting up to search each tent, but found that by now most had been ransacked. As we searched, we could see no one, other than Bernicians drinking the ale they had captured. One of them belched loudly and grinned at me.

"You seen any Welsh running away from here, mate?" I asked the man, not expecting an answer.

He surprised me by nodding amiably. "What? You mean about half a dozen of them along with some women?"

I stared at him. "Yes! Are you serious?" I asked, waving Aedann and Eduard over towards me.

"Yes, of course," the man sounded hurt. "I was just about the first into the camp and saw several jars of beer so I ... ah, acquired them, along with this," he patted a bulging sack which clinked and promised riches within. He was welcome to them − I just wanted to know where Mildrith was.

"Which way?" I asked, urgently.

"Eh?"

"Which way did they run?"

"Oh right, erm ... let me see."

"Hurry man, please," I said, stamping my foot.

"All right, don't rush me," he replied, as he scratched his head and took another swig of his ale and then at last pointed, "That way to the west, towards that forest."

"Thanks!" I shouted, already on the way, followed by Eduard and Aedann.

"Eh?" the man repeated and then belched again, but by then we had left him and the camp behind and headed towards the woods, our feet slipping and stumbling on the scrubby, rock-strewn ground, hope reviving our energy.

The trees were a good couple of miles away, but I thought I could see a few pines or spruce mixed in with what would be the usual oaks and willows. The land had started to rise towards the mountains and we came across the stream that ran through the Welsh camp and followed it back up its course towards the woodland. Totally alone now, we walked across the fields and meadows, so tired that we did not speak. Soon the only sound was the tramping of our feet, the gentle rattling of the equipment swaying on our shoulders and the gurgling of the water in the brook, fed by melted snow in the uplands and now rushing past us over its rocky path.

After half an hour, we passed a small stand of birch trees. When we emerged from the far side, Aedann suddenly hissed at me and nodded with his head to our left. There, about twenty men were coming in our direction, from the south. I turned wearily towards them, drawing my sword then peering that way, my other hand shielding my eyes from the late afternoon sunlight which silhouetted them. Like dark shadows they walked on, not afraid of us, nor stopping to draw their own weapons. Still unable to see who it was, I was about to challenge them, when Eduard suddenly laughed and waved at the men. A moment later, I too saw who they were and felt a huge weight had been lifted from me. First, I saw Cuthbert, walking along with his bow in his hand. Next to him, was the bard Lilla. Finally, I saw the man who I most wanted to see, the man who — these last few days — I had been almost afraid to hope would come: I saw my father.

Eduard cheered when he recognised his friend and ran straight over to give him a huge hug. Cuthbert's face reddened at this, but he was smiling as Eduard stepped back.

"About bloody time you got here. How long did it take you to find the damn Bernician army, then?" Eduard demanded.

Cuthbert looked hurt. "To be fair, most of the fires had gone out by the time I reached them and it was a sod of a long way ..." he defended himself and then halted when he saw that Eduard was winking at me and miming stirring a pot.

"Bastard!" Cuthbert said to Eduard; they both laughed and I clapped a hand down on Cuthbert's shoulder and nodded at him.

"I knew that you would make it, Cuth. Damn well done, all the same."

"Thanks, Cerdic."

I then walked up to my father. He looked tired and drawn: a man not as young as once he was, but Lilla, fresh as ever, was bouncing along beside him.

"Father," I said, "thanks to the gods that you came. It was ... bloody close, I can tell you!"

He studied me, a caring father checking his son, inspecting him for damage, maybe, or perhaps assessing if the last few days had changed him much. I saw him eyeing my various wounds, relief softening his gaze as he registered that none was life-threatening. After a moment he pulled me to him and gave me a hug before letting me go, then stood with one hand on my left shoulder, looking into my eyes.

"I told you I would come, but it took a little longer than I had hoped," he said.

"In fact, it's a fascinating story worth a song; would you like to hear it?" Lilla began, but I interrupted him.

"Another day maybe, but Father: Samlen and Hussa still have Mildrith and they went into those woods," I pointed. "They might be trying to sneak over the mountains by some footpath or ..."

Father's eyes narrowed and I could see that the same thought had come to us both. Samlen could injure us still more this day if he did what he had threatened to do to Mildrith.

Turning to the men who were following him − all that were left from the village and still more from Wicstun - my father snapped out an order. "Right then, men, follow us. Ten of you come with me and Lilla; the other ten go with Cerdic and his friends. We will divide the wood between us."

It was now getting far on through the afternoon and the sun was westering as we again moved across the fields towards the woodland. I was walking in the centre, with my patrol strewn out on either side of me scouring the scrub and bushes for signs of Samlen and his men. After a few minutes, we came across a faint track running through the field towards the woods and we followed it. About half a mile further south, Father and his warriors were matching our speed. We had been gone from the Welsh camp for a good hour already now and as yet had seen nothing except a startled hare, which Cuthbert had immediately shot with an arrow.

"Well, I've got my supper arranged, what about you?" he smirked at us. Tying the hare to his belt he scampered out of range of Eduard's fist. A few minutes later I saw him up ahead, waving at us to catch up. As he was to do often in the years to come, he was scouting in front of us, using his superior stealth and speed to our advantage.

"I think there may be some of those Goddodin in the woods over there. I saw some of that strange blue armour glinting in the trees."

The track continued west climbing towards the mountains. We moved along it until we finally reached the woods. There was quite a bit of undergrowth, but I could see no signs of the fugitives. I turned to look at my friend who, in response to my expression, pointed to the scrub beneath a tall elm tree. Suddenly, there was a yellow-brown flash as the late afternoon sun reflected off something metallic.

The woods were the last bit of cover before the bare hillsides beyond. Perhaps the Welsh were afraid to leave them and to go where we would surely see them. Or maybe they were injured, or even dead. Whatever the reason, we should be able to corner them here, I thought to myself.

"Eduard, take five men and wait here. I will take the other six and move round to the other side of the copse to prevent escape. Wait for my whistle and then move in, fast."

"Fine, Cerdic," my friend said.

Reliable Eduard, not very imaginative, but he could take

266

orders. I led my men around the northern edge of the wood, all the time keeping the glinting armour in sight. It did seem odd that whoever was wearing it was not moving. They must see us, I thought. Beyond the trees, was a ditch, along the wood's edge and I now led my small group along it, with Aedann just behind me and Cuthbert bringing up the rear.

After fifty paces, I halted and we now stood in a line, looking across the woods. I could just see Eduard's bulk through the trees. I whistled a long drawn out note. With a roar – I had never known him do much without a bellow or a roar – he surged forward, leading his half of the patrol through the woods. They were upon the Welsh position in a moment and I expected to hear screams and cries and the noise of battle. Yet, I saw Eduard halt and glance over at me and then bend down. When he came up, he was holding pieces of the burnished armour. They had just been abandoned, I imagined. Unless, it was a …

Trap! Suddenly, from the undergrowth, only twenty paces in front of us, there erupted a half dozen Welshmen. They had smeared mud on their faces and some had stuck leaves and grass in their hair. That and the fact we were looking beyond them, had been sufficient to deceive us. They had few weapons, save surprise, some swords and the odd sturdy branch. That, though, was enough. They rushed at us, knocking us over or lashing at us with branches. Most, I had not seen before, but one I did recognise for it was Hussa who rushed directly at me. His shoulder hit me in the chest and I went down into the ditch, the air knocked out of me. A heartbeat later and he was leaping the ditch and running off towards the mountains.

It took me a few moments to catch my breath and to clamber, mud-covered and winded, out of the ditch. By then, the Welsh were fifty yards away and going fast. Cuthbert, I saw, had blood coming from a cut on his head, but he was still standing, at least. None of the boys were dead, although some groaned and Horsa – a youth from Wicstun – was holding his wrist and wincing as if it was broken. Cuthbert assayed a shot at the fleeing Welshmen, but it sailed far wide of the target.

I saw Hussa turn to check the others were with him and to wave them on past. Then he gazed back at us and on, over the tree tops towards the camp and, finally, the battlefield at Catraeth. For a moment he looked straight at me then, with a wave, he turned and was off. Behind me, I heard Eduard arrive.

"Well, we buggered that up, didn't we!" he grunted. I turned and gave him what I hoped was a withering glare and with a sigh, led the boys off in pursuit.

The ground started to climb much more acutely now and there was little undergrowth and no trees. The fleeing Welsh were still ahead of us and now they were joined from further south by another group of warriors, one of whom glared back at us with his one eye. There then, at last, was the scarred face of Samlen. Aedann hissed and doubled his pace and I did nothing to stop him, for I had seen that Samlen was dragging along the struggling form of my sister.

My father's men closed in on us and reunited now, we pursued the Welsh. We now passed the start of steep, bare-faced cliffs jutting out from the mountain. Our prey had moved into a valley between the cliffs but then, at last, they turned and faced us as it was a dead end and for them, there was now no escape.

Hurriedly, Samlen's men formed up into a shield wall, using the few shields they still had. Behind this, stood Hussa, Samlen and Mildrith. Hussa had planted the Wolf's head banner next to him, maybe trying to goad and taunt us. It was a mistake. It made us angry and gave us just one more reason to kill them all.

Samlen still held Mildrith and now he drew his dagger and placed it against her throat.

"Stop there: or I kill the girl!" Samlen shouted.

"Leave her alone One Eye and fight me like a man. If you win, all of you can leave as free men," I said.

Samlen worked his mourh and spat towards me. "I told you once before, I don't fight slaves!"

Aedann shouted something in Welsh, then stepped forward, his sword and shield ready.

One Eye stared at him for a moment and then replied in the same language.

"Aedann, what's going on?" I murmured.

"I asked him if he would fight a free man of his own race, or die a coward," Aedann answered, sneering at his fellow Welshman.

Samlen growled and letting Mildrith go, he pushed through his men, dropped his knife and drew his sword. Then, I looked again and saw that I was wrong. It was not his blade he carried: this was my uncle's sword – the sword I had come here to retrieve.

"Very well, Eboracii; let us see how well you fight."

Much is said of the value of experience, of how veterans of many battles learn such tricks and see an enemy's moves so often that eventually they develop a second sight and can almost predict and anticipate what he will do next. All this is true, of course, but it is not the entire story: it presupposes that whilst your foe is aiming to kill you, he will choose tactics designed to maximise his own chance of surviving the battle. What Samlen failed to realise was that although Aedann was certainly trying to kill him, he was not bothered about his own survival. This made him dangerously unpredictable.

Samlen advanced on Aedann, swinging his sword in an arc, bracing his shield and taking the time to study his opponent, to learn his weakness. But Aedann did not give him that time: he just charged full on. Samlen took a few moments to react and when he did, he now had to bring his sword back from being held out to his side. He managed it alright, but, with the blade moving so quickly, he could not direct it with any accuracy. Aedann groaned in pain as the sword sliced into his left shoulder, opening a blood vessel which let out a gush of blood. His arm just went limp and he dropped the shield.

The next instant, his momentum had carried him onwards into Samlen and the collision sent him into his enemy's arms. In a bizarre parody of lovers embracing they stood like that for a long moment and then, suddenly, Samlen vomited up blood and fell backwards with a loud crash on to the ground, quite dead, impaled by Aedann's sword. He held it high in the sky, the blade slick with One Eye's blood, and gave out a mighty cry of vengeance satisfied.

"Charge!" my father yelled and started towards the Welsh, followed a moment later by the rest of our men. The Welsh, still stunned by Samlen's death, stood in shocked silence and we cut them down. There was to be no mercy or pity, because we now recognised each one of them. These were Elmetae who had raided the Villa alongside One Eye and watched him kill Cuthwine and the others, whose relatives were in the company and who today avenged their death. These warriors, at least, died quickly on our swords and spears. Only Hussa was left alive. Looking back, I will never be sure quite why I did not kill him there and then, except that for all his betrayal he was still of my blood and that knowledge must have stayed my sword arm.

Then, it was done and Hussa alone stood beside Mildrith. My

sister was crying as she ran over to me and I held her close as she sobbed away her fear, realising she was free again. Father joined us and now I could see that his own eyes were moist. He reached out and pulled Mildrith and me towards him and the three of us stood together, holding each other for several minutes. All this time, the brooding figure of Hussa looked on impassively at this family he was not part of, but perhaps should have been.

Mildrith was laughing and crying at the same time now. "If I ever try and sneak a look at a warrior again, just hit me, alright, Cerdic?" she said at last, reminding me that it was curiosity that had got her into all of this.

I nodded and then tilted my head at Cuthbert and Aedann, who stood nearby.

"I think there are two here, who you won't mind seeing."

Both Cuthbert and Aedann came across. Cuthbert gave a shy smile and Mildrith put one hand gently on his cheek. Aedann suddenly groaned in apparent pain.

"Oh my poor dear, let me see to that," Mildrith said, moving his hand away to examine the wound and then tearing a strip from her own dress to bind it.

Aedann grinned and out of sight of my sister, he rolled his eyes at Cuthbert, who glared back at him. So, not all our battles were over, I realised and idly pondered what the outcome of that little skirmish would be. Chuckling, to myself, I turned away to look at Hussa.

Hussa had dropped his sword and held out his arms.

"Go on, Father ... kill me, too."

Father just walked up to him and slapped him hard across the face.

"Bastard traitor!" he snarled.

Hussa wiped blood away from his lip and glowered back at

271

Father.

"Yes, and as I once said to Cerdic, we all know whose bastard, don't we?" Again he held his arms away from his chest. "Just finish it now. My mother is dead and soon I will be and you can return home as the hero who saved Deira," he said bitterly.

My father looked down at the seax he was carrying, back up at Hussa and then he dropped the long knife and shook his head.

"No, I will not. Enough have died today, besides which, your life is in the King's hands now. You are coming with us ... son," he said and Hussa was led away.

Father bent down and picked up Hussa's sword: the sword I had coveted throughout my childhood and youth. Then, he wandered over to Samlen's body and retrieved his brother's sword from the ground and wiped Aedann's blood off it onto the grass. He then turned and offered them both to me.

"Take one of these, son, you have earned it."

I stared at the blades.

"But, Father ... that sword is yours."

"No ... it was my brother's. He died a warrior and a hero. Today I would give it to you. For this day, it is you who are the hero."

My hand shook slightly, as I reached out and grasped the hilt. My fingers tightened and I took my uncle's blade, the blade of a warrior lord. I held it up, so that it reflected the lingering sunlight.

Then, I glanced across at the other sword – Hussa's sword, which I had watched forged and always wanted to own. Each was a magnificent, glorious weapon in its own way. I studied them both for a moment, then I shook my head and passed my uncle's blade back to my father. He raised an eyebrow and looked at me, puzzled.

"Keep that sword, Father. It has always been Uncle's and then yours. Give the other to Aedann, if you would take my advice, for I already have a sword.

I once heard it said that 'every good story is about a sword'. Well, that may be true, but I now realised that every good sword has its own story. I reached down and drew my own blade. The broad, sharp stabbing weapon that, Lilla later told me, was in fact Roman. It was a gladius and once would have been wielded by a legionary posted to the fortress of Calcaria and later was carried by the armies of Samlen as they attacked my home. It was there I had taken it from the first man I killed. I carried it to Calcaria and used it to free our people. Finally, here at this battle, it was the weapon that killed Owain: the golden King of Rheged. I now held it up high so every man could see it.

"I will call it: Catraeth, in memory of this place, so if I ever have to draw it in battle again I will not forget those who died here."

One of the men had retrieved the Wolf's head banner and proudly carried it back to us. The Wicstun Company had its standard again, so it was time to return to the camp with it. That left just one thing: the amber treasure.

Bending over, I examined Samlen's bloody corpse. His one eye stared at me, but it no longer burnt with his hatred and evil and I did not fear it. Inside his tunic I found what I was looking for: all of my mother's jewellery, save the link from the one earring, which I knew Hussa had sold.

"It is over," I said, handing them to my father. He examined them briefly and then thrust them inside his own tunic.

"No," he said, "not quite over. There is still one more duty."

Then he turned away, before I could ask what he meant.

The sun was setting as we walked back towards Stanwick

273

camp. We were alive and quietly I gave thanks to the gods. I carried the wounds of a warrior, some of them deep and painful, but today I had not been fated to die. Around me lay fifteen hundred men who had not been so lucky. We believe that when we die – if we die as warriors – we go to feast in Woden's hall with the men we have killed now our friends. I looked at Eduard, Cuthbert and lastly, Aedann – walking along one hand clamped to his wounded shoulder – and smiled. Woden's Hall could wait. For now I was glad to share a few more days with my friends, right here, right now.

Soon after we reached the army, the celebrations began. Aethelric welcomed Aethelfrith into Stanwick camp and in the fortress, a victory feast was held. I sensed that we had been present at one of the great battles: a turning point perhaps in the history of our troubled land and indeed we had. There would be no further attempt by the Welsh to cross the Pennines for a generation. Their hopes of driving us into the sea were finally defeated and it had been this battle that planted the dream of a common race north of the Humber. The dark times of division between us, which would plague much of my life, were part of an unknown future. Naïve of what fate was destined to shower upon us we drank ourselves senseless in joy. Bernicians and Deirans celebrated the truth: we were not just Saxons or Angles any longer.

We were Northumbrians.

Chapter Nineteen
Hussa

The following morning, I woke early and, needing fresh air and to empty my bladder, left the hall where I had slept and walked the battlements to watch the sun rise. I was now utterly sick of this place of death and I turned my gaze southwards towards the bridge, Eoforwic and the even more distant Villa.

I did not get my wish immediately, of course. That day and all of the next, we finished burying or burning the dead. Our wounded needed rest and treatment for their injuries, whilst the able-bodied turned their efforts to repairing the camp's walls for defence against a possible further attack; though one never came.

We seemed to be delaying our departure home for no reason that I could discern, but we found out why the following day. Aethelric and Aethelfrith had been involved in long discussions. Harald, Sabert and the other commanders were often seen coming and going into the hall, which the two leaders had taken over. Harald in particular looked furious one night when he came out, but when I asked him why, he would not answer.

There was great secrecy about the subject of their discussions, but rumours will emerge, eventually, in any army. Some men said that King Aethelfrith was keen to invade Rheged and conquer it, taking advantage of its weakness, but that our Prince did not want to. Alfred, from the Wolds swore that he had seen Owain still alive after the battle, walking away from it. I knew this was nonsense, of course, and I told him that I had killed the golden king with my sword and knew he was dead, but in the chaos of battle men can imagine many things. Indeed, one day a tale went round that Eoforwic had indeed fallen to an uprising and that we were about to march there to put the city to the sword.

In the end, we discovered that the issue under discussion was the future of Stanwick camp and the location of the border between Bernicia and Deira. We were shocked to learn that Aethelric had agreed that this border should lie at Catraeth Bridge, a few miles south of the fortress we were in. In other words, Stanwick camp would be left in the hands of Aethelfrith. So, this meant that we had marched all the way here and fought a battle, Deiran blood had been shed, Wallace and hundreds more besides him had been killed; and after all of that, we were simply just giving away the fortress.

Suddenly, the feelings of unity and the dreams of Northumbrian brotherhood seemed foolish. The Bernicians started ordering us Deirans around, acting all self important, as if they were the masters and we their subjects. One day, one of Aethelfrith's house guards called out to Eduard, 'You're a piece of shit!' My friend retaliated, got into a fight with him and broke his nose. Relations in the camp grew tense; soon, fights were breaking out on a daily basis and increasing in severity. Eventually, a man from the Wolds was killed by two Bernicians, but Aethelfrith would not permit them to stand trial, which made us even angrier. It now started to seem as if a battle might be fought between us and our former allies on the very battlefield where together we had defeated the Welsh only a couple of weeks before.

In the end though, Aethelric called to him all the lords and commanders in the Deiran army. He looked frankly exhausted and seemed to struggle to get his words out and when he did speak; there was a tone of resignation in his voice.

"You see, it is simple numbers," Aethelric explained to us. "We have just five hundred men to defend Deira from future Welsh attacks. Aethelfrith has a thousand spears. He can keep a few companies here and still fight on against the Welsh to his west and north, whereas we would be stretched manning a garrison all the way up here. In addition, there are the armies of Elmet, which might come again and attack us one day, from the west. We were victorious here," and now he swept his arm around in a circle, "at Catraeth, because we had allies. But, we would not be able to defend our own home lands if we kept two hundred men here. Bernicia is better placed to watch over Rheged and the pass and release us to guard our western border. I don't like it and I expect you won't either, but there is nothing else to be done."

And so, that was that: a treaty was agreed. The Prince was correct that none in Deira much liked it, but however reluctant, we could see Aethelric's point. Even so, while the victory here had saved Deira from an invasion by the Welsh, we had now given away Stanwick camp to the more powerful Bernicians and many of us questioned the outcome. Had it justified the death of all those who had died? Would Wallace have felt that his sacrifice was worthwhile? Would the families in Wicstun and elsewhere, those whose sons would never go home, find solace in the outcome? Well, to those questions, I had no answer.

There was now nothing to keep us here and with tempers frayed and relations cooling, Aethelric ordered the army to be ready to march the next day. No one complained at that. Aethelfrith came out on that last morning and spoke to Aethelric. Then, the King of Bernicia turned and looked over at us and I found that I did not like his expression one bit. To me, he seemed like a man assessing our strength and abilities. This man and his father had been heroes to us all when we were growing up. I had always imagined him full of courage and valour and he certainly had all that. His eyes, however, told a different story. They showed ambition as well as a lust for wealth, land and power. For the moment, he had been our saviour and our lands were as a result safe, but as we marched away I thought to myself that a man such as that was a dangerous ally and I pondered that it would be all too easy for him to become our enemy. Then, I cursed myself for wasting time with these thoughts. "It's not your problem, Cerdic", I thought. "Enjoy the moment: after all, we are going home."

We did not go straight home, of course. We marched with Harald to Eoforwic and there discovered that Aelle had arrived and set up court in Harald's hall. Aelle held a feast to celebrate victory at Catraeth and to give thanks for our survival. Then, the next day, he summoned a great council, to which I was invited. Lilla was too, of course, but excused himself − saying that he had been invited to play at a special celebration in one of his favourite halls and would see us later. The rest of us sat down to discuss the campaign.

Aethelric talked of the battle and then the negotiations with Bernicia. Frowning as he heard about the treaty, Aelle reluctantly agreed to the arrangement, realising that he really had no choice. But, I got the feeling that he wished he had been there and seeing the expressions on the faces of the nobles, I think many of them felt this too. For, we knew that he would have put up a bigger fight than his son did.

Then, Aelle called Father and me forward and we stood side by side in front of him.

"It's time for some reordering of my realm," he said. "Lord

278

Cenred, your action in persuading Aethelfrith to come to our aid saved the army at Catraeth and − as a result − our land. Lord Wallace died bravely saving my son and I honour his memory. But now, Wicstun needs a new master. Wallace left no heir so to you, Cenred of the Villa, I grant the estates of Wicstun and the title of Lord of the South Marches."

My father must have known that this was likely, because he did not act surprised, unlike me − gawping at my father like an idiot.

"Thank you, my Lord, I'm honoured," Father said, in a hoarse voice and I could tell that the often gruff man was touched.

"Cerdic, son of Cenred of the Villa, I have heard the words of the Lords Harald and Sabert who have sung your praises." I looked at Sabert in surprise and Aelle saw the glance and smiled. "In particular, Lord Sabert has said that it was your insistence that you stay and your unfaltering faith in your father's arrival, that saved the army. More than that, your defence of the gate at Stanwick camp at the critical moment and the slaying of Owain enabled the Bernicians to join a battle, rather than have to fight Owain's army after he had slaughtered you all."

I nodded at Sabert and for the first time, he smiled at me.

"So, it is with great pleasure and with your father's permission, that I grant you the title of Lord of the Villa, under your father's overlordship."

My head spun at that news. I was a lord now. Was it that many days since I was, more or less, a farm boy? I was unable to find a word to say, so I just bowed. As I came back up, my father placed a hand on my shoulder.

"You make me proud, son. Cuthwine would have been so, too."

How my life would have been different if Cuthwine had

lived. Would he have taken command of the company in Elmet? Would it have been he who fought Owain at the gates of the fortress of Catraeth? Then, would it have been my brother standing here in front of the King, confirmed as the new Lord of the Villa? At that moment, I realised that I would have given up all of these triumphs and willingly passed the glory to him, if only he was alive today.

"Now," Aelle went on, his voice suddenly stern, "there is one more matter we must attend to."

I was not surprised when Hussa was led out, his wrists bound tightly behind his back. One of Aelle's house guards pushed him down and he was made to kneel in front of the King.

Aelle then called my father to give an account of all that Hussa had done and went on to summon other witnesses who confirmed that Hussa had been seen alongside Owain and Samlen and was in fact Samlen's trusted lieutenant.

Finally, the King turned to my half-brother.

"Have you anything to say in defence, before I pass judgement?"

Hussa just glared at him and said nothing.

"You understand that you stand accused of treason and that the penalty for betraying your country is death?"

Hussa spat on the ground at the King's feet.

"My country?" he asked, "What has my country done for me? I had more honour and reward in Elmet and in the service of Owain and Samlen, than I ever had here. Here I was just an unrecognised bastard son, whilst there I was a lord."

Part of me could understand how appealing that must have been. To have left behind the past, full of anger and rejection and taken on a new life would have seemed intoxicating. Yet, almost two thousand people had died these last few weeks. How much of that blood was on Hussa's hands, I wondered.

"Very well, I judge that you are guilty of treason and will be executed by hanging. Your body is to be left to rot in the open, as a warning to others."

As Aelle declared his fate, Hussa visibly paled, but still he glowered defiantly back at the King.

In the hall, there was now utter silence. Then, next to me, my father stirred. He glanced at me then he moved forward to stand beside Hussa. I stared at him, wondering what he was doing.

"Sire, I wish to claim the right to pay weregild for this man, in lieu of his punishment."

The lords in the hall gawped at my father they, like me, shocked by this unexpected statement. From the expression on his face, Hussa was as stunned as the rest of us and just stared in confusion at his father: the father who had never acknowledged him, who had repeatedly rejected him and who thought him a traitor and yet now stood by him – a condemned man, guilty of treachery.

What did my father hope to achieve by this?

Sabert coughed, breaking the silence. "Cenred, why do you do this, what is this man to you?"

Father did not hesitate to answer. Until now, only a few men knew – or had realised – that Hussa was his son. Of the Lords of Deira, only Wallace had been aware. Now, he chose to confess to them the truth.

"Hussa is my son," he said simply.

Sabert's eyebrows went up in complete surprise. Harald's expression was that of a man who had just heard the answer to a riddle and now realised that he really knew it all along. Aelle, on the other hand showed no reaction. Had he known it after all, or was he just very good at hiding his reactions? My father looked at the King and spoke again.

"His mother and I ... had a brief relationship one summer seventeen years ago. She was beautiful and I was weak. It was ... intense, for as long as it lasted. But then I realised it could not go on. In the end, I was forced to choose between my wife and the family I had made with her and Hussa. I realise now that this was the wrong choice and I was weak: I should not have been made to choose between them. I should have recognised Hussa years ago. Then things would have been different ..." He paused and I knew he was thinking of my mother, who had insisted he make that difficult choice.

Aelle sighed.

"A man makes his own choices, Lord Cenred. Hussa made his and nothing that you say excuses what he has done."

"Perhaps that is so, Sire. But, he is still my son."

Aelle nodded.

"Weregild though ... it's for murder, theft and so on. The law and our customs do not allow it for treason."

Weregild was blood money. If a man killed or harmed another or caused damage to property, he could prevent punishment by compensating the victim. Our kings defined, in various codes of law, how much it all cost and the lords then enforced it. But, as Aelle said, treason was never included in these lists.

"The King decrees the law, Sire. You can decide if it may be included and if so, how much."

Sabert spoke again.

"Cenred, even if the King chose to allow this, how can you value the safety of a kingdom, how do you define its worth?"

Aelle nodded.

"Lord Sabert speaks truthfully, Lord Cenred. To dissuade offenders, the fine must match the crime. It would be a fine of the order of thousands of shillings."

"But, you will allow that the kingdom needs such money, at a time like this: to repair the damage of the war and to rearm and equip the Fyrd," my father suggested and Aelle nodded.

"There is no denying that."

"Then, for treachery to a kingdom, I offer as weregild a kingdom's treasure."

With a flourish, he pulled out my mother's jewellery.

Aelle looked at it and pursed his lips, staring at the amber treasure for a long time before speaking.

"I once gave that to your brother as reward for saving the kingdom," he said at last.

"Then let me give it back in payment for his nephew's wrong doing," my father answered.

Aelle was silent again, but this time his eyes were not focused upon the jewellery, but somewhere else and just as on the day of the great council in his own hall, weeks before, he seemed to be thinking back over the years to another war: another battle. Finally, he nodded.

"So be it, but I will not permit a traitor to remain in my kingdom. Hussa, I commute your sentence to exile from Deira during my lifetime. My heirs will decide if that sentence prevails after my death. You will leave Deira within two days. If after that time you are found within its bounds, you will be declared an outlaw and any man can kill you, lawfully."

Hussa was shaking now and seemed to be in a mix of conflicting emotions. He was staring at Father as if he did not know what to make of him.

"You may escort your son to the border," Aelle said softly, "this council session is ended."

I went to join my father, but he shook his head and then held up his hand, bringing me to a halt.

"Wait here for me," he said and then turned away, glanced at Hussa and pointed at the door.

Hussa shuffled that way, escorted by two warriors and followed by my father. At the door my brother turned and looked at me for a moment and then nodded briefly, just the once. What did that look mean? Was it an apology, or was it a threat that the next time we met, I would not be so fortunate.

Then, he was gone and I was left staring at the door, not sure if what had happened was right or wrong. Right for Father, perhaps, but maybe wrong for everyone else. Aelle passed me and glanced at my face.

"Don't blame yourself, Lord Cerdic – for Hussa, I mean. A man makes his own choices and he made his," he said. "You and your father have served me well and I am sure you have many future battles to prove your worth," he foretold.

So there it was, a prediction about my future: Cerdic as a warrior lord. There was a time when Lilla's poems had set my soul aflame, when all I dreamed of were the glories of battle and of winning a name and land, of slaying the kingdom's enemy and becoming a hero of the sagas. As I thought back upon them, I realised they were not visions I wanted anymore. No, the events of the last few weeks had changed all that.

If I was honest, I had been terrified when we got into battle. A lot of young men from both sides had died on Catraeth field. Only a few days before, they had been alive and probably full of the same dreams I had. Like them, my dreams had died and I had simpler ones now. Now it seemed that a hero's heart did not beat within my chest and I realised that all I really wanted was to return home and settle down to domestic life. Whatever Aelle said, I believed my fighting days were over. It was time to go home to the Villa, to my family and, I thought tentatively, to Aidith.

Father and Hussa had departed Eoforwic within minutes of leaving the council. They had ridden north, out of the city and up Dere Street. Father was gone for a couple of days and when he did return, all he would say is that he had seen my brother to the border at Catraeth, where Hussa crossed the bridge. Of what they spoke on the way, or how they had parted, he never said a word.

When he did return, he clapped me on the shoulder and I could see the tension finally draining from him.

"Now it is, at last, over!" he said with smile, "let's go home."

Yes, it was over and the next day we left Eoforwic. Firstly we went as far as Wicstun, with the rest of the company. Now the cost of the war came home and showed itself in the anguished sobs of mothers who had lost sons, wives who had lost husbands. In all, of the eighty-five who had belonged to the Wicstun Company, sixty still lived, though many were badly wounded. Twenty-five, including Wallace, were dead and those losses hurt the small town and all the villages around it. Numbed by the deaths and exhausted by the weeks of raids and war, there was relief rather than joy over the victory. So it was, with polite acceptance rather than celebration, that the townsfolk welcomed Father as the new Lord of Wicstun. I think we were all glad that there was no suggestion of feasts or days of ceremony. We stayed just the one night in Wictsun, then father summoned the villagers, Mildrith and me for the final journey home.

As Father led us down the road from Wicstun, we came over the last rise and could see the Villa and the village. He stopped a moment and then laughed out loud and I realised that it was the first time I had heard him laugh since my brother Cuthwine had died. We all halted and looked at the sight that greeted us and I felt my heart suddenly fill with joy. For there, ahead of us, was the little world I was born into. Those fields, woods and cluster of buildings were so familiar to me that they were like parts of my body. Now, after all the blood and horror there it was, at last: home – we were home.

Father had sent ahead word of our coming, so Mother had learnt of our return a day before and the villagers had hurled themselves into frantic preparation. The last of the spring blossoms were all used up in great garlands decorating the barn. A bonfire roared on the ground outside it and strips of bright cloth streamed from all the huts.

We rushed down the path towards the barn but, when we arrived, we were surprised to see no one. In fact, the entire settlement seemed deserted. Then, I heard a giggle from one of the village children hiding in the barn and a moment later the doors were flung open and all the village women and children burst out, laughing and smiling.

Sunniva almost knocked me over as she hugged me, then she rushed on to embrace Mildrith. Mother was just behind her, laughing and crying at the same time. Mildrith came back and moving past me, she surprised Cuthbert with a kiss on his cheek. My friend went red with embarrassment. He glanced to see if this had been noticed and saw Eduard and me watching him intently, grinning like idiots, as well as Aedann whose face was wrinkled into a puzzled frown. Then, I felt someone kiss my own cheek and I turned to see Aidith standing there, her hair braided with ribbons and wearing a dazzling yellow gown and looking simply stunning.

"Welcome home, Cerdic," she whispered. I could find nothing to say and just stood there nodding stupidly.

Suddenly, in the barn, music could be heard: a jaunty little tune played on a lyre. We all went in and found that it was Lilla playing. The smile on my father's face at that moment was priceless.

"I thought you said you had to play at a feast in your favourite hall," Father said to him.

"Yes well, I do get so very bored at councils. Besides which, Hrodwyn sent a message to me, asking that I be here when you arrived ... and I decided to come early and practice ... this is, after all, my favourite hall," Lilla said, gesturing with his hand at the barn.

My father beamed and reached across and pulled my mother to his side. Then, laughing, he waved us all into the barn for the feast.

To all men, just like nations, there are golden times. Moments that for all their lives they will think back to as an ideal. To some it will be their earliest memory, to others it is times of their glories and triumphs and others still, their first love. For me, looking back through the haze of the long years through times of sorrow and hardship, it was nights such as these, filled with joy and music and surrounded by friends and family whom I loved, that are my golden times.

Of course, I may be a little biased, for on the night of the great feast, Aidith found me after we had all drunk far too much mead and ale. She had listened with a mixture of horror and pride at Lilla's tales of my battles and even though I denied most of what he said, it was clear to her that I could so easily have died and that I might have been one of those poor souls who now lay beneath the soil of Catraeth field. That night, she took me to a dark corner of the hayloft behind the great barn, from where laughter and music could be still heard coming through the night air. Then, having both learnt just how fragile life was, feeling a desperate need to simply enjoy the moment and with any inhibitions relieved by the mead, she pulled me down on to her - and it has to be said that I offered no resistance.

A few weeks before, the last spring of our childhood had ended with a night of horror and blood that made the children we were into man and woman. This summer night ended in warmth and pleasure and we celebrated the fact that we were still alive and young by giving ourselves to each other.

All my life, I had wanted to become a warrior, inspired as I had been by the poems of Lilla and the stories about my uncle. Yet, my dreams of glory had turned into the blood and ashes of a battlefield. I realised that I did not find joy in the fighting or the victory: rather, it had all seemed horrific beyond words. I still honoured my uncle, but I had been glad to get home and I now assumed that I was destined to be a farmer. I believed that I could live out my life in obscurity, farming the land and filling my free hours with Aidith's company.

This though is where this story started. I said then and I feel it now, that looking back from old age, when the faith of Christ has replaced the old religions of my fathers, I can recall many times when my friends and I appeared to be at the whim of powers beyond our understanding. Today, we talk of the will of God. In those far off days it was the machinations of the gods or a man's 'wyrd' or fate that affected his destiny. A man prayed to the gods, put his trust in fate and life would go well: unless of course he was fey − unless he had been chosen or doomed to follow some other path.

I still am not entirely sure I agree with all that. It implies that nothing we do has any effect, that in the end we are all merely pieces on the game board of the gods; just pawns pushed around by Loki. I will accept that most folk just live and die with little impact on and little affected by the world about them; but some of us, at least, are more than that. We become part of the world, help to shape it and mould it. You can tell we lived, because the world changed whilst we were alive.

Whatever the truth: the will of man, the plans of the gods or the chances of fate, I was a fool to believe that the world had finished with me just yet. No, Loki had not cleared away my piece from his board.

Not me, nor my friends Cuthbert, Aedann and Eduard. Not the bard Lilla or the teacher Grettir. All were still in play, as was Aethelfrith and Aelle.

Then, Loki laughed ... and put one more piece back on the board.

His name was Hussa ... and he was still in the game.

The End

Historical Note

The period of history following the departure of Roman troops from Britain in about the year 416 and lasting until the reign of Alfred the Great almost five hundred years later, represent the most poorly documented in the history of Britain. Enormous changes overtook the Island. Large parts of the country passed from the domination of one race to a completely different one. Place names, history, culture and language were swept away. Invasions, battles and wanton destruction raged across the land as never before, or since.

In this time, there would have been heroes and villains. Legends would have arisen. Folk would have spoken with familiarity of battles and warlords, as we today talk of celebrities and sports teams. Amongst all this, normal people lived normal lives. People were born and died. They lived and loved, as we do today.

And yet, we know almost nothing of this time. Most records that do exist date from a period decades or even centuries after the events they record. The greatest record of the age, The Anglo Saxon Chronicle, was probably started by Alfred the Great. Some of the events mentioned in it occurred five centuries earlier. That is like a modern man writing an account of the Battle of Bosworth or the Spanish Armada. Clearly, the monks who wrote the Chronicle referred back to earlier manuscripts that do not now exist, but we have no idea how authentic they were.

In short, researching this book has led me to conclude that no one can write a fiction on this period without a great deal of guesswork and improvisation. Deira, Bernicia, Pennine, Rheged, Elmet and the other realms mentioned did exist and did interact, by and large, as I have written. Aelle was king of Deira. Aethelfrith was certainly a powerful and ambitious king of Bernicia, as was Owain of Rheged. If I have made any of them harsh and merciless, this is probably fitting for the times.

I have simplified the succession of Bernicia. Dependant on which source you read, three of Aethelfrith's older brothers or uncles were kings before he suceeded or possibly he succeeded directly from Aethelric. Maybe Aethelric was "Firebrand" who fought on Lindisfarne, or maybe it was his son or brother. I took the view that if I was confused, so would a reader be. In any event, I wanted to use one of the names for a major character: Hussa.

Looking at Catraeth there seems no doubt that a battle of some sort did occur around the year 597 or maybe a little earlier. Surviving records imply that it was a counter attack by the British against land newly conquered by the Saxons. It seems certain, that Aethelfrith and his Bernician army was involved, although Deira's part in the battle is less well recorded. As for the battle itself, the only event that is documented is the charge of the Goddodin Cavalry. This does appear in the poems of Aneirin but I have to confess that I have paraphrased the bard's words a little. The rest of the battle is purely guesswork. Stanwick Camp does still exist and it is possible to walk along the earthworks and to get a feel for the size of the structure.

The existence of the England we know today is strongly and rightly linked to the victories of Alfred the Great and his Kingdom of Wessex over the Vikings in the ninth century. Yet, three hundred years before Alfred's time, it was the creation of the powerful kingdom of Northumbria and its emergence as the dominant power in Britain for about a century, where we can see the roots of that England.

This was the Kingdom of Bede, the great chronicler of the late 7th. and early 8th. centuries and author of *Historia Ecclesiastica Gentis Anglorum*: 'The Ecclesiastical History of the English People'. It is also the land of the great kings, Edwin and Oswald, as well as the location of the Council of Whitby that established the form that the Christian Church in England would take: a form that lasted – more or less unchanged – until Henry VIII broke away from Rome some 900 years later.

One day, the Vikings would sweep it all away, but by then the mark left on the history of England by the golden age of Northumbria, could not be erased. The journey to that golden age started at Catraeth, but there are many dangers, many battles and times of terrible peril before that era arrives.

It will take heroes like Cerdic and his friends to make sure it all happens.

Further Reading

Kings and Kingdoms of Early Anglo Saxon England: Barbara Yorke/ Routledge
Anglo-Saxon Food: Ann Hagen/ Anglo Saxon Books
Childhood in Anglo-Saxon England: Sally Crawford/Sutton Publishing
The English Warrior: Stepehn Pollington/ Anglo-Saxon Books
Anglo-Saxon Weapons and Warfare: Richard Underwood/Tempus
Warriors of the Dark Ages: Jennifer Laing/Sutton Publishing
An English Empire: N.J. Higham/ Manchester University Press
The Age of Arthur: John Morris/ Phoenix
The Anglo Saxon Chronicle: Various publishers

Places to Visit

Sutton Hoo, Woodbridge, Suffolk. This is an ancient Saxon Burial Site.
West Stow, Bury St Edmunds. Recreated Saxon Village

I would recommend attending events where Regia Anglorum appear. (www.regia.org)

Regia Anglorum strives to re-create an accurate live image of the life and times of the folk who dwelt in and around the Islands of Britain during the Viking centuries - mostly from Alfred the Great to the reign of Richard the Lionheart. They perform re-enactments throughout the UK . More info on their website.

The Northern Crown Series Book Two
Child of Loki

A divided land ... a divided family.

The Battle of Catraeth has been won and Cerdic's homeland is safe ... but for how long? The Northern British were crushed but yet more enemies have risen to replace them.

Soon Cerdic and his friends must go to war again - against the Scots and Picts north of Hadrian's wall. He goes to help his country's allies - the Bernicians - under their great warlord, Aethelfrith.

But what is Aethelfrith's true design? How ambitious is he and how far will he go to fulfil his dreams? And what is Cerdic's treacherous half brother, Hussa up to in these fierce wild lands?

All Cerdic wants is to be left to live out his life in peace.

But Loki, it seems, has other ideas.

Read on for a sneak peek at Child of Loki

Chapter One
Loidis

Loidis was in flames. It was the price Elmet must pay for choosing the losing side. I, Cerdic, once heard Abbess Hild talk of forgiving one's enemies: she said that a man should pray for those who curse you and bless those who mistreat you. These were Christ's words and we should heed them, she implored us. For, they were words of love and words of peace.

But this day was not a day for peace or love. This was a day for vengeance and blood. Elmet chose to back Owain and his great alliance of the Northern British tribes. Together they attacked my land and my people - the Angles. They raided Deira, killed my brother and kidnapped my sister. Then they took their army and joined Owain at a place called Catraeth. There they hoped to destroy my land and my race for ever.

But it was we who prevailed. We Deiran farmers and towns-folk from the Wolds and Moors and the lands along the River Humber held on against the odds until our brothers - the Angles of Bernicia - had marched from the North and fallen upon the enemy.

There, at the great Battle of Catraeth, we destroyed them. The tribes from Rheged, Strathclyde and Manau Goddodin had been crushed. So now we returned to our neighbour - to Elmet to make them pay for the hurt they had done us.

That at least was what Aelle - our king - had ordered. He wanted recompense from Elmet's King Ceredig, and punitive steps taken to ensure he could not easily attack us again. For my part I had seen enough blood and death at Catraeth to last a lifetime. I would have been content to stay at home with my family and Aidith, my woman. But Aelle was our King, and my father, Cynric, was Earl of the Southern Marches. Our family's lands around the village of Cerdham lay in his domain so when he called out the Wicstun Company that spring, a few months after Catraeth, he expected me, the Lord of the Villa to obey the summons.

So we went - ten men and boys from the village - led by myself. Amongst them were my three friends: Eduard - tall and broad-shouldered, a fierce warrior, utterly loyal and a true friend; Cuthbert, my other boyhood companion - short and delicate, yet agile and as much a master with the bow as Eduard was with his axe; and Aedann, the dark-haired, green-eyed Welshman, who had once been my slave and was now a freedman sworn to my service. With us went the rugged old veteran Grettir - our teacher once upon a time and still full of the wisdom of a man who has seen many battles.

We left the village of Cerdham with its hovels and huts and left too the Villa - the decaying old Roman house that my grandfather had captured and made into our family's home. Off we went with the rest of Aelle's army - six companies from the South of Deira - and invaded Elmet. We marched hard and fast, striking deep into the Welsh land and, before he knew we were coming, their King, Ceredig, was staring down at us in horror from the wooden palisade around his city of Loidis.

Aelle's orders had been strict and Earl Harald commanding us followed them to the letter. There was no offer of peace from Harald, no olive branch held out and no chance of reprieve. Not yet. Not until we had smashed our way through the city gates and burnt the houses that lined the main street.

I am an old man now and I have been in many battles and

many fights, but despite all the sights I have seen, I will never get used to the screams and cries for mercy from the innocent. The gods blow their trumpets and the Valkyries ride forth to choose who is to be slain and lead them to Valhalla, and men cheer and do battle for the sake of glory or wealth or honour. Yet it is the children and the women who suffer while we men wallow in blood.

So it was that day. Vengeance might sound a fine thing to demand when you stand over the grave of your brother and smell the smoke of your own home burning. But see how you feel when it is someone else's brother, son or daughter who lies at your feet, their home burning whilst you stand nearby, holding the torches that kindled the flames.

Yet it had to be done, did it not? They must be made to regret their attack and be prevented from doing it again. It was us or them; and frankly, when you have seen hundreds die you can harden your heart to the cries of the innocent. Or at least you can try to....

A little later, Eduard, Cuthbert, Aedann and I stood with our men amongst the Wicstun Company in a square at the heart of the city. Smoke from the smouldering hovels and the stench of burning flesh wafted across to us, but I tried to ignore it. In front of us was a long hall: Ceredig's royal palace. Lined up between us and it were two hundred Elmetae warriors, shields held high and spear points sharp and glowing red in the firelight. They were the King's last defence and we and two other companies were forming up in a shield wall to attack them. The rest of the army was elsewhere, ransacking the city and putting it to the torch.

"This is it, lads. One last attack and the campaign is over," Harald shouted. "One last attack and then we can all return home and forget about war."

"If you believe that you will believe anything," I heard Eduard mutter, but loud enough that many of us heard it and chortled wryly. Yet, we all hoped it was true. It was what gave us the strength to carry on. Maybe Harald was right. After all, the armies of Owain and his allies were scattered or dead. With Elmet suppressed too, who else was there to threaten us? I gripped my shield tighter, checked the balance of the spear in my right hand and waited for the order to advance.

Harald blew one sonorous blast on his horn and we were off. Behind us my father and his huscarls followed and over our heads our company's standard flapped in the gentle spring breeze - the running wolf visible through the drifting smoke.

A few arrows flew back and forth above us - but not many for apart from Cuthbert we had brought few archers along with us and the Welsh had only a handful themselves. Nevertheless, one arrow found its mark somewhere amongst the company for I heard a curse over to my right. Glancing that way I saw a man from Wicstun tumble out of the shield wall, blood streaming down his chest and an arrow shaft protruding from just above his collar bone. He slumped onto the ground and sat there, face screwed up in agony, each breath laboured and painful. Then he was forgotten as the army moved forward.

We were thirty paces from the enemy, who now locked their shields together, each one overlapping the next. Then they brought their spears down so they pointed towards us and with a clattering of ash staves on oak boards, we copied their move.

Twenty paces away now and my gaze fell upon one Elmetae spearman directly in front of me. In truth he was barely a man and from the faintest wisp of a beard on his chin and the gangly thin arms and legs I surmised that he could not have been above fourteen years old. His dark green eyes looked haunted and his gaze darted this way and that. I had seen that look before at Catraeth on a hundred faces and knew without a doubt that today he was in his first battle. Next to him and older was a gruff veteran with scars down his cheeks and bulging upper arms. His eyes showed none of the fear in the young man's eyes. Instead hatred and bloodlust lingered there.

Ten paces away and the spears of both armies interlaced each other like the fingers of a man bringing his hands together. Then the shields crashed together. The shock of the collision sent a judder up my left arm and it was all I could do to keep hold of my shield. Unbalanced, I stepped back just as a spear point lunged at me, missing my throat by only an inch. Recovering my feet, I thrust back, realising as I did so that my spear was aimed at the young boy's neck. Maybe I hesitated for just a second, for it never reached him: the grizzled old veteran at his side hacked down at my ash stave with his sword, snapping it in two and leaving me with a useless stump. He then brought the sword round aiming to take out my throat with the fearsome edge. I was saved by Aedann who, standing on my left, took a step forward and drove his spear into the veteran's left shoulder. The enemy gave a roar of pain and recoiled. The youth, meantime, drew back his own spear preparing to thrust it forward again. In his eagerness and his panic he fumbled, dropped it and then bent to recover it.

Panting hard, I took advantage of the reprieve and reached down to my baldric, grasping the hilt of my short stabbing sword. I had taken this blade from my first foe, whom I had slain during the raid on the Villa. It had served me well: it was with this sword that I had killed Owain, the golden king of Rheged and it was in honour of that battle that it earned its name:

29

'Catraeth'.

I dragged Catraeth up above my shield just as the youth advanced again, screaming as he thrust his spear at me. I leant to one side, letting the spear point go past and then following up, hacked over the top of the shield and felt the edge cut through tendon and bone deep into the boy's arm. He let out a howl of agony and fell to the ground, shield and spear abandoned as his hands reached up to stem the flow of blood from the wound.

To his right the veteran roared in anger and then hurtled forward, his own wound forgotten, slamming his shield against Aedann's own, knocking my Welsh companion back through the rear ranks. Without pausing, the enemy stepped over to me and kicked hard against my shins. With a shout of pain I too tumbled to the ground.

Above me the light was blocked by the huge figure of the grizzled veteran standing astride me, his face a mask of rage, his shoulder pouring blood that dripped down onto my upturned face. Yet there was something in his features that reminded me of the young man I had just cut down. It was then I realized that the youth must be his son. Thirsty for revenge and consumed by anger, the old man swung back his sword and prepared to finish me.

"One last attack and then we can all return home," those had been the words of Earl Harald just minutes before. They resounded in my head; hollow now. But then again, maybe he was right. But if so I would not be returning home to live in peace.

No, instead I would be going home to be buried ...